THE BOY IN THE PHOTO

BOOKS BY NICOLE TROPE

My Daughter's Secret
The Boy in the Photo
The Nowhere Girl
The Life She Left Behind
The Girl Who Never Came Home

THE BOY IN THE PHOTO

NICOLE TROPE

GRAND CENTRAL PUBLISHING

New York Boston

This book is a work of fiction. Names, characters, places, and incidents are the product of the author's imagination or are used fictitiously. Any resemblance to actual events, locales, or persons, living or dead, is coincidental.

Grand Central Publishing
Hachette Book Group
1290 Avenue of the Americas, New York, NY 10104
grandcentralpublishing.com
twitter.com/grandcentralpub

First published in 2019 by Bookouture, an imprint of StoryFire Ltd.
First Edition: June 2021

Grand Central Publishing is a division of Hachette Book Group, Inc. The Grand Central Publishing name and logo is a trademark of Hachette Book Group, Inc.

The publisher is not responsible for websites (or their content) that are not owned by the publisher.

Library of Congress Control Number: 2020949420

ISBN: 978-1-5387-5434-4 (trade pbk.)

Printed in the United States of America

LSC-C

Printing 2, 2021

For D.M.I and J

THE BOY IN THE PHOTO

PROLOGUE

She can feel the blood rushing through her veins. The incessant thudding of her heart in her ears drowns out all other sounds, and her chest heaves as she tries to get enough air inside her. She is running now, running with no real purpose, no idea where exactly she is trying to get to—just running. The space is too big, too filled with locked doors, hidden corners, and lurking shadows. There are too many places he could be. How could this safe space have suddenly turned so vast and threatening? Why does nothing look familiar?

Her breath comes in pants, faster and faster. Panic has taken hold. Sweat trickles down her back. Her legs start to ache.

She knew this would happen, didn't she? She tried to dismiss it, to talk herself out of it, but she knew. She knew.

Where is he?

Where is he?

Where is he?

CHAPTER ONE

When the call comes Megan is trying—and failing—to feed her daughter. There is rice cereal on the tray of the high chair, rice cereal all over Evie's face, and rice cereal on Megan's hands; but so far none of it seems to have been swallowed by Evie, whose little tongue pokes out indignantly every time the spoon comes anywhere near her mouth.

"I give up, baby girl," says Megan, laughing as she wipes her daughter's face.

Evie smiles at her.

Megan's phone starts ringing, and she glances down, seeing it's Michael. A rare middle-of-the-day call.

"Hey, babe, what's up?" she asks as she lifts Evie out of the high chair and puts her on the floor on her back. Evie immediately flips over and begins trying to get up on her hands and knees.

"Megan, they found him," says Michael, dispensing with the pleasantry of "hello."

"Found who?" she asks, watching Evie rock back and forth in the crawling position. She is only days away from being able to move, keen to put babyhood behind her despite being only six months old.

Megan assumes that Michael must be talking about someone from one of his latest cases. Mostly shrouded in secrecy, they are sometimes mentioned over dinner when some of the information is already out in the wide world for speculation and horror. She finds the stories he tells painful to hear but she feels she must listen. She must give the heartbreak of others her attention. Her own pain has strengthened her ability to empathize with those who find their lives shattered in an instant and dwarfed by grief. But he has never called to update her during the day, preferring to talk to her over dinner, use her as a sounding board.

The news is on the television and Megan glances at the screen, where a picture of a young man flashes and words scroll beneath his genial face: missing backpacker Steven Hindley from England. Megan looks around for the remote so she can turn up the sound in case this is the person Michael is talking about, and she experiences a flash of alarm that someone so young may have met a terrible end. She watches as a young woman with short pink hair tells a reporter, "He, like, loved Newcastle, you know, said he wanted to visit every part of New South Wales. He said he wanted to go to a rave here. Maybe he's just back in Sydney and hasn't contacted anyone."

Megan turns down the sound. Newcastle is not Michael's jurisdiction. Michael doesn't work missing persons anyway, not anymore.

"They found…" says Michael and then he stops.

Megan runs through their conversation last night, imagining her tall, broad-shouldered husband at his desk, tapping his pencil to make the *rat-a-tat, rat-a-tat* sound. The sound signals anxiety, signals the fact that he feels a little out of control.

It could be an old case. Despite now working with serious crimes, he still looks into his old missing persons cases when he can. Closure brings him relief, regardless of the outcome. It could be one of the cases he's working on now. They discussed a woman whose husband beat her up and left her for dead, and one about a driver who hit an old man, then left him to die.

She becomes aware of the silence at the other end of the phone, and without the slightest warning, a prickling sensation crawls up

CHAPTER TWO

Six Years Ago

Monday, May 20, 2013

Megan slaps at the alarm clock, hitting it off her bedside table, stopping it from letting her know that she has, once again, hit the snooze button. She grabs her phone from the side of the bed and peers blearily at the screen. It's only seven twenty. Not as late as she thought, but late enough.

She curls herself into a ball, groans a little, and finally flings back the covers and leaps to her feet.

She can hear the television is on; morning cartoons blare around the small apartment, bouncing off the walls. Too much wine last night. Too much lonely always leads to too much wine. She knows she will eventually get used to the late-night silence that pervades the apartment, and maybe even learn to enjoy it, but last night it had made her feel trapped and intently aware of her separateness from the rest of the world. The wine had helped. One glass had made her feel better, two glasses had made her feel optimistic about the future, three had made the comedy on television hilarious, and then, without her noticing, the bottle was done.

"All I want to do is love you, Megan. Is that too much to ask?" She hears the words he spat into her ear, his fingers bruising her jaw. Pushing aside the memory, she washes her face, acknowledging that a lonely bottle of wine and a thumping headache are easier to deal with than her ex-husband Greg's suffocating, obsessive, controlling company. His version of love cannot be recovered from with some acetaminophen, washed down by a cup of strong, bitter coffee and a liter of water.

"Daniel, turn that down," she shouts as she grabs tracksuit pants and a warm sweater from the wardrobe, suitable for the school run. It's not like she'll get out of the car anyway. She can't bear to face all the mothers, not when she's feeling like this.

A quick glance in the mirror makes her wince. The circles under her eyes are dark enough to look like bruises. She really needs to drink more water, start exercising, and generally get her life together. She shakes her head at herself. "You're doing okay," she whispers to her reflection, and she's immediately cheered by the way her brown eyes light up a little. She pulls her long, curly, black hair into a ponytail and smiles at herself. "You're doing okay."

The affirmations, recommended by a website filled with advice for people going through divorce, made her feel stupid in the beginning, but on days when she questions what has happened to her life, what has happened to her, they help. They really do.

In the living room, six-year-old Daniel is dressed in his gym clothes. Bare-chested, his ribs protrude, fighting with his collarbones for angles in almost comical opposition to his chubby cheeks. He is slumped on the couch, spooning cereal into his mouth. *How can someone who never stops eating be this skinny? I should look into supplements*, Megan thinks as she appraises her son.

"I can't find my gym clothes." Daniel doesn't take his eyes off the television, where a talking dog is flying through space.

Megan tears around the apartment, looking under the couches and in the bedrooms, opening the washing machine and dryer and finally finding the top, neatly folded on top of the clean laundry. "Daniel, it's sitting right here. If it was a snake, it would have bitten you."

"But it's not a snake, Mum, it's my gym clothes." He grins. Four missing front teeth, but still beautiful. A rush of love fills her and she kisses each chubby cheek. "I'm watching, Mum," he protests.

"Sorry, here, lean forward and put down the cereal for a second." Megan pulls the top over his head and he obediently threads his arms through. "Now go and find your tracksuit top, will you?"

"I'm sitting on it. Now you have to pack my lunch."

"I know, Daniel, I'm getting a little tired of you telling me what to do," she snaps, instantly regretting it. *How can my mood change this quickly? I'm doing okay, I'm doing okay.*

She takes a deep breath. "I mean, I know, baby. I know what I have to do to get you ready for school."

Annie, the school psychologist, says he keeps telling her what to do because he needs to feel he's in control of something.

"It's a coping mechanism. Divorce can make children feel very insecure," the earnest young woman had reported to Megan. "Daniel is a sensitive child who needs to feel that he can manage this change. He's not being rude, he's just making sure you aren't late or don't forget something."

"I understand, I do," Megan had replied. "But sometimes it feels like he's trying to mother me. I'm struggling to feel in control of my own life too, and being told what to do by a six-year-old only heightens that."

"This must be very hard for both of you," Annie had said, focusing her sympathetic gaze on Megan, who found herself tearing up at the psychologist's kindness.

"Yes... it's been... just horrible."

"Does Daniel get along with his father?"

"They do, I mean, sort of. It's funny to see them together because they both have the same curly brown hair and hazel eyes, like carbon copies on the outside, but inside they couldn't be more different. Greg was always..." Megan had paused. She hadn't wanted to say "a bully" because she hadn't wanted to paint that picture for the psychologist.

She finds this juxtaposition of thoughts about her ex-husband difficult to deal with. She would like to announce his sins to the world but she's acutely aware that as Daniel's father, he needs to be spoken of carefully to protect her son. How she sees Greg isn't how Daniel sees him. She wouldn't want Daniel to see his father like that.

To her, Greg is a bully, an emotionally—and sometimes physically—abusive man, a nightmare of an ex-husband. To Daniel he is a hero, a joker, a friend to play with.

"Greg was always the loud kid at school, the sporty one, you know," she had explained to the psychologist. "He had lots of friends and he played for every team. Daniel is more like me: quiet and he's very artistic."

"Oh, I know, I've seen his paintings hanging in the hall at our art shows. You teach art, don't you?"

"Yes, although I haven't had much time to do my own work lately. But hopefully sometime soon."

Annie had leaned across the desk, covering Megan's hand with her own slightly rough one. "I'm sure you'll get back to it very soon. You and Daniel are going to be just fine."

Megan had been oddly grateful for the words. From a stranger, they seemed to carry more weight than from her mother or her brother, Connor, or his husband, James.

"Everything is packed and ready," says Megan, remembering the psychologist's platitudes. "Are you ready for a great school day?"

"Ready!" shouts Daniel.

At the school drop-off she gets out of the car, just long enough to hug Daniel.

He grins up at her. "Have a good day, Mum, enjoy your art stuff…Look, there's Max, Max, Maxie," he calls and he runs off without looking back.

"Love you," shouts Megan to his back. Three children turn around. She could be speaking to any one of them. She spots Olivia, Max's mum, who gives her a thumbs up and holds her hand up to her face, miming "call me" as she pulls away from the drop-off zone.

Back at home, Megan tidies and sips coffee as she gets ready for work. She's starting the day with a new class of people from the senior living facility. Megan loves these art classes. They are all so supportive of each other, all so excited to be there. There's no competition, no comparisons. They are all past that, at an age where merely being alive is cause for celebration. They are joyous to be around.

Her hours at the art studio pass quickly, and over lunch she gives silent thanks for Mr. Pietro and his support. When he'd first heard her news he had said, "As many classes as you want, my darling, you just tell me. Divorce is a terrible thing, but sometimes to stay married is even more terrible."

She had loved Mr. Pietro in that moment, loved him for understanding without her needing to explain just how hideous things had become.

Her boss had never indicated that he was aware of what was going on at home, but sometimes he would bring a cup of tea into her studio and say, "I thought something hot and soothing would be nice. I think this morning was, perhaps, not that good a morning."

"Oh no, I love my classes," she would reply quickly, panicked that he thought she wasn't happy in her job. It was, after all, the place where she could forget that she had been labeled a whore over breakfast for wearing red lipstick.

"I mean this morning at home, Megan," he would reply quietly, taking off his little round glasses and polishing them. Even though she wanted to tell him he was wrong, it had been easier, on days like that, to simply nod her head.

At the end of the day she stands outside the school, watching the primary-school students tumble out of classrooms, laughing and talking, greeting parents with enthusiastic hugs as though they have been apart for years. Even at three thirty, the light has already started to change as they see out the last month of autumn. Megan wonders how her first winter in the flat where she and Daniel have had to move will go when it's dark by five o'clock in the afternoon. She worries about feeling claustrophobic in the small, stifling space after having had the vast expanse of her garden to enjoy.

"Megs, over here," she hears. Olivia is dressed for court with her hair tightly wound in a bun and wearing a pants suit that only seems to accentuate how small she is.

"I thought you'd be in court all day?"

"Nope, the whole thing degenerated into complete chaos with the husband swearing at the wife and the wife's mother standing up and threatening to kill him, so it was all adjourned with stern instructions from the judge for everyone to learn how to behave. Honestly, you would think it was an episode of *Suits* the way these two are acting."

"I wish you could tell me who they are."

Olivia brushes her fingers across her lips. "No way, Megs. It's all strictly confidential, but you would have seen their photos in all the tabloids. Anyway, the good news is that I get to pick up Max. Roy wants to take us out to dinner."

"Lucky you. Celebrating something?"

Olivia looks down at her high-heeled boots and her face clouds. "We're going to start trying IVF."

"Oh, babe, I'm so sorry you have to, but it's a good thing, right? You'll be pregnant in no time and complaining about back pain and nausea."

"I guess," agrees Olivia. She looks up at Megan. "The two of us, hey? We really need a few good months."

"If Greg would just stop emailing and texting me constantly, I would be happy."

"He still doing that?"

"Yep. Still hoping I'll come back to him. It's been two months since we signed the parental orders and finished mediation. I thought he would have given up by now but he keeps telling me how much he's always loved me, how much I've hurt him, how I don't deserve to have a child because I've broken our family, and the latest is, 'You'll know this pain one day.' I know it's all just idle threats but it still gets to me." The words emerge with a flippancy that Megan does not feel.

Her mother had tried to reassure her that it was all just hot air and anger from Greg, that all he was doing was trying to scare her and that she shouldn't take any notice of him at all. But Megan worried that it was more than that, that Greg was angry enough to do something to really hurt her or Daniel.

"Hang in there, babe," says Olivia, dragging her away from her thoughts. "He'll find someone else to control soon enough. There'll be some young thing who has no idea what he's really like, and she'll be swept off her naive feet."

"Just like I was. Poor thing," Megan says, thinking about the charm of Greg's attention and flattery, his beautiful eyes, his ability to make her feel like the luckiest woman in the world. "I imagine she'll be swept away by the smile and the sports car as well. I feel like I should warn her."

"Not your problem. Oh, hey, Max."

"Hi, Max," Megan says to the dark-haired little boy. "Where's Daniel?"

Max shrugs. "Mum, did you know that an ant can carry ten to fifty times its body weight?"

"Really?" Olivia smiles. "Fascinating. I'd better get him home and changed, Megs. I'll call you tomorrow."

Megan waves goodbye to Olivia and Max and looks back at the kids pouring out of the school. The stream has slowed to a trickle now. Megan sighs. Daniel will be somewhere staring at a bird in a tree or an overfull garbage can or a piece of paper scrunched up on the floor. He dawdles and wanders, finding everything he sees fascinating, if he's not with Max, who hurries him along. Megan waits, tapping her foot. When the high-school students start funneling out ten minutes later, her irritation grows.

She sighs, giving up on waiting. She walks into the school, drawing curious glances from any teenager who can be dragged away from their phone.

It takes her ten minutes to cover the primary school, walking quickly and peering into any unlocked classrooms. When she finds herself back where she started, panic starts to rise inside her. She does another lap of the school, panting and sweating, fear making her mouth dry. Daniel is nowhere. Primary-school students are not allowed onto the high-school section of the school, and regardless of what might have caught his attention, Daniel would not have disobeyed that rule.

Muttering, "Where are you, Daniel?" she runs to the administration office, bursting into the reception, startling the school secretary, Mrs. Roberts, who calls the students "luvvy."

"My son, my son Daniel," pants Megan.

"Ooh, darling, just calm down now, what is it?"

"My son Daniel, Daniel Stanthorpe from first grade. I can't find him. I can't find him anywhere."

"My goodness, oh my goodness. You just sit yourself down now. I'll call . . . I'll call Mr. Nand. I'm sure the little mite is somewhere—you know children. Maybe he's hiding, playing with a friend?"

"No, no, no." Megan shakes her head vehemently. "I've looked. The primary-school kids are gone. The high-school kids are nearly all gone as well. He's not here. He's not anywhere."

Mrs. Roberts picks up her phone and has a whispered conversation.

Down the hall, a door opens and Mr. Nand, the principal, strides out. "Mrs. Stanthorpe, I understand you can't find Daniel," he says. His tie is royal blue and his suit crisp and neat.

Everything's going to be fine, Megan thinks. "Actually, it's Ms. Stanthorpe," she says. "I wanted to go back to my maiden name after the divorce but Daniel . . ." She shakes her head. *Idiot, idiot, why are you telling him this?*

"I'm sorry, Ms. Stanthorpe. Please don't worry. I'm sure he's somewhere. He's a bit of a dreamy one, quite the little artist. Maybe he's in the art classrooms at the high school. I know the final year students are having a display of their work this afternoon."

Relief floods through her. "Of course, of course." She smiles.

"I'll just see if I can get hold of his class teacher; maybe she knows where he might be. And Alice, could you call up to high-school reception? See if the lad is just getting some inspiration."

"Oh, yes, yes I'll do that."

Megan sags in her chair while Mr. Nand looks up the cell number for Daniel's class teacher.

"Oh, Jenny, yes hello, it's Peter. I'm sure it's nothing to worry about but Ms. Stanthorpe is here, Daniel's mother. She can't find Daniel."

Megan watches Mr. Nand nod once, twice, the office lights glinting off his rimless glasses. "Yes . . . yes, I understand. Okay, I'll tell her. Just keep your phone on and nearby, will you, in case we need to speak again."

"Ms. Stanthorpe, Ms. Abramson said that Daniel was picked up by his father at the end of the day. She said your hus—ex-husband was standing outside the classroom when the final bell rang. Daniel seemed really pleased to see him and she assumed that he had arranged with you to fetch him."

"Oh," says Megan because she cannot think of anything else to say. "Oh."

She pulls out her phone and calls Greg. She waits for it to go to voicemail and leaves a cheery message, straining to sound normal. "Hey, Greg, it's me. I didn't know you were picking up Daniel. Give me a call, okay, so I know what time you'll have him home." Then she rings his landline at the flat he has only just leased. "This number is no longer in service. Please check the number before calling again."

She calls his cell again. Voicemail. She rings the landline again after double-checking the number. "This number is no longer in service. Please check the number before calling again." She does this for ten minutes, one number after the other while Mr. Nand and Mrs. Roberts watch her. Fear clawing at her, she looks up at the principal. "He wasn't supposed to pick him up. He's not answering the phone and it says his landline's not in service anymore. I think…I think I need to call the police." She can feel the thrum of her heart in her neck and beads of sweat prickling her body. She takes a deep breath, trying to stop herself from panting. *Daniel, Daniel, Daniel*, repeats inside her head.

"Oh, surely not," says the ever-optimistic Mrs. Roberts.

"Call the police, Alice. Tell them we have a missing child. Tell them it might be a case of parental abduction." Mr. Nand's face is grave. He fiddles with his tie. "I'll check the procedure on this," he says before going back to his office.

"There's a procedure for this?" asks Megan, looking at Mrs. Roberts as she puts down the phone.

"Oh yes, luvvy. You know there's a lot of divorce about these days and it can get a little complicated. The police are sending over two officers. They'll be here soon."

Megan drops her head into her hands. "One day you will know what this pain feels like," she hears Greg say, taunting her.

"What have you done, Greg?" she whispers. "What have you done?"

She looks up again. "Thanks. I'll just call my mum. I'll tell her to go to my apartment and wait in case they turn up."

"There you go, I'm sure that's exactly what will happen."

"Yes, yes, I'm sure," Megan replies robotically before going outside to stand in the afternoon sun. She calls her mother, Susanna; she explains once, explains twice. She struggles to get the words out, to make sense, as though just by saying them she makes what's happening real. She takes one deep breath after another, trying to calm herself, but her heart will not be slowed, her body will not be comforted.

"I'll call Connor and James. You need to call Greg's friends and maybe ring his parents?"

"His parents are in England, Mum."

"Of course. Is there anyone in Sydney?"

"He has a cousin in Adelaide."

"Well, call them then. Call whoever you can and we'll all keep trying his cell phone. Maybe he'll pick up if he doesn't recognize the number. It's so like him to do something this selfish. He has to know that you'd be worried sick."

"I'm sure that's exactly why he's done it."

"Oh, Megan, I'm sure it will be fine, don't worry. Daniel will be safe home in bed tonight but you probably need to tell the school that Greg is never allowed to pick him up without your permission."

"Obviously I need to do that." *Why didn't I do that before?* She has worried over every visitation Daniel has had with his father, counting the minutes until her child is home, opening her front door every time she hears voices. She has worried about the access visits but she has not thought to worry about school. How could she have been so stupid? But Greg had never, in all the years they were married, picked Daniel up from school. Not once.

"Don't snap, darling. I'm sorry, I'm just worried."

"I know, Mum. I'm sorry, I'm just worried too."

"I'll be at the apartment in a few minutes."

"Okay, don't forget your key."

Megan calls Greg's cousin, Les, in Adelaide. She phones his friends Will and Kyle. No one has heard from him in weeks. *Why wouldn't they have heard from him? What does that mean for Daniel?* He used to have a boys' night out at least once every couple of weeks when they were married, telling her, "These are my best mates. I'm not just going to stop going out with them because I'm married."

"But don't you talk to him every few days?" she asks Kyle.

"Sometimes, I just figured he was busy."

Busy doing what? What has he been busy doing?

When the police officers arrive, the unreality of what she is going through makes Megan want to laugh. *This can't be happening, can it?*

"Can you start from the beginning?" asks the young, ginger-haired man after he has introduced himself as Officer McGuire and his partner as Officer Wong. Megan starts at the beginning, detailing everything, focusing on the patch of ginger-blond hair on Officer McGuire's chin that he missed while shaving this morning.

"Do you have a parental order?"

"We do, we signed those a couple of months ago. Greg is supposed to have him every Saturday night."

"And is that all?"

"Yes." Megan feels judged by the constable. She can see him deciding that she has been difficult about visitation, that she wants to keep Daniel away from his father. A bubble of frustration rises inside her.

"It's what he wanted, what he asked for," she explains, feeling the need to justify herself. "I thought it wasn't much but he said he has to work so he can't see him during the week."

"Fair enough," says the officer. Megan can see him taking sides already, concluding that she's just an angry mother whose ex picked her son up without permission. *You have no idea.*

"And have you tried to contact your ex-husband?"

Megan swallows words about the "bleeding obvious" and instead turns her phone around so he can see exactly how many times she has dialed Greg's phone.

"Sorry, but I needed to ask."

"The landline's been disconnected."

"And have you called his work?"

"I... No, I didn't think to do that." Hope flares in Megan at the thought that she might not be at a dead end.

"What does he do?"

"Something in IT... I think he markets cyber security software to big companies—at least he was doing that the last time we talked about his work."

"How long haven't you spoken to him for?"

"We've lived apart for a year now. We don't exactly have polite conversations so I try to limit contact to text and email."

"And why is that? Has he ever been abusive toward you?" Officer McGuire waits patiently for her answer while Megan considers how to explain Greg's behavior.

She hadn't thought it was abuse, even when she had physical evidence on her body. Even when she was dotted with purple and blue and yellow bruises, she had never classed it as abuse. But now that she has read more, has opened up to Olivia, she has allowed herself to admit it: it was abuse. During her marriage, she spent a lot of time questioning herself. Maybe she was just too sensitive, as Greg accused her of being. Maybe she was misinterpreting the things he was saying. Maybe she was being difficult for no reason. The sinister nature of Greg's emotional manipulation made Megan doubt herself beyond what she thought was possible, and Greg would argue, convince her, that it was love and not abuse. And when it did get physical, it was always an accident, a mistake. Like when he grabbed her arm too tightly or prodded her with his pointed finger or shoved past her so quickly, she fell back against the wall. He had explained those times away with, "I didn't mean to do that," or, "You shouldn't have been standing so close to me," or, "You know I'm not like that." And so, she had dismissed even those times, had dismissed everything until finally, finally it was all too much.

She chews on her lip as the officer studies her with watery green eyes. She knows if she answers "yes" and Greg returns with Daniel, she will be accused of being paranoid. Greg will rant at her about her attempts to alienate him from his child. She can picture the scene, and despite the sneer on her ex-husband's face, she welcomes it because it would mean that Daniel was here and safe. But if she says "no," they might drag their feet. They might leave it until it is too late.

"Yes," she finally answers the officer. "Yes, he was. He never wanted to get divorced. He blames me for breaking up our family."

Officer McGuire nods. "Do you have his work number? Officer Wong will give them a call. People tend to respond faster when it's the police."

Megan hands her phone over to the officer, who takes it and walks toward Mr. Nand's office.

"Does your son by any chance have a cell phone?"

Megan shakes her head, knowing that on her list of things to do for her first free day is to look into getting Daniel a cell phone. But she doesn't want to have to explain herself to this young man. She was going to get around to buying him a phone so they could speak when he stayed at Greg's house without her having to talk to Greg. It was something she was going to do.

Officer Wong walks back over to where Megan and Officer McGuire are sitting.

"The human resources manager says he quit his job a month ago."

"What? A month ago? He never said anything. Why wouldn't he have told me?" Her heartbeat ramps up again. *Something is wrong, something is wrong, something is very wrong.*

Megan watches as the officers and Mr. Nand exchange glances full of meaning, as though they have been here before, seen this before. Officer McGuire looks at her with sympathy.

Please don't look at me like that. Tell me he'll be home soon. Please, please, God, don't look at me like that.

"I think we need to get you to speak to a couple of our detectives from the missing persons unit. It would be best if you came into the station with me."

Megan stands up. *So, this is real. This is happening. Greg has taken our son and disappeared. Where are you, Daniel? Where are you?*

Megan cannot remember much of the rest of the day. She knows Detective Kade has kind brown eyes and that the stripes on his blue shirt began to dance in front of her eyes when exhaustion took over.

The first thing she had done, as the detective listened in, was to call Audrey and William, Greg's parents in the UK.

"Audrey, Audrey, it's me, it's Megan," she had started.

"Megan who?"

At any other time, Megan would have laughed at Audrey's banal attempt to put her into her place, to make her understand that she was no longer part of the Stanthorpe family, but at that stage she had been trying to control her own growing hysteria and had responded sharply, "You know who I am, Audrey. I'm calling because I need to know if you've heard from Greg at all. He's picked Daniel up from school and I can't get hold of him."

"What do you need to get hold of him for? He's fetched his son from school. I should think most women would be grateful to have an involved husband—sorry, ex-husband."

"Audrey, I can't explain it all to you now but he wasn't supposed to collect Daniel. The police are looking for them and I need to know if Greg has called you, if he's told you anything."

"Well, I'm sure whatever conversations take place between me and my son are private, Megan. You no longer have any right to know what Greg is thinking."

Megan had sighed in exasperation. "I have a right to know because he has my son, Audrey. This is very serious. The police are involved. Greg is going to get into a lot of trouble if he doesn't bring Daniel home to me now. I need you to call him and tell him he has to bring my son back."

"I will do no such thing. How do I know you're not making all this up just to cause trouble? I know about you, Megan, you and your family of meddlers, always trying to hurt my son. I don't know who you think you are, but you certainly can't call here threatening me with the police and expect to get any help."

Megan had opened her mouth to reply but Audrey had already hung up the phone. The detective had tried to call back, hoping that Greg's mother would respond to a different number and the voice of a policeman, but Audrey wouldn't answer the phone.

Megan had closed her eyes and been able to see her former parents-in-law sitting at their tiny kitchen table over a pot of tea and exactly two slices of toast each. She knew that Audrey would take a sip of tea, then dab her mouth with a linen napkin and pat her gray hair that was tightly scraped back into a bun. She knew there would be very little conversation about what had just happened except for William occasionally saying something like, "The nerve of that woman."

After that there had been forms to fill in, which she did to the tune of Detective Kade's tapping pencil—a sound that had set her on edge and eventually made her ask him to stop.

"Sorry," he'd said, his brow furrowed as he ran his hands through his chocolate-brown hair. At some stage, a recovery order had to be handed to the court in which she detailed why Daniel needed to be returned to her. "Isn't it obvious?" she'd asked. "I'm his mother."

"I know it seems ridiculous, but situations get complicated. The courts have to look at every possible eventuality."

"Do you think he'll hurt him? He won't hurt him, will he?" she had pleaded.

"I wish I could give you the answer you're looking for, Megan, but I really have no idea. In my experience, if he wanted to . . . hurt him in any way, to punish you for the divorce, then he would have called you to let you know he had him. The fact that he hasn't contacted you is a good sign."

That's a good sign? Megan had thought. *How can that be a good sign?*

When she gets back to her apartment hours later, what feels like years later, her parents are waiting for her. When she fits her key into the lock, she prays that Daniel will be sitting on the couch, talking to his grandfather about his day. She forces her mind to accept this with absolute certainty, despite knowing that her mother would have called her to tell her Daniel was home. When she opens the door and only her parents are there, the reality hits her.

"Oh, Megan, oh, darling," her mother says, leaping up from the couch for an encompassing embrace.

"How could this have happened, Mum?" Megan replies, eyes filled with tears.

"We'll get him back." Her father's low, rumbling voice puts an end to any possible hysteria. "We'll get him back even if I have to kill the bastard."

Megan calls Olivia, filling her in with a trembling voice. "I'll check in with someone I know who deals with recovery orders, make sure this one is fast-tracked," her friend says.

"Thanks, Liv."

"He'll be home soon. Your idiot ex is probably just trying to scare you. He'll bring him home stuffed with sugar so you'll be up all night dealing with him."

"I hope so, Liv, I really hope so."

An hour passes. Then two hours, then three.

"Connor and James went past his building," her mother reports after she speaks to Megan's brother. "James managed to speak to the landlord. He never lived there, Megan. He lied."

"But I don't understand, why would he lie?" *What have I missed? Why didn't I know? What is happening? Oh, Daniel, baby, where are you?*

Her father shrugs; her mother wipes her eyes. "Surely he'll bring him home soon."

Another hour passes, two hours, three hours and then it is midnight.

"Go home, Mum. You and Dad need to rest."

"We'll stay here with you."

"No, please, don't worry, just go home and rest. The detective said I need to go back in the morning. They've put out an alert."

"Okay, then. Try to get some sleep, Megs, just rest on the couch." Her mother wraps her arms around her and holds tightly. Megan doesn't want her to let go, but eventually her mother steps back. "Rest," she says, planting a kiss on Megan's forehead.

"I will," Megan replies as she sees her parents to the door.

After they have left, she calls Greg's cell over and over again, finally dropping into an exhausted doze with the phone clutched in her hand.

*

In the morning she wakes with a start, worrying she has overslept and that Daniel will be late for school, only to realize that Daniel is not in the apartment, not in his bed.

He is gone. He has been taken by his father. She curls herself up, holds her cushion against her mouth, and screams until her throat burns.

CHAPTER THREE

Daniel—six years old

It's Daddy. Daddy, Daddy, Daddy.

"A special surprise," Daddy says.

Daniel loves Daddy, loves him more than anything. Daddy lets him watch as much TV as he wants to. Daddy lets him eat chocolate for breakfast and fries for lunch. Daddy likes to play Xbox and he doesn't care about bedtimes. Daddy is the best and Daniel knows he's sad that he can't see him every day.

"It's not my fault," Daddy has told him. "I love Mum and I want to live with you and her so we can be together every day, but Mum won't let me."

Daniel feels mad at Mum sometimes because she won't let Daddy live with them, but sometimes he loves her as well. Before Daddy went to live somewhere else, Mum used to cry in the bathroom. Now she doesn't cry, but he misses Daddy. A lot of the time he's not sure what to think or to feel. He wishes he was bigger so he could understand about Divorce. Divorce is a big ugly word and he doesn't like it at all. Divorce makes Daddy sad and Mum cross. Divorce is bad.

Daniel jumps up and Daddy catches him and Ms. Abramson says, "Aren't you a lucky boy to have your daddy pick you up?" and Daniel laughs because Daddy is the best.

"Chips!" he shouts because Daddy always buys him hot fries, all salty and crunchy but soft inside.

"Whatever you want, my little man. Whatever you want."

CHAPTER FOUR

Evie moves an arm forward, followed by a knee, and then she repeats the process. Megan notes somewhere in her brain that her daughter has just made her first attempt at crawling and that she would like to take a video to show Michael, but there is a ringing in her ears that is so loud it has almost paralyzed her. In the kitchen she slumps onto the floor and presses the phone against her ear.

"How?" she asks because she cannot think of anything else to say.

"Apparently he walked into a police station in Heddon Greta and told them who he was."

"What?" She is trying to breathe but her body doesn't seem to know how to do that. She cannot get her lungs to expand enough. She pants like she remembers doing in labor with Evie.

"Okay, Megan, I need you to calm down."

"I am calm," whispers Megan. *Concentrate, calm down, think straight, listen. Daniel, Daniel, Daniel.*

"You sound like you've just run a marathon. I don't want you to hyperventilate. Just take some deep breaths. Where's Evie?"

"She's here, she's... I think she's crawling. She just started crawling." Megan inhales deeply, finally, and holds it for a count of five before letting it out slowly.

"That's... that's great. She's getting so big... I wish I was there. Are you okay, Megan, are you still with me?"

"I'm okay. I'm here. Where's Heddon Greta?"

"It's a town just outside of Newcastle, in New South Wales."

"In New South...? You mean here in Australia? Not in the UK?"

"Yes, here."

"But I thought he was in the UK. You said, everyone said, that Greg must have taken him there and then just disappeared. You had records of him getting on a plane, you had witnesses, you had..." Megan's voice rises as adrenaline floods her body.

"I'm sorry, Megan... You have no idea how sorry I am. I can't believe we've... I've let you down like this but we were wrong."

"You were wrong?" A simple statement of fact. The words cannot convey the magnitude of such a mistake. What if she had known he was in Australia? What if? How different would her life be now? She would have never given up on finding him. She would have knocked on every door across the country, renewed her appeals on Facebook and television, talked to police in every state. She would not have given up.

"We were wrong. He did go to the UK and he did disappear for a short while but sometime in the past six years he must have returned. He's been living in a small town called Heddon Greta; they've been living there together. It's about half an hour from Newcastle. It's a small town with a three-man police station and some stores."

"So, he's still there now? What did he say? Is he okay? Where is Greg?"

"Sorry, Megs, right now I don't know much more than that."

"Heddon Greta," Megan repeats, as if that will make what she is hearing any more plausible. It doesn't.

Evie has crawled forward a meter and finds herself unable to move anymore. She shouts, "Gaah," furious with her uncooperative body, and then she begins to cry.

Megan stands and goes to pick her up.

"Megan, are you still there? Are you okay?" asks Michael.

"I am, I'm still here but I have to feed Evie and put her to sleep. I can't... I can't do this right now, not with her crying. I'll put her down for her nap and call you back."

"Do you need me to come home? I'm getting up now. I'm coming home."

"No . . . don't worry, I just need to get Evie into her bed for her nap and then I need to know, I need to know everything. How do you—"

Evie shrieks in her ear.

"I'll call you back and you can start at the beginning."

"Okay . . . but if I don't hear from you in an hour I'm coming home."

"I promise I'll call you. I will."

In the rocking chair in Evie's room, Megan watches her daughter drink. Evie reaches up as she feeds to touch Megan's black hair and pat her cheek as if she senses her mother needs comforting. Her big brown eyes blink slowly as she grows closer to sleep. Megan bites down on her lip. She wants to scream or cry or something but the endless ringing in her head is still bothering her, and what she mostly feels is utter confusion. *How has this happened? How did I not know he was so close?* "Daniel," she murmurs, earning a smile from her daughter, who has no idea of the existence of her big brother. Relief floods her body as Evie succumbs to sleep.

Over the last six years she has imagined thousands of scenarios in which her son is found, in which he comes back to her. At first, she thought it would be simple. The police in the UK would go to the house where Greg's parents lived, Greg and Daniel would be there, Greg would be arrested, and she would fly over and collect her son. That scenario kept her going for weeks despite the evidence to the contrary, despite Greg's parents denying having seen him, and the police confirming that there was no evidence of them having been at their house. As the years passed the scenarios changed with time. She imagined that Greg would get tired of raising his son, that he would remarry and have other children and simply send Daniel back to her. She imagined that Greg would call one day, apologizing and apologizing, and they would meet and discuss joint custody. She pictured a car accident where Greg would die but her son would miraculously be fine and his details would be found on the missing persons database.

What she has not imagined is this scenario—this scenario in which, after years of hoping, praying, and then grieving, she has found a place to put him in her mind so that she can move forward with her life. This scenario in which she has another child and has basically given up all hope of seeing her son again until he is eighteen and hopefully makes the decision to contact her again—only for him to return. She has not prepared for this. How can he have casually walked into a police station and told them who he is after all this time? Why has he never told anyone before? Where has he been? Why has he never tried to contact her if he has been in Australia? Why has no one recognized him from all the photos that the media and police sent out over the years?

Evie is deeply asleep in her arms and Megan stands up and lowers her gently into her crib, covering her with her wrap and placing her soft doll next to her to play with when she wakes up. She straightens up and looks around Evie's room, with its light-pink-colored walls and tumbling bunny decals. When Daniel was a baby his room was painted white with a yellow border because they didn't find out if he was a boy or a girl before he was born. Greg hadn't wanted to know, and even though Megan had, the choice had not been hers to make. "It's my first child, Megan, don't ruin this for me," Greg had hissed.

It's my first child too, Megan had thought but had been wise enough not to say. She knew the result of a quick comeback, knew the rage it would engender.

Megan scratches at her neck. She has managed months now without thinking about Greg, without hating him with a visceral heat, but here he is, right back in her brain.

She goes back to the kitchen to get her cell phone as the ringing slowly fades away and more questions begin to form in her mind.

"How do they know it's him?" she asks Michael when he answers his phone. There was a boy four years ago who was found in an abandoned house in the UK. He was the right age. He had curly brown hair like Daniel did, and people had seen him with a man who looked like Greg. The man had disappeared and it was assumed that the little boy had gone with him, leaving the house empty for months until the council turned up to begin clearing the home for demolition. That's when they found the boy's body.

Megan doesn't like to think about those few brutal days as she waited for pictures to come through official channels, refreshing her email again and again in the hopes that those few seconds would mean the photos had arrived, and then the suffocating heartbreak as she waited again to view the body via webcam because the images were not clear. He would have changed, she knew that, and the child's body was badly decomposed. But on the webcam, it was obviously not Daniel.

Megan remembers how long she sat crying, how much she drank, filling her glass with acidic white wine over and over as she tried to find a way to rid the image of the unloved little boy from her mind. She'd stayed in bed for a week, unable to eat, unable to sleep, pulled back to the first dark days after Daniel disappeared. Now, she knows she cannot go through such a thing again, so when Michael doesn't immediately answer, she repeats, "How do they know it's him?"

"He told them his name. He told them that Greg Stanthorpe was his father and then he told them he's been living in a house and that there had been a fire."

"A fire... Is he... Is he okay?"

"According to the officer I've been speaking to at the Heddon Greta station, he seems physically fine. He wasn't wearing any shoes or a sweater. His feet are pretty messed up but not as bad as what she would have expected for someone who walked at least ten kilometers. He has blisters and some cuts but he's basically okay, so she thinks he may have hitched a ride with someone at some point, although he denied it when they asked him. She and her fellow officer are looking into that. He won't answer any questions about how he got there. He told them a few things and then just clammed up. He just repeats his name any time they try to question him further."

"Is he hurt? Has he been hurt?" Shock floods her body at the thought of her son in pain.

"No, just the blisters and cuts on his feet according to her. But she has no idea how he would have made the journey without help because he lived somewhere in the middle of some bush, in what was basically a shack, apparently."

"A shack?" Confusion ripples through her. "How do they know where he lived?"

"He explained it to them and they were able to find it. It's on the edge of a state forest, owned by someone who lives overseas and doesn't want to sell it."

"Maybe Greg dropped him off, maybe he didn't want to take care of him anymore?"

"No... no, they don't think so."

"Why? What do you mean?"

Michael grows silent and Megan hears the pencil's rapid beat as he tries to find a way to tell her what he is about to tell her.

"Daniel told them Greg was dead, that he burned in the fire."

"Oh... God, is he sure, are they sure?" She is surprised by an instant and overwhelming feeling of guilt as she remembers how many nights she has lain awake in the last six years, her mind churning with the words, *I wish you were dead, I wish you were dead, I wish you were dead.*

"Right now, they don't know. When the local guys found the shack, they discovered that it had been burned down. Completely obliterated, really. A woman who lives on a property nearby reported that she saw fire and smoke and she heard one explosion, which may have been a gas bottle, but she assumed it was back burning going on in preparation for summer."

"But there are no explosions in back burning."

"They're not sure if she did or didn't actually hear an explosion. She's nearly ninety and prone to confusion. An explosion would explain the condition of the house. She said the fire went on for a while, maybe a few hours, and the smoke was beginning to bother her—but again, she thought it was back burning. That night there was one of those major storms that just goes for hours and hours. The rain must have put out the fire and there was nothing left by the time they got there. It's hard for them to tell right now without an investigation if there are human remains in the house or not." He whispers the last few words.

Megan feels bile rise in her throat, and she sees the decomposed body of the little boy on the webcam again. The image will never leave her. *It's not Daniel, it's not him, not him.*

"Could Daniel be wrong? Could Greg still be alive?"

"Officer Mara in Heddon Greta says Daniel seems certain that Greg is dead."

"He told them his father's dead... just like that?" *No child should have to utter those words*, she thinks, tears rolling down her face.

"According to Officer Mara, he was very distressed, hysterical when he began talking about it. They've calmed him down now and he's just stopped talking. It must be a reaction to the trauma."

Megan closes her eyes and sees her son at six. She mentally wraps her arms around him, shushing him, soothing him. *I'm so sorry you're sad, little man, my beautiful boy. I'm so sorry your heart is broken.*

"So, Greg is... he really is dead?" Megan needs to make sure she has heard correctly. She wants to feel sorry for Daniel's loss, but her relief that her son is fine, that he has not been hurt, makes this impossible. Her deepest, darkest wish has come true and it has brought her son back to her. It has brought her little boy home. She won't feel guilty about it.

"Well... yes. I'm sorry, Megs. I'm sorry."

"Why are you sorry? He took my son from me, *stole* my son from me." She is suddenly furious, sadness morphing into anger.

"He was Daniel's father."

Megan bursts into tears, listening to Michael trying to calm her down as she howls into the phone, sobs ripping through her body.

"I'm coming home," he says eventually.

"Yes," she chokes, "please come home."

When Michael arrives twenty minutes later, Megan is curled up on their bed, looking at a picture she has on her phone of six-year-old Daniel. In it he is watching some bubbles being blown by an entertainer at a party. It had been a science party for one of his classmates and they had made their own colored bubble water as one of the activities. Megan had arrived to pick up Daniel, finding him gazing rapturously at the different-colored bubbles floating in the air. Instead of calling to him she had taken out her phone and snapped a photo, wanting to preserve the wonder in Daniel's eyes. She has looked at this image every day for six years—every single day. The pure joy on his beautiful face has made her cry more times than she could ever count.

"Evie?" asks Michael as he sits gently on the end of the bed.

"She's still sleeping," murmurs Megan, not taking her eyes off the photo.

Michael slips off his shoes and slides next to her. He wedges a pillow behind his head and Megan shuffles over to him, resting her head on his chest, feeling calmed by his familiar smell and the sensation of his arms around her. She wonders at the way the universe works. If Daniel had never been taken, she would never have met Michael. She would never have known her strong, gentle husband and they would never have had baby Evie. On that first devastating afternoon when Michael had stood up from behind his desk in his office, she had looked up at the tall, broad-shouldered man, noting his dark brown eyes, and she had thought, *You will find him. You will find my son.*

So much suffering has led her to where she is now. She would never wish Michael and Evie away, and she can only be grateful that Michael was the detective she spoke to on that terrible day all those years ago, but she has missed six years with her child, her son, her boy.

"I think this is for real," Michael says, squeezing her hand.

"I'm afraid it's not," replies Megan, a tremor in her voice. There have been false alarms over the years, aside from the little boy in the abandoned house. Daniel and Greg have been sighted in the USA, in Mexico, and in China, but there were never any records of their passports being used.

The private detective she'd hired in the UK had never closed the case, and every six months or so he would send her a bill for work he claimed he was doing until Megan married Michael and he put a stop to what he said was a "useless waste of money."

"*I'm* a detective," he'd assured Megan. "I'm good at what I do," he'd said gently. "Even though I no longer work with missing persons, I promise I will always keep the case open. I will never stop looking for him. But from what I can see, this guy isn't doing much except writing a one-paragraph report every six months and then charging you for each word."

Everyone in Megan's family had said more or less the same thing. "He's a con artist," her father repeated whenever Megan called to tell him that the detective had a new lead. There was a boy in London, a boy in Beaconsfield, a boy in Castleford. But it was never Megan's boy. "He's taking your money," her father had said, "money you don't even have, and he's doing nothing at all. He could be making all of this up."

"You don't know that, Dad. Tomorrow he could find him or next week he could find him or next month. If I give up now, then who is going to look for my son? Who will search for Daniel?"

It had taken days and days of Michael pointing out the obvious mistakes the detective was making before Megan had agreed to give him up. She had struggled to accept that no one would be actively looking for Daniel anymore. Every day when she woke up, her first thought was always, *This could be the day they find him. This could be the day he comes home.* Firing the private detective meant that she could no longer open her eyes with that thought. She felt she was losing him all over again. Giving up hope was tantamount to giving up on him.

But then something else had happened, something that made Megan toss and turn through nights riddled with guilt. Once she had worked through the pain, the agonizing pain, she had found a way to finally accept what had happened. She hadn't seen her son for five years by then. In the beginning each breath had hurt, each passing hour had been impossible to bear, and the idea of a whole day without seeing her son was horrifying. But when Michael convinced her to stop paying the detective, some tiny part of her had also felt a sense of relief. There was nothing more she could do—she had to get on with her life and hold on to the hope that one day an adult Daniel would walk back into her life.

She'd prayed every night for her missing child, for him to be found, for Greg to be treating him kindly and raising him well. She'd prayed for Greg to love his son enough for the both of them, and it was only by remembering how much Greg loved Daniel that she was able to find comfort in her son being with his father. On the internet, she'd found a group of people who understood her experience. Her close relationship with two of them had helped her as much as her friends and family.

"I have a picture on my phone—are you ready to see it?" Michael asks, tearing her away from her thoughts.

Megan closes her eyes. "I'm so afraid, Michael. I'm scared to believe, only to have my hopes dashed. I'm terrified of going through that again."

"I know, Megs, but to me the photo looks a lot like the age progression image we have on the fridge, except his hair is much longer. And I have to ask myself why anyone would want to say he's Daniel Stanthorpe if he isn't. What would be the point? There would be no reason for a stranger to have any information on him. His case hasn't been in the news for years. I honestly think this is him."

"Okay," says Megan, inhaling deeply. She sits up. "Show me." She tries to temper the hope flaring inside her, tries to force herself to approach the picture with logic, but she cannot stop the feeling from taking over her body.

Michael hands her his phone. The photo has been taken in a room with a leather couch and a picture of a landscape on the wall. There is a window and a box of tissues on a chipped coffee table. Megan studies each of these things carefully, managing to studiously avoid looking directly at the skinny boy sitting on the couch, for fear that it is not her son. When she feels that she will see the room in her dreams, she finally looks directly at the boy. She starts with his hands, noting the long, tapered fingers and bony wrists, and then she moves her eyes over the rest of him, seeing his long, wavy brown hair, his full lips, and his eyes. His eyes that look brown because of the flash of the camera but that she knows, as she examines his whole face, will take on a green hue in the sun. Hazel eyes. Such beautiful, wide, hazel eyes that were always full of wonder for the world.

The boy in the photo is not smiling. He doesn't look angry or unhappy. He simply looks detached, as though his picture has been taken when he is thinking about something else entirely even though he is staring directly at the camera. There is a slight pull in her full breasts, a sensation that she experiences when she looks at Evie and it's nearly time for her to feed. Her body recognizes the boy even though he looks nothing like the picture Megan has in her mind, despite the age progression photos pinned to her fridge.

"I think it's him," she whispers, hearing the words, believing the words. "I think it's him." She covers her mouth with her hand and then bites down a little on one of her fingers as she nods her head. "It's him," she repeats, dropping her hand, "it's him." Tears splash onto her chest. The impossible has become possible.

"Okay," says Michael. He reaches forward to take the phone from her but Megan finds herself unable to let go as if she can somehow hold onto the truth of his existence if she just keeps looking at the picture, drinking in every detail. She sniffs and takes the tissue Michael has handed to her.

"Oh, sweetheart," he says. He leans back against the pillows on the bed and places his hand on her knee, squeezing a little, and they sit in silence for a few minutes while she gazes at the photo of her son. Her Daniel. Finally, Michael takes the phone gently from her hands and forwards the image to her phone. When Megan hears the text notification, she grabs her phone and opens up the picture, and when she sees it is there, she feels her shoulders slump forward, relieved that the photo has not disappeared into thin air, stealing away the evidence of her son's existence.

"If we leave soon, we can get there before six," says Michael.

"Yes," replies Megan, still staring at the picture.

"Babe, I need you to get up now. You need to get organized so that we can go," he says gently, softly.

"What if I had said it wasn't him?"

"We still would have gone to make sure. It's only a two-hour drive and you would have needed to give a DNA sample anyway, although I'm not sure if they're set up for that there. And I think you should call your parents. Tell them what's happened and ask if they can have Evie for the rest of the day. Then let's check that you've expressed enough milk for her."

"Okay," agrees Megan, unable to comprehend the practicalities. This is one of the things she has come to rely on Michael for: his ability to bullet point any situation so that it can be managed. She will follow his instructions because she can't think for herself right now. She gets off the bed and goes to the kitchen, pressing her mother's number as she opens the fridge to check her milk supply.

"Mum," she says when her mother answers.

"What's wrong?" asks her mother, Susanna, displaying her ability to notice even the slightest change in Megan's voice.

"They found him," says Megan.

"Oh God... no," says her mother.

"No... no he's fine... he's fine," she says, and for the first time since Michael called her, she experiences a rush of pure elation through her body. "They've found Daniel, Mum." She starts giggling and, even without knowing all the details, her mother joins her as they celebrate the return of the boy they both love and adore and have missed for six long, torturous years.

CHAPTER FIVE

Megan feels a fluttering in her stomach somewhere between excitement and nausea. She and Michael have made the two-hour drive largely in silence. She has spent most of the time staring at the picture of Daniel on her phone, occasionally running her fingers over his face, a smile on her own.

Michael had tried to get her to talk about how she was feeling but she couldn't articulate what was going on in her head. Finally, he had turned on the radio and they had listened to a report on the missing British backpacker. "Mr. and Mrs. Hindley have flown in from England and they are deeply concerned about their twenty-five-year-old son," the reporter had said.

We never stop worrying, Megan had thought. *We mothers can never stop worrying.*

Her thoughts have careened wildly from certainty that everyone has made a mistake and the boy is not Daniel to absolute belief that her child is safe and will be sleeping in his old bed, set up and waiting for him, in her house tonight.

"Will they let me take him home? They have to let me take him home, don't they?"

"I think they will, Megs. I'll make sure of it."

She has tried not to dream up a pretty picture of family reunions and her and her son cuddled up close on the sofa sharing a pizza, but the images have flashed through her head uninvited anyway. As a new mother, she had often imagined what her child would be like as he grew. She had prepared herself for an awkward adolescent and a surly teenager, had promised herself to always remember the vulnerable baby in her arms.

When Greg had taken him, he hadn't just taken her son in the present; he'd robbed him from her in the future as well. It was not something Megan could ever have forgiven him for. She has wanted, many times over the last six years, to see Greg in jail for what he has done, but she knows that even if he had been found, he probably would have escaped a jail term. Greg would have argued that she'd agreed to let him take Daniel overseas, that she'd signed forms so he could get him a passport. Greg could be charming and convincing when he wanted to be. Megan knew that better than anyone. She had found herself easily persuaded out of her own opinions and thoughts for years.

In the car she has made a list of questions to ask Daniel, and then has abandoned that list and exhorted herself to let him lead the way. She has also decided that when she gets to the station the officer will say, "Sorry, that child's parents came to pick him up an hour ago." Or, "Sorry, his father who we thought was dead came to get him and they've disappeared again." When Greg picked him up from school and left the country with him, he made the impossible possible, and so now Megan knows that even the most ludicrous thought in her head may very well eventuate. She has had to learn the hard way.

But now the drive is over and she and Michael are standing outside the same small room where the photo of Daniel was taken. The door is closed but Megan knows it's the same room. She can almost feel her body pulling toward it as her heart races.

It is after five and the winter sun has disappeared, leaving a chill in the air, but she is sure she's not shivering from the cold. Heddon Greta is as small as Michael described it. They have driven through kilometers and kilometers of forest filled with pine trees and layered green bush. There are no people anywhere and Megan assumes they have been driven inside by the cold. The empty street has an eerie, postapocalyptic feeling to it, as though some disaster has caused all of the residents to disappear.

In the police station, three officers are sitting at a desk, each drinking a beer. The workday is over but Megan fights the urge to tell the woman and two men that what they're doing is inappropriate under the circumstances. All three look up as she and Michael walk in. The two men quickly return to their beers.

A young Asian woman in a starched police uniform with perfectly pleated pants stands up and quickly walks across the floor. "You must be Megan Stanthorpe," she states, smiling a little.

"Yes," answers Megan. But Stanthorpe is not her surname, not anymore. She glances at Michael, who nods. He understands.

"I'm Officer Mara, we spoke on the phone," continues the woman, holding out her hand to Michael.

"Thanks for waiting for us," Michael says as he grasps her hand.

"No problem. This way." She walks over to the door and opens it slightly, allowing Megan to look inside. Megan puts her hand over her mouth, not wanting to call out to her son before she's had a chance to look at him. Her body is shaking, her heart racing. *What if it's not him? What if it is him? Will I recognize him? Will he recognize me?*

The boy, Daniel, is sitting on the couch absorbed in a game he is playing on a cell phone that reminds Megan of an old phone she had years ago. He bears only a passing resemblance to the computer-generated image she was given by the police only a month ago. He has always been portrayed with short, brown, curly hair and the boy sitting on the couch has long hair halfway down his back. The tangled curls give him a feral look as though he has been living in the bush for years, which for all Megan knows he may well have been. At six, his face—despite his skinny body—was round, slightly chubby with cheeks she used to cover in kisses. Now his face is elongated with sharp, angled cheekbones as though the lengthening of his body has continued past his neck.

Megan feels a tightening in her breasts and hopes she won't leak. She has left Evie with her mother, who took the child wordlessly, her eyes filling with tears, unable to say anything.

"Ready?" asks Michael. He places a hand on her shoulder, and as he takes a deep breath, she does as well.

She nods even though she is not ready, and as she looks at the boy on the couch, she realizes that she could never really be ready for her son at twelve years old. He has been six years old in her head for the last six years, and that is the Daniel that she would like to see sitting on the couch now. That boy she would recognize. That is the boy she has missed. The Daniel that was stolen from her.

Officer Mara goes into the room and sits down on the couch next to him. Megan cannot hear what she's saying. He doesn't take his eyes off the phone but he begins to nod as the officer speaks, and then when she points at Megan, he finally lifts his head and looks at her. She stands up straight and then pats her hair without meaning to. Her son is almost unrecognizable from the little boy he had been. Even sitting down Megan can see that he is probably taller than her now. Greg is—was—over six foot, and when Daniel was born Megan had hoped that he would not just share his father's eye color and wavy hair but also his height. Now she can see that this is the case and her heart aches once again for all that she has missed. He will be thirteen soon. He had been taken three months before his seventh birthday, exactly three months. He has been gone for six years, one month, and four days. And now he is sitting on a couch in a police station, looking at her.

His childhood is over. She watches as he reacts to seeing her and wonders if she looks older to him. At thirty-eight she has just begun dyeing her black hair to cover the gray, and she knows that even though she had Evie only six months ago, she is thinner than she was before he was taken. She has been carrying around the image of her six-year-old son all this time and he has probably been carrying around an image of a much younger woman. Perhaps he has even forgotten what she looks like, her face fading from his memory with each passing year. Megan can feel she is holding her breath as her son looks at her.

Daniel stands up and walks over to the door and Megan moves quickly to be there.

"Mum... Mum... Mum." His voice catches in his throat, deeper, somewhat husky—almost the voice of a man. Megan can hear the tears he is holding back. She can do little except nod. Her eyes fill and her throat closes and she opens her arms.

"Hello, my beautiful boy," she whispers.

He looks at her for a moment and then he steps into her embrace, bends a little, and lays his head on her shoulder. He smells different—the thick odor of smoke clings to him—and he looks different, but for some reason he fits right where he should, despite his height and his age and everything that has happened.

"There, there, baby," whispers Megan as she rubs his back in circles the way she did when he was a newborn. "There, there." Megan lets go of the breath she has been holding and feels a lightness enter her body, as though she has not just let go of the breath she was holding in this moment but the breath she has been holding for the last six years. *Six years, one month, and four days.*

They stand together as night falls. Megan does not let go until Daniel pulls away a little.

"I've missed you," she says, encapsulating six agonizing years into three simple words.

"I've... missed you too."

Megan cannot remember exactly what he sounded like at six years old. She has some videos on her phone but she has not watched them in a year or two. Pictures are easier to bear.

"You're so tall."

"You're not," he says and then he smiles. His even, white teeth remind her that on the day Greg took him, Daniel had looked at her and proudly shoved his tongue through the gap where his four front teeth had been.

"I can feel the new ones, Mum."

"Better make sure you brush them every night so they'll be strong forever," she had replied. *Did Greg make him brush his teeth twice a day? Did he stand next to him and say, "Make sure you get the back ones?" Oh, how I missed watching you brush your teeth.*

Daniel looks at Michael, who is standing a little behind Megan.

"Hey, Daniel, I'm Michael. I'm your—"

"He's my husband," Megan jumps in, hearing the awkwardness in his voice.

"I'm pleased to meet you finally."

Daniel stares at Michael's large, outstretched hand for a moment until Michael drops it back down to his side. His eyes narrow and his face flushes a little.

"You're bigger than I thought you'd be," Daniel says to him.

"What do you mean?" asks Megan.

"I mean, I thought if you got married again it would be to someone like Dad. Someone tall and thin but he's . . . he's bigger than Dad."

"He's not like Dad," Megan says, four words filled with so much meaning.

"No, not Dad at all," agrees Daniel, and his lips curl a little as though he finds this idea disgusting.

Megan is struck by his behavior and she finds herself realizing with a thud that although the past six years have been difficult, often intolerable, things will not be much easier now. The skinny adolescent before her may be nothing like the six-year-old she lost. He is nearly a teenager. He has been living in the bush with his father and no one has any idea for how long. She cannot fathom the things he may have seen or the experiences he has had. Who is he now? And will he still love the person she is today, the way he did when he was six years old?

"I think we should get home before it gets too late," she says brightly.

"I'll sort out the paperwork," says Michael, leaving Megan and Daniel to stare at each other.

"Your hair is really long," she comments.

He touches his hair as though this is something he didn't know.

"Do you want to sit down for a bit while Michael finishes the paperwork?"

He nods and they move back to the couch. "What game were you playing on the phone?" Megan asks. All her prepared questions seem to have vanished. She cannot think of a single thing to ask him.

"*Snake Xenzia*."

"Is it... is it a game you've played before?"

"Yeah. I only have a couple of games on this." He starts another round of the game.

"Oh, that's your phone. How long have you had it?"

"A while. It was only in case of emergencies so I could call... Dad. I thought I broke it when I was running. I dropped it on the ground but that other policeman, his name is Gary, see that one with the beard? He put it back together, except I lost the SIM card. I don't know where it is." He hangs his head and Megan watches him play the game for a few minutes until she sees "game over" flash on the screen. She would like him to look at her but can sense his discomfort. It is easier to stare at the small screen. She holds her hands clenched in her lap, preventing herself from touching him in case he doesn't want to be touched. She lifts one hand a little—*Maybe I should put my arm around him*—but then drops it. *What will I do if he pulls away?*

"Why were you running, Daniel?" she asks softly, noticing a light gray streak of soot under his chin and the acrid smell of smoke on him.

He shrugs his shoulders, his gaze focused on the screen, as he starts a new game.

"We can get you a new SIM card," she says.

"I only had one number on it," he says, starting another round. "It was only to call Dad. I won't need to call him now."

"Oh, baby," whispers Megan.

He doesn't look up from his game. "It's an old phone," he says as his fingers press the keys, making the snake move as it chases apples around the screen. "I've seen lots of much nicer ones on the computer. Some people have hundreds of games on their phones but I was only allowed two. I wasn't allowed any games on the computer either."

"Why?"

"Rots your brain, turns you into a mindless zombie. Our computer got burned. It was old but it still worked. It got burned though."

Megan studies her son. He is obviously repeating something that has been said to him again and again over the years. Greg's thoughts have become his thoughts. She knows how that feels, how easy it is to just train yourself to think and say what Greg needs you to think and say. She wonders if Daniel fought against that as hard as she did, but then she realizes that he is a child. He wouldn't have been able to fight at all.

How will she navigate the minefield that is his return? Because she knows it will be a minefield. There is so much she doesn't know, so many questions she wants to ask but probably shouldn't. She doesn't want to say the wrong thing to him but she has no idea what the right thing to say would be. There's a lot of information on the internet about how to survive your child being taken from you but very little on what to do if he comes back. *Don't think about that, just breathe him in. See him. Here he is.* She cannot stop her eyes from roaming up and down his body. He has a wart on his thumb and a cut on his hand. He has two pimples on his chin and freckles over his nose and cheeks. His skin is darker than it was, as though he has spent a lot of time in the sun. His feet are filthy and covered in Band-Aids.

"Are your feet sore?"

He stretches his legs out and stares at his feet as though he is seeing them for the first time. "I have blisters and some cuts. A stone went into this heel but I got it out," he says, pointing.

"I'll take a look when we get…home, put some cream on for you."

"My feet are tough. I don't like wearing shoes."

Megan remembers buying him his first pair of school shoes, remembers him running up and down inside the shop. "They make me feel big and strong, Mum." *Why would he not like wearing shoes? What kind of life has he been living?*

"I'm sure they are," she says, and finding herself unable to resist touching him, she leans forward to hug him again but he flinches and moves back.

She tries not to feel hurt by the rebuttal. "This must feel really weird."

"It is. You look…you look older, not how I remember you. You're thin."

She smiles, nodding, and wills herself not to cry. *He remembers me.* "I run a lot."

"You never used to like running."

"I like it now. Do you like… running?" Megan feels like she is on an awkward first date. The language she and Daniel had, the easy way they spoke to each other, their mutual understanding is no longer there.

"Off to bed, little monster."

"Raah, monsters don't need to sleep."

"Monsters who like Nana's chocolate cake do."

"Okay, only after story time in your bed."

She searches her mind for another question to ask him as he starts another game.

"I don't like sports," he says to her.

"No, you never did. Do you still like to draw?"

"I haven't done that much. Paper is expensive and so are proper pencils." His face clouds and his eyes dull. At two he had stood next to her at a small easel and copied her as she painted a simple cat, a house, a tree. An old T-shirt of hers had hung from his neck to his toes, covered in paint because he kept touching the colors and then wiping his hands on the shirt. "I do a cat," he had said seriously, and she had watched as he'd drawn a circle but placed the triangle ears floating somewhere above the head. He had loved creating from the very beginning. She feels an ache inside her that he has lost this passion.

"I have lots of stuff you can use."

"I don't care about it that much anymore," he mumbles, and Megan's stomach sinks.

"All done," interrupts Michael. "You just need to sign some stuff and then we can go." He is standing at the door with Officer Mara.

"I won't be long and then we can go home," Megan says to Daniel.

"My home burned down," he states as he stands up. "It burned to the ground. There's nothing left... nothing at all."

"There's always something left," says Officer Mara.

"What could be left? My dad burned up in that fire!" says Daniel, his voice rising.

"Well... there will be bones," she replies, forgetting who she is speaking to. "Oh, no." Her hand flies to her mouth and her eyes widen as she hears her own shocking words. "I'm so sorry, I shouldn't have..."

Megan stares at the officer, unable to believe what she's just said.

"You won't find anything, nothing at all," Daniel says.

"It's true that they can always find something, Daniel, but it's not something you need to think about. It's going to be okay, it really is," says Michael quietly.

"No, no," repeats Daniel, shaking his head.

"We don't need to discuss this, not now. Now we're going home," Megan says, watching his face crumple as though he is suddenly feeling the enormity of his father's death. She knows that this terrible realization will strike him over and over again for years and she wishes she could steal away his pain.

"No, no," he mutters, sniffing and wiping his eyes.

"I know, baby, I'm so sorry. I know how hard this must be for you."

"But not for you because you hated him anyway. I bet you're glad he's... dead." As he whispers the last word, there is no anger in his voice, no acrimony behind his words. It's as if he is making a casual observation. The tears are gone.

Megan flinches and she looks at Michael and Officer Mara, who cannot hide the dismay from their faces.

"I think you need a good rest tonight, Daniel, maybe talk about all of this tomorrow," the officer says brightly. A deep red suffuses her face.

Megan wants to feel sorry for her but her horrifying words were unacceptable. How could she say such a thing? How could she have been so reckless?

"Yeah, tomorrow," agrees Daniel. His eyes return to the screen and he lowers himself back onto the couch.

Megan follows Officer Mara and Michael over to a desk where the officer Daniel has referred to as Gary is sitting. He hands her a pen and wordlessly points out where she needs to sign.

"Did you ever meet his father?" asks Michael.

"I didn't meet him but now that I've seen pictures, I realize I saw him around. You met him a couple of times, didn't you, Gary?" says Officer Mara.

"Yeah, I think they've only lived here for six months or so. He came into the pub and put a sign up for his handyman services on the corkboard a few months ago. We started talking and he asked me if there was any work around. I told him I'd put the word out. Saw him in the pub once or twice after that, shared a beer, but he wasn't a big talker."

Michael nods. "Did he ever mention Daniel?"

"Nah, mate, he told me he was staying out in the bush in that cabin owned by some guy who lives overseas. He's never here, but I didn't put two and two together until the kid told us where it was. The owner is gonna be pissed. We're bloody lucky that the volunteer fire guys had done some back burning and that it rained pretty soon after the fire started, otherwise we would have had a massive bush fire on our hands."

"He never said he had a child?" asks Megan. "Never mentioned his son?"

"Sorry." Gary lifts his hands up. "I've called the local school as well. He never went. No one knew your son existed. I thought the bloke was a loner, you know, like one of those guys who drifts from place to place, doing not much at all. We get a lot of drifters through here and lots of backpackers—we're looking for one right now... Steven Hindley. Stupid buggers think they're ready for the Australian bush but they never are. They have no idea."

"Thanks, that's all done," says Officer Mara, taking the pen from Megan, and they walk back over to the little room where Daniel is sitting, still playing the game. Megan thinks about all the games her niece, Lucy, has on her iPhone. Greg was obsessed with technology. When they were married, he always had to be the first person to have the latest phone or television. She remembers him waiting in line for hours for the latest iPhone more than once. He also managed to while away hours on his Xbox. Megan can't imagine him giving up all the games that he claimed helped him relax. He obviously purposefully kept Daniel away from a smartphone and a computer so he could keep him isolated, in the dark, separate from the outside world and any chance he may have had of finding his mother. He would have looked. She is sure he would have looked for her if he could have.

"Are we going now?" Daniel asks when he sees them.

"We are. Got everything?"

He nods.

"Don't forget the charger," says Officer Mara.

Daniel bends down and unplugs the charger from the wall.

"It was all he was carrying," whispers the officer to Megan. "The phone was broken because he said he dropped it. Thankfully Gary managed to put it back together again but he's lost the SIM. We did try and look out for it when we went to find the house, but we didn't see anything. He showed me some stuff on the phone. There are lots of pictures of him and his dad."

Megan bites down on her lip, thinking about all the years of pictures she's missed.

"Let's get going," says Michael. "Ready to go home, Daniel?"

"I need the bathroom."

"You know where it is," says Officer Mara.

Megan watches her son slouch off.

"Greg never told anyone he had a son," Megan murmurs.

"He was hiding," says Michael.

"There are people I know now who don't know that I have a son, and Greg never told anyone he existed. It's like we both just wiped him out."

"That's not what happened; you didn't do that at all, Megs. You never stopped looking for him and neither did I—that's why we were contacted so quickly. The case has stayed open," says Michael.

"But that's what it feels like." Megan runs her hands through her hair. *How have I let this happen? What kind of a mother am I?*

"He hasn't exactly been talkative," Officer Mara says. "Someone will need to come out to you at some point and talk to him about what happened, but so far all he's told us is where he lived and his name and a few other basic things. He doesn't seem to want to answer any other questions. He may be in shock—I wanted to get the local doctor to look him over but he's been out at one of the remote properties all day. Maybe get your own doctor to see him. We also need to get a DNA sample in case we find... something, which we haven't managed to do because we're waiting for kits to be sent from Newcastle. It's important that you do that as soon as you can at one of the local hospitals when you get back to Sydney. The coroner will need that information. I've given Detective Kade the details, but of course he knows the procedure so I think it's okay for you to take him home."

"We'll sort it out," Michael says.

Daniel ambles back over to where they are standing. He is holding his phone and his charger in his hand but something has been stuffed into the pocket of his pants.

Michael says, "What have you got there, mate?"

Daniel looks down at where Michael is pointing. "Nothing."

Michael doesn't say anything; he just keeps looking at the bulging pocket.

Daniel sighs and puts his hand in the pocket. He pulls out what can only be described as a crude knife.

"What's that?" Megan asks sharply, stepping back, away from him.

"Daniel!" says Officer Mara, and she also takes a step back.

He looks at the knife in his hand as though he was unaware of its existence. "It's my knife, I made it. It's my knife."

"You need to put that down, Daniel," says Michael quietly.

Daniel is not holding the knife in a threatening manner but the fact that he has it, that he has had it all along, frightens Megan. He looks around at the assembled adults. The knife looks like it was carved out of a piece of wood with a blade inserted in the middle.

"Why do you have a knife?" asks Michael. He seems very calm, very controlled, and for a moment Megan wonders why he's not panicking, but then she realizes that he needs to remain calm so that Daniel stays calm. Her son seems bewildered by the reaction of the adults around him.

"Can I see it?" asks Michael, and slowly, Daniel lifts his arm and hands him the knife. It has an intricate pattern of crisscrossed black lines covering the handle. The blade looks like it's been forced in and has probably come from a box cutter.

"It's very interesting—how did you make the design?" asks Michael. He holds on to the knife tightly and Megan watches her son, watches his body language to see if he will try to get the knife back, but his shoulders slump and he makes no attempt to reclaim it.

"I used wood, heated it in a fire, and burned them on," says Daniel. Megan can hear some pride in his voice at the achievement.

"Who . . . who taught you to do that?" asks Officer Mara.

Daniel looks at her. "No one," he says finally.

"I'm afraid I'm going to have to take that, Daniel," says Officer Mara. "It's illegal for you to carry a knife. Why didn't you tell me about it before? Where have you been keeping it?"

"In my pants," he says. "It's mine. I wanted to show you," he says quietly, looking at Megan. "I made it and I wanted to show you."

Megan nods, unsure of what to say. The knife is clearly an artistic project to him. He wanted to show her that he was still doing something creative. She wants to tell the officer that Daniel should be allowed to keep the knife but that's obviously impossible.

"I'm sorry, you can't keep it," she says.

He looks down at his feet and shrugs.

"Right, home time," says Michael, forced cheer in his voice.

Daniel sweeps his eyes up and down Michael's body. "I live with my mum now," he says. And then he walks toward the front of the police station and out the door.

CHAPTER SIX

Tuesday, May 20, 2014

One year since Daniel was taken

Megan is woken by her cell phone. She ignores it, burrows under the covers, licking her dry lips. She could use some water, some coffee, something. She knows it will be her mother on the phone, knows that the fact that she has ignored the call means Susanna will be getting in her car right now to come and check on her daughter. Her mother has just turned seventy-five. She should no longer have to offer this level of care to one of her children. Megan can feel guilt over her behavior gnawing away at her, but it is nothing in comparison to the agony of *this* day.

I can't bear it.

I can't bear it.

I can't bear it.

Last night she had prepared for today with two bottles of wine, meaning to sleep through most of it, but now her mother has called and she is awake and thirsty and engulfed by misery. She flings back the covers and silences her phone.

It's 8 a.m. Too early to be awake, too early to be dealing with this.

She gets up, uses the bathroom and then stands in the kitchen, greedily drinking a glass of water when she hears her mother's key in the lock.

"You didn't answer your phone."

"I was asleep, sorry."

"I was worried."

"I'm not going to off myself, Mum. I got drunk and overslept, that's all." Megan watches as the brutal words cause hurt and pain. Susanna doesn't like to think about what Megan has dubbed, humorously she thinks, "the night of the sleeping pills." She hadn't meant to take so many, she is sure; she just wanted to be able to sleep for more than an hour without waking again. She is certain she would have just had a very long sleep if her mother hadn't come by and found her sprawled on the couch. The trip to the hospital was unnecessary. "I only took six pills," Megan had stated at the time.

"Yes," the emergency room doctor had agreed, "but you were only supposed to take one and you mixed them with a bottle of wine."

Now, Susanna looks pained as she examines her daughter. "Is alcohol the solution then?" she asks. Megan can see her getting ready to deliver one of her "you have to be strong for Daniel" speeches.

"Please, please don't lecture me, not today, not now."

"I'm not... I'm sorry, that wasn't what I came to do. I know you've taken the day off so I wanted to know if you'd like to go out for the day. We can go to a movie or shopping? We could have lunch at that Italian place you like."

"I'm sorry, but I don't think I can cope with much except going back to bed."

"Megan, I know this is a hard day..."

"It's been a hard three hundred and sixty-five days—a hard year, Mum. Today is just a reminder of how hard."

"I miss him too. We all miss him but you're doing so well now. You're back at work and out of bed. I know this is going to be a difficult day, but I don't want you to let it overwhelm you."

Megan scratches at her arm. Sometimes she wants to lash out at her mother, spit scathing accusations. Her grief stirs itself up into anger with little provocation. *You told me to try and be nice to Greg. You told me to keep it cordial. You told me you didn't see any reason why I shouldn't let Greg get Daniel a passport so he could take him to visit his parents.*

As quickly as the impulse to hurt her mother flares, it disappears and guilt takes over, and she regrets ever having the thought. She was the one who signed the papers to allow Greg to organize Daniel's passport—she is the one to blame.

At the time she had said, "I think he's too young to travel overseas without me, Greg."

"So, my parents don't get to see him ever again? Isn't it enough that you've taken my son from me, that you've broken up our home? You're going to deny him his grandparents too?"

"Greg, please."

"Just let me organize it, Megan. Nothing will happen until you say he's ready. I want to be able to tell my parents that they'll see their only grandchild again. Please, Megan, please let me just do this." His voice had flipped from aggressive to low and seductive, reminding her of the Greg she had been desperate to marry. His voice used to send shivers up her spine.

"Fine, Greg, okay, I'll sign the papers, but he's not going anywhere with you until I say it's okay."

"Of course not, not until you say it's okay."

Thinking about Greg's parents makes her burn with anger as she remembers the call she made to them one year ago today, remembers how she was dismissed by Audrey.

Only weeks after Daniel had been taken, a letter had arrived from her former mother-in-law, sent, it seemed to Megan, to almost gloat over the pain she was suffering. Megan had read it in her bed, unwashed and greasy-haired. As she'd read and reread Audrey's words, she had felt herself sinking into the mattress, wishing that she could simply close her eyes and disappear. There was no way she could find the energy to refute the things Audrey had written, and she knew that this was part of Greg's plan because that had always been part of Greg's plan. You could only say, "But that's not what happened," so many times before you ran out of energy to counter every argument and just subsided into silence.

Dear Megan,

I thought it best to get in touch with you by mail rather than on the phone. I find things tend to get misheard and misconstrued in a phone conversation, which is something that doesn't happen when the words are written down and cannot be disputed.

I want you to know that I speak for both William and me. I also want you to know that when Gregory told us the two of you were getting married, we were over the moon, and you know how delighted we were when Daniel was born. I am just sorry that we never got to see him more than we did. I know that Gregory wanted to come and visit every year but that you said it wasn't good for a child to travel so much. That's possibly true when they are young but I couldn't help feeling that you didn't want to share our grandchild with us.

I have to say that I wasn't surprised when Gregory told me about the divorce. We have always been very close, my son and I, and I know he had been unhappy for a long time. Being a wife and a mother and taking care of your husband and son was the most important job you had, but over the last years of your marriage you made Gregory feel that he was unimportant, that he was not wanted, and that he was only there to provide financial support for you and Daniel.

I always encouraged Gregory to try and be understanding of your needs, even though he knew I believed you were not treating him the way he deserved to be treated. He is, as is his father, a bit of a difficult man—but it is up to us women to use our ways and means to always make the men in our lives feel wanted and loved.

When Gregory took Daniel, I am sure he did it as a cry for help. You didn't just break his heart, Megan. You shattered it. He never stopped loving you, regardless of the way you treated him, and I am sure that if you had reached out to Gregory with love and acceptance, he would have been persuaded to bring Daniel home. Instead you sent the police to our home to accuse us of hiding Daniel from you. What kind of a person does such a thing?

You have no idea of the humiliation that William and I both felt when police turned up on our doorstep and demanded to search the house. They went through all our rooms and William's computer and our cell phones. I know that Gregory thought something like that would happen. He is a very clever man and no doubt wanted to protect his parents. Because of that he did not contact us and he still has not contacted us. I don't know if we will ever hear from him again. Do you understand what you've done? You have broken Gregory's heart and tried to take his son away from him, and you have left him with no other option but to take Daniel away from you. In doing this you have not only taken my grandson away from me, you have taken my son. Do not be confused, Megan. This is all your fault and you have brought the most terrible grief to William and myself.

There is little else I can say about this except I now regret ever telling Gregory that you would make a wonderful wife and mother. You clearly have been neither.

Please do not, under any circumstances, contact me or William again or I will be forced to go to the authorities.

Audrey Stanthorpe

She had known, as she went through the letter again and again, that Greg was telling Daniel lies about her, just like he was telling his parents lies about her. She had no doubt that he'd told lies about her to every person he'd ever met.

She had been too stunned to respond to Audrey's letter for a few days, but in the end she had because she knew it was possible that there would come a day when Greg contacted them. She labored over at least six letters—handwritten because Audrey hated email—in which she explained the truth about her marriage to Greg in the hope that Audrey would understand that Greg had painted her and their marriage in a horribly biased light. She kept writing until she received one final, two-line letter.

Please stop contacting us. We will no longer open your letters.

Megan wonders now how much Greg must have laughed at her naivety when she signed the forms to get her son a passport. She wonders how she let herself be manipulated, time and time again.

In her bedroom, her phone rings again.

"It will be Connor or James," Megan says. "Please answer it. I really don't want to speak to anyone."

Her mother leaves the room to get the phone.

"Megan," she says, returning and holding the phone out, "it's Detective Kade."

"Oh, oh God." A rush of nausea, a thrill of anticipation.

"No, Megs, it's nothing about Daniel. He's just phoning to find out how you are. He's just checking in."

"Just checking in?" Her body fires up with rage. "I don't need him to check in. I need him to find my son. Find my son, just find my son." Her throat cracks as she shrieks in the direction of the phone. Her mother colors, puts the phone against her ear. "I'm so sorry, it's a challenging day. I'm sure she's... grateful for the call."

"Stop speaking for me!" Megan yells and then she stomps to her room, a teenager in the middle of a tantrum. Her head is pounding. She wants to scream until she has no voice left. He's been gone for a year. One whole year. *Where are you, Daniel? Is your dad being kind to you? Do you miss me? Is he treating you well? Do you think about me? Do you cry for me?*

Megan flings herself down on her bed and opens her laptop, accessing her "Find Daniel" blog. Her comments section is filled with messages of support from those who know what day it is.

A month after Daniel was taken, Olivia had suggested starting a blog. It was meant, Megan knew, to be something tangible she could hold on to and maybe something that would eventually get her out of bed and back to walking around in the world.

"Think of it as an online diary, Megs, just someplace to put your thoughts down and maybe connect with other people going through the same thing."

"Why would I want my pain out there on the internet for everyone to gawk at?" she had protested.

"There will be other parents going through the same thing, other people who know exactly how you're feeling." Olivia had been standing in Megan's bedroom at the time, asked to come over by Megan's mother.

Just find a way to get her out of bed, Megan had imagined her mother saying to Olivia.

Megan had known that she smelled and her hair was a mess but she hadn't cared. It had been a month since Greg had taken Daniel, and the first few weeks of press and intense police involvement were over. Megan's emotional plea for Greg to return their son had been on every television channel for nearly a week. She had stared out at the camera with her parents behind her. "Please, Greg, I'm begging you, just bring him home and we'll work this out." A women's magazine had run a story with an awkward picture of her clutching Daniel's Billy Blanket and looking grief-stricken. "Just bring back my baby," the headline had screamed—words that Megan had not used.

Daniel's photo had been shared on Facebook twenty thousand times. Strangers had sent Megan information about child recovery teams, ex-military men and women who were trained to fly overseas and snatch your child back from the abducting parent.

"If it comes to that, we'll find the money to pay them," her father had assured her.

Every day had brought new leads—or supposed leads, because nothing led her to her son. But the news cycle was always hungry for fresh stories, and soon her search was mentioned in the news bulletin and then it was just a line at the bottom of the screen and then her story was no longer of interest. Everyone, it seemed, had other things to get on with.

Megan had known by then that Greg had left the country with Daniel to go to the UK. And she knew that he had never shown up at his parents' house—or at least that was what they said. No evidence of Greg and Daniel being at the home of Audrey and William Stanthorpe had been found; the trail was cold and they had simply disappeared. She'd known all these things but it had seemed to her at the time impossible to comprehend. How could a man and a child simply disappear? The father of her child, her baby boy?

The blog she had begun had helped her come to terms with that unbelievable fact. It had put her in touch with other mothers and fathers who knew exactly how easy it is for people to disappear.

Now she reads through the messages from brokenhearted mothers and fathers who also have a day this year where they mark just how long it has been since they've seen their child.

"Thinking of you on this sad day."

"Wishing you the best for today. Sending you courage."

"Hoping you have the strength to survive today."

What else can you say to someone who has had their child torn from them, and not by a stranger but by the person who was supposed to love them?

She opens Facebook, looking for messages from the only two people she really wants to hear from: Sandi and Tom.

As the months passed, messages and contact on her blog had slowed down quickly, and only a handful of people were left messaging her.

Sandi's first message had captured the way she was feeling so clearly that Megan had wondered if they had known each other in another life.

"*Believe that he can feel you missing him. Believe that when you touch his things you are sending your love to him. Believe that he will always remember how you raised him and loved him and that he will take comfort in this. But most of all believe that he will come back to you, regardless of what the police and the people around you say; believe it with all your heart. The bond between a mother and her child is the strongest there is. He will come back to you. And whatever you have to do to get him back—be open to doing that. He will come back.*"

Megan had thanked Sandi for her message, swiping tears away as she did and adding her as a Facebook friend so they could speak privately. This woman understood her, and she knew she needed her in her life.

Tom's message was different but no less personal and profound. Megan had been reluctant to speak to a man at first, firmly entrenched in the idea that because Greg had done this terrible thing, all men were capable of only terrible things. At one point she had even felt herself pulling away from her father and Connor and James. But Tom had made her aware that there were fathers who had lost their children, and that their hearts were as broken as hers was.

"*I know that you will go into his room because I go into her room. I sit on her bed and then I lie down and hold the soft, ragged doll that she used to sleep with, and what kills me is that my wife didn't take it with her. I don't know how my little girl has been sleeping without her doll, without her Jessie. I hate to think of her missing her doll as much as I hate to think about her missing me.*"

Megan had felt Tom's pain even through her own. Greg had left Daniel's security blanket—the blanket he had named "Billy" when he was three—behind, and for the first week she had cradled it next to her head, wondering how he was able to sleep without it, imagining his tears and Greg's frustration that she feared could turn violent. His Billy Blanket had been by his side since he was a baby. On the same day he'd been taken from his mother, he had been taken from his security object. How frightening the world must have seemed to him on that day. The thought tortured Megan as the weeks and months passed.

She had added Tom on Facebook as well. His Facebook picture was of his daughter, Jemima, a child with tumbling gold curls and wide blue eyes, laughing at the person taking the photo.

Most of the parents used Facebook photos of their children as their profile pictures, a banner to show the world what was missing in their lives. Sandi's was of her two daughters: slim, dark-haired, dark-eyed little girls with gentle smiles.

Today both Tom and Sandi are online. Both of them have messaged her.

"Hey, Megan. I just wanted to let you know that I'm thinking of you today. I know how hard it's going to be. I wish I could give you some advice on how to get through the first anniversary, but I personally took to my bed with a bottle of Scotch. I woke up hours later and then threw up for the rest of the day, so not really ideal. I'm here if you need to talk. I know how this feels. I know how badly you would like it to be over. I know."

Megan smiles a little as she reads Sandi's message. She'd tried wine instead of Scotch last night, but she'd certainly had no intention of getting out of bed. She would like to speak to Sandi but she knows that her friend gets into trouble for sitting on Facebook during working hours. Sandi lives in Brisbane, in the same house she used to live in with her family.

"I sleep in Bella's bedroom one night and Tasha's bedroom the next," Sandi has written in past conversations. *"I don't know if I'll ever be able to go back to my own room. They've been gone for*

three years now and their rooms have stopped smelling like them, but I still need to sleep in their beds, put my head where they used to put their heads. They were ten and twelve when he took them and they've both had to have their periods without me. I don't know why that bothers me so much out of everything—maybe because I had already planned ways to celebrate their becoming women, and now they're locked in a country where it's so difficult to grow up as a young woman."

Sandi's ex-husband took her two daughters to visit their grandparents in Lebanon and never came home. Because Lebanon is not part of the Hague abduction convention, there is no agreement between Australia and Lebanon for the authorities to help get them back to her. It means that she is stuck, without her children.

Tom is online as well. Tom is often online. He rarely sleeps, not since his wife Leah took his daughter and disappeared somewhere in India two years ago.

"I don't know why she went there," Tom had written when he and Megan began chatting. *"I spent a month over there visiting every major city and every hotel I could get to, showing them pictures of Leah and Jemima, but nothing ever came of it. I finally ran out of money and had to just come home. I feel like I failed her, like I failed my little girl."*

Megan reads Tom's message from today, which is simply, *"Thinking of you."*

"Hey, thanks," she types.

"Oh hey. I didn't know if you were going to be online today."

"I wasn't going to. I was planning to sleep all day and just pretend that it's not a full year since I've seen my son, but my mother woke me up and then she came over. I can hear her tidying up the kitchen. I yelled at her, so I feel awful."

"Don't feel bad. Just put it down to a bad day. Do you know what makes me feel better when it's the anniversary of when Jem was taken?"

"What?"

"I think about the good times we had as a family. I think about the times we went on vacation or on picnics, times when we were all happy."

"I find thinking about that stuff hurts too much and it's all tainted now because I wonder for exactly how long Greg was planning to take my son from me. I wonder if, even long before the divorce, he knew it was something he would do. Although that thought is better than believing that me asking for a divorce caused me to lose Daniel."

"Greg didn't want the divorce?"

"God no."

"Leah didn't either."

"But you can't live with someone who makes you unhappy, can you?"

"I don't know, Megan, I really don't. Maybe if I had... I don't know, agreed to try again, she would have felt that I was at least trying, and if we still got divorced, she wouldn't have been so angry."

"You can't blame yourself, Tom."

"But isn't that what we do? In the middle of the night when we miss our kids, isn't that all we can do? Maybe it was my fault. I could have been a better husband. A better father."

"I don't know. I just know that I thought this would get easier with time but it hasn't. It's worse, it's harder."

"I hear that. I hope you make it through the day. I'm sending a hug."

"Thanks, Tom xx."

After saying goodbye, Megan closes down the computer. She doesn't want to speak to anyone else. She curls herself around her pillow, wanting to cry but mostly feeling angry. God, she is so angry. Angry with her parents, who told her to keep the divorce civil; angry with the police in the UK for being useless; angry with the police in Australia for being equally useless. Most of her fury is saved for Greg, and some nights she can feel it burning inside her. She wants to tear his head off; she wants him to die in a fire, to suffer for what he has done. And the rest of the anger is directed at herself.

Megan knows that she sometimes forgets, wrapped in her own grief, that there are others who miss her son. Megan's father and Daniel had been in the middle of a chess game they hadn't finished. A year later, the chess pieces remain in position, ready for Daniel's hands to make the next move. Her mother dusts them carefully, one at a time so that they remain in the right places. "Sometimes he just sits at the board and stares at the pieces," she has told Megan. "He hates that he cannot fix this for you, that he cannot find his grandson and bring him home."

Megan gets off the bed and goes to find her mother in the kitchen, where she is packing plates into the dishwasher.

"Maybe I'll shower and we can go to a movie," says Megan.

Her mother smiles at her and Megan can see the shine of relieved tears in her eyes.

"I'm ready when you are. Maybe afterward or tomorrow you can call Detective Kade and apologize for yelling. You want him to keep looking, to always keep looking."

"I want the whole world to keep looking, Mum. The whole world."

CHAPTER SEVEN

Daniel—seven years old

Daniel is sitting up on his knees on the chair so he can look out of the hotel window. There are lots of people in the street. There are lots of children going to school. Some are holding hands and some are shouting at each other. Two boys are kicking a soccer ball to each other as they walk. Daniel watches as the ball hits the leg of an old man. He shouts at the two boys but they just laugh, pick up the ball, and run down the street. Soon he can't see them anymore and he wishes he was with them.

The sun is shining and if he puts his hand against the glass, he thinks he can feel some of its warmth. It's nearly summer, which is funny because in Australia, it's nearly winter.

He hasn't been to school for a whole year now. One whole year. At first, he hadn't minded because he was with Daddy and they had so many adventures. They'd gone from city to city to city, on and off an airplane and on and off an airplane over and over again. Sometimes he forgot what country they were in. Daddy shows all the people at the airport Daniel's special new book and tells them that his name is Daniel Ross. Daniel has to stand quietly when Daddy says this because now, he can't be Daniel Stanthorpe anymore but sometimes he whispers, "Daniel Stanthorpe, Daniel Stanthorpe," to himself, just so he can remember.

"It's to keep you safe," Daddy says.

Daddy makes him read every day and he teaches him math and science stuff. They visit a lot of museums in every country they go to. Daddy knows everything about everything.

Behind him in the bed, Daddy is snoring. He likes to stay awake at night to look at his computer but Daniel is not allowed to look at the computer or at Daddy's phone—not ever. That's the most important rule of their adventure.

On the first night of their adventure, on the airplane, he had asked where Mum was. At first Daddy hadn't seemed to hear him but Daniel had kept asking and finally he'd said, "She's tired of taking care of you. She says you make too much mess and she needs a break."

That had made him cry and cry and he had promised to be better, promised to tidy up his room.

"She doesn't care, Daniel. She doesn't care about anyone but herself, but I will love you forever and I will never get tired of taking care of you," Daddy had said. "I told her she can call you and talk to you if she wants to. If she doesn't, you know she doesn't want to be your mother anymore."

Daniel has been listening and listening for Daddy's phone to ring, but even when it does, it's never Mum. She doesn't want to be his mum anymore. That makes him feel full of sadness inside. Sometimes the sadness leaks out and he can't help it and he cries and cries. Sadness is heavy and gets caught in his throat. He wishes he could just make it go away.

The adventure had been fun at first. There was so much to see and do, and he got to see Granny Audrey and Grandpa William. Granny Audrey had been so happy to see him she had cried and said, "Look at you, just look at you." She had toasted him crumpets and smothered them in jam and then helped him have a bath and get into bed, and all the time she had talked and talked about how he was just like his father had been when he was a boy, with the same smile and the same eyes. She had sat on his bed for ages, reading stories from a book called *The Big Book of Boys' Stories*. He had been afraid that he wouldn't be able to sleep without his Billy Blanket but eventually he had drifted off, listening to her voice, feeling safe and warm even though Mum wasn't there.

But the adventure is not so much fun anymore. He's tired of always having to take his clothes out of the suitcase and of never being allowed any toys because they can't take them with them. He wants to go home to his Billy Blanket and his Cookie Monster poster and all his Legos. And he wants Mum; he can't help wanting her even if she doesn't want him.

Daniel watches a little brown dog sniffing around a small clump of bushes on the side of the road. This place is called Holland. Daddy told him that twice already so he's trying to remember it because Daddy gets angry if he doesn't remember. He's also trying to not think about Mum because if he talks about her or asks about her or cries for her, Daddy shouts.

"After everything I've done for you, you ungrateful little shit. She didn't want you anymore—don't you get it? She said she'd had enough of having to deal with you."

His mum doesn't love him anymore and that makes him so, so sad. He wishes he would have been a better boy so she could keep loving him. His daddy says he should hate his mum for not wanting him anymore, but even though he tries very hard to hate her he still misses her and he misses Billy Blanket and he misses Nana and Pop and Uncle Connor and James and Max. He misses Max a lot because they were both learning how to play *Minecraft*, and now he knows that Max will be better than him because Max is probably still allowed to go on the computer but Daniel must "never ever touch it."

If he touches the computer then the police will come and get them and they will send him home to Australia. He will be sent to live with a horrible family who would hurt him and make him eat yucky food because his mum doesn't want to take care of him anymore.

"Maybe I can live with Nana and Pop?" he once said to Daddy.

"They don't want you either. No one in that family does. I'm the only one who truly loves you, Daniel, the only one."

He is hungry but he won't wake Daddy up. He gets angry if he's woken up. He touches his cheek because he can feel he's crying again and he's not allowed to cry. He is not allowed to be "weak." But sometimes it's hard not to cry when there is a ball of sadness inside him all the time. He wishes he could make it go away but he can't. He's almost used to it now and he knows to only cry quietly so Daddy doesn't hear him.

He wipes his face. He needs to be strong and he needs to be grateful that Daddy loves him. He can't cry. He has to be strong and he has to be grateful.

CHAPTER EIGHT

As they climb into the car together, the news is on the radio again. "Steven Hindley," begins the reporter before Michael turns it off.

"Wait, don't do that," says Daniel.

"Did you want to hear it?" asks Megan, and she turns the radio on again. The announcer has moved on to speaking about house prices.

"No," he says, his arms folded tightly across his chest.

Megan looks at Michael and turns off the radio again.

The trip home is conducted, mostly, in silence. Silence from Daniel but not from Megan, who tries to ignore what feels like a simmering, angry heat coming off her son from the backseat of the car. She understands how he feels. They took away his knife and he has nothing left, except the phone, that belongs to him. Even she doesn't belong to just him anymore. He had no idea he was coming home to a new stepfather, to a new man in her life. *How will he feel about all the other changes to his world?*

"I've missed you so much," she says and then bites down on her lip to stop herself from asking, *Did you miss me too?*

"Everyone has missed you," she says brightly. "Nana and Pop and Connor and James and Lucy—you remember Lucy? She was only two when you... She's eight now and such a big girl."

At each of Lucy's birthday parties over the last six years, Connor had toasted Daniel with the words, "He'll be here next year," and in the last couple of years the words had simply disappeared into the singing of "Happy Birthday" without the power to make Megan clutch at her stomach to keep the nausea at bay.

"Do you remember Lucy, Daniel?" Megan asks.

"No."

"Oh... well I'm sure once you see her... although she looks so different now, she spends so much time on her phone playing games that Uncle Connor says..."

Michael puts his hand on her knee and she knows he's telling her to try and avoid prattling on but she doesn't seem to be able to stop herself. The questions stream out of her.

"How long were you in England?"

"How long have you been back in Australia?"

"Have you been going to school?"

"Did you have your own room where you lived?"

"Do you play any sports? Not sports, you don't like sports. Do you play a musical instrument?"

Daniel doesn't reply. He sighs and occasionally grunts. She subtly wipes away a stray tear and determinedly looks out of the window, biting down on her lip. He's here, he's back. This is everything she's wanted for the last six years.

"I live in a different suburb now. Well, Michael and I do. And Evie." Megan laughs and even to her own ears she sounds slightly hysterical. "I almost forgot about Evie. You have a sister, Daniel, a little sister."

"A sister," repeats Daniel. "I have a sister," he says but it doesn't sound like a question.

"Yes, a sister."

"How... how big is she?"

"She's six months old."

"Yeah but how... big is she?" he asks again.

"Big enough." Megan laughs. "She's really heavy."

"Really heavy," he repeats and then he subsides back into silence.

"Yes, and we live a couple of suburbs away from where you and I used to live. It's a really nice house. It has a big garden and a pool and I even have a room to use as a studio—you can use it too if you'd like. If you want to start painting again, I mean, but you don't have to, of course."

"Megan," says Michael quietly.

She scratches at a small stain on her pants, thinking desperately of something else to say.

Michael covers her hand with his. She leans her head back against the headrest and closes her eyes, and she is reminded of the first time she met Michael in his office. "I will find him for you," she remembers him saying as he wrapped a large, warm hand around her cold, clenched fist. "I will find him." Now she knows that he should never have said those words. He was not allowed to promise things he didn't know he could deliver, but he has told her that—despite doing his work for years—he had found himself profoundly moved by her.

"You looked so completely lost and I could feel your love for Daniel in the air, like a mist. I just wanted to help you, and when I looked at you, I had that feeling that people talk about when they say 'love at first sight.' Even though you'd been crying, even though I could actually hear you grinding your teeth, you were the most beautiful woman I'd seen in a long time. I shouldn't have touched you, not even your hand, but I just needed to feel your skin. I'd never believed that love or infatuation could hit you like that. I thought it was all bullshit for movies and television, but I felt it when I looked at you."

The memory fades and Megan opens her eyes, blurting out another question. "What do you like to eat, Daniel?"

"Fries," he says.

She turns around to look at him and he looks back at her, looks through her, observing himself being observed. Goose bumps rise along her arm and she turns around again. "Oh look," she says, "McDonald's. I think we should stop. Are you hungry, Daniel?"

"Yes."

Megan's heart skips. She can feed him; that she can do. "What would you like to eat?" she asks as they stand in front of the brightly lit signboard, peering up at the choices while all around them families talk and laugh and yell at each other.

"Fries."

"And what else? How about a burger?"

"Burgers are expensive," he says, and for a second Megan hears Greg's voice: "Living is expensive, Megan—you don't know that because you don't pay the bills."

"Oh," Megan replies, flustered. "You can have one—they're not too . . . too expensive."

He looks at the floor. "I would like a burger." He lifts his head and looks directly at her for a moment. "Please."

Megan would like to buy him one of everything on the menu.

She finds herself unable to eat anything, content just to stare at him, admire him, while he is distracted by the food.

"You must have been hungry," she says quietly as he wolfs down his food, and he shrugs his shoulders.

"I need the bathroom," he says, looking at a family with a toddler strapped into a high chair, banging a plastic spoon on the tray.

"I'll show you," she replies, rising out of her seat, but he jumps to his feet and holds his hand out to indicate she should stop.

"I'm fine," he says and he turns and walks toward the bathrooms at the back of the restaurant.

Megan stares after her son. "What's wrong with him?" she asks Michael.

"Trauma," he replies. "His father has died, which would be horrifying enough but there was also the fire. We don't know how the fire started and what happened after that. We don't know if he tried to save Greg. We don't know anything, and until he tells us, we have to tread carefully. I know how hard it is, but we have to try, Megs."

"I don't know what to say to him. I don't know what to even say."

"I wish I could tell you, but I think maybe talking about everyone in the family is probably a good thing. I know he doesn't seem to be listening but I think he is. I know it's hard but try to relax a little. Maybe don't ask so many questions—he doesn't seem to want to respond."

"But how can I relax, Michael? Just look at him. He's obviously battling with emotions and I can't help him. I used to be able to help him with everything. I was the person he came to, and now he won't even look at me for more than a few seconds."

"It's natural that you would want to get him to open up to you, but you have to be patient," Michael says.

"He's not your child, Michael, you have no idea," she snaps.

Michael shakes his head slowly, sadly, and Megan can read the wounded look on his face. She's being unfair. In her desperation to get something from her son, she's attacking her husband and it isn't what he deserves. He has listened to her talk about Daniel for years, not just as a detective but as a friend, a lover, and a husband.

"I'm so sorry," Megan gasps and she drops her head into her hands.

"Babe, babe, don't, it'll be fine, just relax, it'll be fine," Michael whispers, squeezing her shoulder.

Back in the car she manages to keep her questions and comments to herself.

"Are you sure you want to pick Evie up tonight?" asks Michael as they approach the outskirts of Sydney.

"Yes, absolutely, I want us to all be together." She is aware of herself wishing for a magic wand so she can make her family immediately whole again.

Michael pulls up to a stop outside her parents' flat.

"Where are we?" asks Daniel.

"This is Nana and Pop's flat. I'm just going to get Evie from them. Do you want to come in and say hello? They would really love to see you."

"My grandparents don't live here."

"That's because they moved. They wanted an ocean view so they sold their house. It's a lovely flat—why don't you come in and see it?"

"My grandparents," he says slowly, "don't... live... here."

He slumps down in his seat and folds his arms.

"I think everyone is tired, Megs. I'm sure we'll all feel better tomorrow," says Michael.

Megan nods and slowly gets out of the car.

"I'm sorry, not right now. I'll call you later and explain," she says to Susanna when she asks to see Daniel.

Once she's buckled into her car seat, Evie stares at her brother.

"This is Daniel, Evie."

"This is Daniel, Evie," Daniel repeats, pitching his voice high.

Megan feels a ripple of shock run through her. She struggles to think of what to say, unable to believe that he has imitated her the way he has. Once again, she chooses silence as the best option.

"We're here," she says cheerily as they pull into their double garage.

Daniel's sigh is long and loud.

"It must be strange to have a little sister you didn't know about," she says once they're all inside, standing awkwardly in the kitchen as though they are trying to acclimatize to a new country. Michael is holding Evie. It's nine o'clock and Megan wishes the heater would hurry up and warm the room. The cold makes the house seem bigger and more sterile than it is.

"Half-sister," states Daniel, his tone flat. "A real sister would have come from you and Dad."

"Yes..." says Megan, unsure of exactly how to respond. "Come this way, Daniel," she says, holding out her hand to him.

He glances down at her hand and then very slowly clasps both of his own behind his back.

Megan laughs self-consciously. "I suppose you're a bit old to hold hands, aren't you?"

"I'm twelve. I'll be thirteen on the twentieth of August."

"Of course, I know more than anyone when your birthday is, Daniel," she replies with a smile. "You're too big to hold my hand, I know that. I just wanted to show you your room."

"I don't have a room in this house. I had a room in the house with the blue roof and the water fountain out the front, and then I had a room in the small flat with the old man who lived downstairs and liked to play the trumpet, and then I had a room in the old house in the bush but that's gone now. It burned down."

Megan looks at Michael, who is holding Evie. The baby's normal exuberance has been hushed by the strange boy with the long, curly hair.

Daniel has spoken more in the last minute than he has in the last four hours.

"That's right," Megan finally says because Daniel has fixed his flat gaze on her. She wants to laugh with relief because with just a few words Daniel has indicated to her that he remembers things she has been talking to him about, but she also feels tears forming because the memories are recited without emotion. It is simply a list of places Daniel has lived in and lost, and that breaks her heart.

"When you were little," Megan continues, "we did live in the house with the blue roof but I had to sell that house, and then we lived in the flat and now I live here with Michael and Evie. But don't worry, I brought everything from your room at the old house, all your toys and books and...I suppose you'll be too old for a lot of it but I thought you might like to decide what you want to keep and..." Megan finds herself unable to keep speaking. Daniel doesn't appear to be listening to her. He looks as though he is simply staring at her mouth, watching her lips form words. He has barely blinked and his hazel-eyed stare is disconcerting enough to make the hair at the back of her neck stand up. Every now and again his gaze darts over to Evie. He doesn't smile or try to engage with her; he simply stares at her.

"How about I show you your room and we can find something for you to sleep in?"

"These are my pajamas," says Daniel, looking down at himself. His tracksuit pants have a hole in each knee, and the T-shirt he is wearing may have started out white but is now a washed-out gray. Over it he has a cardigan given to him by Officer Mara. It's a man's cardigan, swamping his skinny frame.

"Okay, well, tomorrow we can go shopping and get everything new. That will be fun, won't it?" Megan asks, conscious that her voice is too high-pitched, too desperate.

Daniel nods at her again. She walks up the stairs and then down the passage to the room she has had set up for him for months. When she and Michael married and bought this house, she had thought of keeping all of Daniel's things in storage, but when she was nearly eight months pregnant with Evie, she found herself standing in the empty room and gasping for breath. The space was supposed to be filled with her son's things. Keeping everything in boxes felt like he was dead, and she still needed someplace to sit and think about him, someplace to be with all the stuff that defined his six-year-old self.

When Michael had come home from work that night, he'd found her attempting to put together Daniel's blue racing-car bed, her huge belly getting in the way.

"Please don't tell me not to do it," Megan had said. "I can't explain it, but I can't breathe until his room is ready for him. He's too old for this bed now, I think, but..."

"I wasn't going to tell you not to do it," Michael had replied. "I was going to tell you to give me a minute to change and I would get my drill."

When it was finally done, Daniel's room looked almost identical to the way it had looked in the flat where they had lived together. There was a Cookie Monster poster on the wall and a stack of Legos in a box under the bed. His collection of superheroes stood ready to defend on his bookshelf, and next to his bed, *The Lion, the Witch and the Wardrobe* was waiting with a bookmark at chapter three, which was where she had read up to with him the night before he was taken.

Michael had put his arms around Megan and said, "You're not replacing him, Megs. You haven't given up, we haven't given up. He'll be back one day. We're still looking for him."

Now, Megan opens the door to the room that has been waiting for Daniel and then she steps aside and lets him walk in first. The clothes he is wearing have a weird smell about them—not just smoke but something unwashed—and Megan cannot wait to take them away and throw them in the garbage, although she is unsure if this is a good idea. He has lost everything except for the clothes he has on and his old phone and charger—can she really take them away from him too?

It was too late in the day to do anything about shoes, but she knows he can probably borrow a pair of flip-flops from her that will at least allow him to walk around the shops tomorrow. *Where are his shoes? How could he not have had shoes? And if he doesn't like to wear them, will he agree to buy some new ones?*

She would like to sit him down and wash his feet and examine the cuts and blisters, but she is reluctant to touch him again until he relaxes a little. She can see the tension in his neck and across his skinny shoulders. An image of him as a baby in the bath, his soapy pink body covered in bubbles, comes to her, his unselfconscious kisses and hugs, his habit of twirling her hair in his fingers as he fell asleep and she lay next to him. They were so physically connected. His tangible separateness right now is painful.

Megan watches her son look around the room. Inside she feels her heart race and flutter as she wishes that she could rush him to the shops and fill his room with things he would like and his wardrobe with clothes that would fit him so that she could wake up tomorrow and call him for breakfast and enjoy the sight of him sitting in his pajamas in front of the television as though the last six years had never happened.

Daniel stands in the middle of the room and turns in a slow circle. Occasionally he spots something that is obviously familiar and lifts his hand and starts to move toward it, but then he quickly drops his hand and resumes the slow circling.

"Do you remember?" asks Megan.

Daniel nods and stops his circle to look at the bed. A duvet and Transformer-themed sheets are on the bed, and on top of the pillow is Daniel's Billy Blanket. The blanket she'd wrapped him in to feed him when he was a baby, the blanket that had become necessary for sleep. She had held Daniel's Billy Blanket at night for months and months, devastated that he did not have his comfort object, and she had willed him to feel her touching it, touching him.

Megan knows that the boy staring at his car bed is Daniel, but as she watches him peruse the room, she can't help wanting some further sign that this is the boy she remembers. She knows he's been through a lot, that he must have missed her terribly, and the thought of him crying for her has kept her awake not just for months but for years—and here he is. But at the same time, here he is not. The child in front of her is essentially a stranger, and she needs something from him, something that she knows is unfair to want but she needs it nonetheless.

Daniel walks toward the bed. "I'm too old for a blanket," he says slowly, but he climbs onto the bed that he barely fits in now and curls up around the blanket. He drags his cell phone from his pocket and holds it as he falls asleep. He is filthy and he smells but his sleep is so deep and so instant Megan cannot bring herself to wake him.

She stands and watches him for a few moments, unsure of what to do, and then she moves quietly out of the room, turning off the light as she goes. In the morning she will show him the years of wrapped birthday and Christmas presents stacked up in the bedroom cupboard and let him open them and decide what to keep. In the last few years she has bought him a new electronic device every year, unsure which one he would prefer. She hasn't thought about the money wasted, only about wanting to be able to give him a gift from all his missed birthdays when she saw him again. Each year she has baked a cake, and her family has come over and she has lit candles. They have sung "Happy Birthday" to him and blown out the candles together. In two months' time Daniel will finally, finally be able to blow out the candles for himself.

CHAPTER NINE

"He's exhausted," she says when she finds Michael trying to pat Evie to sleep.

"He must be."

"I'm not sure how we're going to do this, Michael," she says with a sigh, picking a fussy, still-awake Evie up out of her crib, and sitting down with her in the rocking chair so she can feed her to sleep.

"We'll do it the way everyone does anything: one step at a time. I've called your mum. She says she can take Evie for the day tomorrow so you can spend time with him. I think we'll need a new bed and..."

"And?"

"He's going to need to see someone, Megs, about what happened, about being taken and then about the fire and losing Greg. There's a lot going on inside him. It's going to be quite a while until the investigation is complete. I don't know how much there is to find. If there was an explosion of some sort and then the fire burned for some time, they may only be able to find fragments of bone. Those will have to be identified with DNA from Daniel or dental records if they can't get any DNA from the bones. It's a long process. A funeral would help bring closure but we're a month or two away from that."

"Of course, but he might be okay. We'll get him into school and get him a whole lot of new things. It'll be exciting for him. We can have a party to celebrate that he's back. I can invite Max and Olivia..." She stops speaking, aware of how ridiculous she sounds. She cannot erase the last six years with a party and a visit from his best friend.

"Slow down, Megs. You don't know how he's going to be or who he's going to want to see. I know it's hard to hear, but you don't know him really."

"But he's my child, Michael. I know him."

"Of course, of course you do, but maybe try to take this slowly. He'll settle in soon, I'm sure. You haven't eaten anything for hours so while you get Evie down, I'm going to order a pizza. I'll get two in case he wakes up."

"Okay," agrees Megan quietly, suddenly so exhausted she can barely think.

As Evie's eyes close, Megan struggles to make sense of the boy sleeping in the too-small bed in the room next door. What has he seen in the last six years? What has he heard? Where has he been? What has happened to him? Who is he now? Michael is right: she doesn't know him at all really.

When the pizza comes, she finds herself hungry, realizing that she hasn't eaten since breakfast.

Michael pours her a glass of red wine. "You won't have to feed Evie until tomorrow morning, will you?"

"No, and I need this." She takes a sip and closes her eyes, willing her shoulder muscles to relax. "I wonder if he still likes pizza," she says to Michael.

"What kind of kid doesn't like pizza?"

"True." She smiles.

Michael's phone rings. "Kade here," he answers. "Oh yes, hello, Detective Wardell. I didn't expect to hear from you so soon, just a minute." Michael covers his phone with his hand. "It's a detective from Newcastle, she wants to talk about Daniel," he tells Megan.

"Put her on speakerphone."

"Go ahead, Detective," he says, hitting the speaker button.

"I just wanted to touch base with you about Daniel Stanthorpe, your..."

"My stepson," says Michael, and Megan flicks him a smile.

"Yes, your stepson. I'm a little concerned that you took him home from Heddon Greta. Officer Mara really shouldn't have allowed that. I wanted to begin the interview process. It's also very important that we get a DNA sample from him to confirm his identity and to use it with what we found at the scene of the fire."

Megan shakes her head. She knows her own son. That's enough. It should be enough.

"What did you find there?"

"We've only just begun."

"I'm aware of that. Has a fire investigator been out there?"

"Yes. She was there for most of the afternoon."

"And?"

"She has found human remains, bone fragments mostly. She's going through the scene very slowly so she doesn't destroy possible evidence."

"Just bone fragments?"

"And part of a skull. I think they're going to have to extract DNA from what little there is of the bones and teeth. That could take a few weeks at least. Amanda, the fire investigator, said the bones are black-burnt, meaning DNA is probably highly degraded. Until the pathologist gets there, we won't know if any nuclear DNA is left. They may have to use mitochondrial DNA analysis. We need to get some dental records as well because that's probably our best hope for a positive ID. I think we'll end up bringing in a forensic anthropologist. There's really very little left."

"Oh God." Megan's hand shoots up to her mouth as she feels nausea rise.

"Jesus, Megs, sorry—I shouldn't have let you hear that," says Michael.

"Oh, I do apologize, Mrs. Kade," says Detective Wardell, "I didn't realize you were listening in."

"No, it's fine... I just can't think of him... burning, it's so hideous. What if Daniel had been in the fire?" She thinks about the knife her son had been concealing, about the black lines he had burned into the wood. "He could have been hurt," she says.

"But he wasn't, Megs, he's okay, thank goodness. Listen, Detective Wardell, I told the officer we would provide a DNA sample as soon as possible. We needed to come home, we have a young baby who my wife needed to feed, and she wasn't going to leave Daniel there overnight. He's been through enough."

"I understand, Detective Kade, but it's very much against protocol."

"Yes, well, it's done now. Don't blame Officer Mara. They only had a couple of officers there at the time so she wasn't to know. Daniel not being there is not hampering the investigation, Detective, and it's not like we live in another state. I strongly believe that after everything he's been through, he needs time to settle in and recover a little. Children do better in interviews when they feel safe."

"Yes, but he's old enough to give us a fairly accurate reporting of what happened, and the investigation is going to be difficult."

"I understand that."

"We need to know why he wasn't hurt."

"Jesus," spits Megan.

"I'm sorry, that sounds terrible. Of course it's better that he wasn't hurt, but it is strange that he's not burned in any way, unless he wasn't in the house, but only near it when it caught fire. Perhaps I could come to Sydney tomorrow to conduct an interview."

"No," says Michael.

"But it's really important—"

"Detective Wardell," Michael enunciates her surname with exaggerated care. He scrunches his face and wraps his hand tightly around his wine glass. "I am very aware that you need to get as much information as you can from him. I can assure you that you will have a chance to interview him once he's a little settled. My wife needed to take her son home. She has waited six years for him to walk back into her life. I can assure you that we'll get the DNA sample done and then we will give this child, because he is just a child, a little time to adjust to an entirely new life."

"Okay then, sir. Have a good night. We'll be in touch soon."

Michael ends the call. "You know, they're right, Megs, we probably shouldn't have taken him home."

"Yeah, well, as you said, it's done now."

"You'll have to stop off at one of the hospitals to give a sample. If you can, do it first thing tomorrow and take those forms with you when you go."

"Yes, sir," says Megan with a smile.

"Drink your wine," Michael says, laughing.

Megan does, and as she finishes her pizza, she allows a peaceful lightness to descend. Her son is home. Daniel is home.

CHAPTER TEN

One day since Daniel's return

Megan is in the kitchen feeding Evie some apple and rice cereal mixture. She had peeked into Daniel's room when Evie had woken up, holding her dark-haired daughter on her hip, seeing him sprawled on the bed, one foot dangling off the side. As she'd looked at her sleeping son, she'd decided that it was best to let him rest while she got Evie ready to drop off at her mother's.

In truth she had looked in on him all through the night, getting up to get a glass of water or go to the bathroom or soothe Evie back to sleep; she had not been able to resist opening the door to his bedroom to simply reassure herself that he was there. He was actually there. She could not believe the miracle of his presence, could not believe that each time she opened the door, she could make out his shape curled in his bed. The racing-car bed was no longer empty. She remembered that in the first few weeks after Greg kidnapped him, she would wake up and stretch in her bed while running through all the things she needed to remember for the day, only to be hit with the crushing realization that there was nothing she needed to do for Daniel because he was not there. She had shed rivers of tears, and now he was there, right there. It was incredible.

Her own sleep had been light and troubled. She had sunk into nightmarish scenes where Daniel was burned alive in the shack in the woods and Greg had survived to tell her that he had finally taken her son to a place he could never return from. When she'd woken up, she had felt only sheer relief that her despised ex-husband was the one who was gone. Then she had felt sick and guilty because Daniel had lost his father.

"What did Detective Wardell mean when she said the bones were black-burnt?" she had asked Michael just before she fell asleep.

"You don't want to know that, Megs. I don't want you to think about it."

"Please, Michael."

Michael sighed. "Bodies burned in a fire can be well preserved, meaning they've been protected by something falling on them or they've been under something, or they can be semi-burnt or black-burnt or blue-gray-burnt or blue-gray-white-burnt. It's pretty much what it sounds like: degrees of burning from the least to the most. If they're well preserved or semi-burnt, it's easy to get DNA from them, but if they're black-burnt or worse, it becomes more difficult. The DNA can be highly degraded. That's why this process is going to take a few weeks."

"But they know it's Greg—Daniel told them, he told us."

"They need a formal identification. It's the same with Daniel: they know it's him and you've confirmed that, but they will still use DNA. They don't simply take people at their word. They'll probably get you to try and remember who Greg's dentist was so they can get some dental records as well. They need to try and determine how exactly he died."

"He got burned in a fire. Isn't that how?"

"Maybe, or maybe he was dead before the fire started."

"What?"

"It's all just supposition, Megs. I'm not saying I know anything. That's what the investigation is for."

Michael had closed his eyes and fallen asleep almost instantly but Megan's mind had been crowded with images of burned flesh and bones. She had been grateful for Evie's early-morning cries saving her from any more dark dreams.

*

As she feeds Evie she listens for some movement from Daniel's room, but so far she hasn't heard a thing. She is desperate for him to wake up, so excited that she feels like she is the child.

"You like that, don't you, darling, yes you do, you do," she says to Evie, who is having a lot more success with solid food this morning.

She is relishing every moment of Evie's babyhood. Finding out she was pregnant two weeks before her wedding to Michael had been surprising, but she had gone from shock to delight in a matter of minutes. She had kept the news for their wedding night, sure of Michael's ecstatic reaction. "Champagne," he had said, picking up the phone to call room service at the small bed-and-breakfast in the mountains where they were staying. "A very small glass of champagne for my beautiful bride, who is giving me the gift of a child."

She turns in her chair to grab a cloth off the counter to wipe Evie's messy face, and Daniel is standing there, almost on top of her. Her shriek of surprise makes Evie cry. "Oh, oh, I'm sorry, I'm sorry, baby," she says, standing and picking Evie up and bouncing her as she wipes her face. "It's okay, look, it's just Daniel, it's Daniel."

"Just Daniel," he whispers.

He stands very still, watching her coo and comfort Evie as she tries to get her to calm down. He stares first at Megan and then at Evie, without seeming to register either of them at all.

Finally, Evie allows herself to be comforted and seems contented with a teether in her high chair. Megan turns her attention to Daniel, reaching out for him, wanting to hug him, but he steps back quickly. She drops her arms, feeling physically rebuked—but looking at him standing in her kitchen, dressed in his filthy clothes from the day before, she is unable to resist some form of physical contact. She steps forward and gives his shoulder a squeeze.

"Hello, darling," she whispers. "Did you sleep well?"

"I was tired," he says.

"I'm sure you were. Yesterday was a long day."

"Long day," he repeats as though he is just learning the words.

Megan finds herself flustered and uncomfortable so she smiles inanely at him until he looks away at some pictures on the wall.

"That one was in the house with the fountain," he says, and she turns to see a picture of four-year-old Daniel in his paddling pool.

"Oh yes, it was." She's surprised that he has remembered something from so long ago. "You loved that paddling pool. I think you spent more time in there than anywhere else during the summer."

"The paddling pool was in the garden."

"It was," agrees Megan, finding herself slipping into the same monotone he is using.

"If you hadn't made him get divorced, we would still live in that house." The words are not accusatory, simply factual.

"Um . . . I suppose we would."

"Yeah, we would."

She would like to explain to him, as she had done many times before he was taken, sugarcoating the truth, the reasons for her and Greg's divorce. But standing and looking at her twelve-year-old son, she realizes that his first morning home is not the best time for that. She decides to focus on getting the day started instead.

He has slept right through from the night before, without any more food or a shower, and as he stands in front of her, rooted to one spot in the kitchen, she notes the sour, unwashed smell coming off him along with the dark, burned smell from the fire. His feet are still filthy and she is worried about bacteria getting into his cuts.

"Would you like to shower or eat breakfast first?" she asks brightly.

Daniel meets her eyes for a moment and then he focuses on the fridge behind her. "Whatever will make you happy," he murmurs.

"Oh…" Megan begins but then she stops. The simple words are familiar. Familiar and frightening. "Whatever will make you happy," was a favorite choice of phrase for Greg.

And just like that, her ex-husband is in her head. He could be standing in her kitchen looking at her with his almond-shaped eyes that on his son are more green than brown in color this morning. She can feel him assessing her, judging her from behind his son's eyes.

She reaches out for her kitchen counter, needing something to hold on to, gripping it tightly as she tries to control her emotions. That phrase…Those words were Greg's way of leading her into a trap. "Whatever will make you happy," he would say, seemingly uninterested in whatever decision she was about to make, and then, without fail, over and over, she would find herself falling for the idea that her happiness was all that he wanted, whether it was a simple discussion over what kind of takeout to order or something more complicated like whether or not she should go back to work when Daniel started preschool.

"I really feel like Chinese," she would say to Greg if they were discussing what to have for dinner.

"Really?" he would ask as though the idea was a startling one. "You do know how much salt and sugar is in Chinese takeout, don't you? I would have thought that with the weight you're battling, you'd want to cut down on that sort of thing. I mean, it's not something I care about but I did think it mattered to you. You go ahead and do what suits you though, whatever will make you happy."

Megan would find herself backtracking, apologizing for her appalling choice and almost begging him to make the decision of what they would have. Usually she would end up with a small serving of sushi while he would get a burger and fries. Before her divorce she had lived in a house she didn't like, driven a car she hated because it was too big, and never had a vacation to a destination she wanted to go to. She had worked for only a few hours a week despite wanting to work more, and she had never bought an item of clothing unless she had received his approval for it. But everything she did had seemingly been her choice because Greg had always said, "Whatever will make you happy."

No matter how many times she reminded herself that it was a trap, she still stepped right into it, wanting to believe he had genuine intentions, not wanting to see him for the man he truly was. The one time she had confronted him about it, he had called her paranoid. "I only want to make you happy, Megan—how could you ever doubt that? You're my life, my love. How could you not know that?"

As the years passed, she understood, logically, how she could doubt that, but it had taken her a long time to make the move she knew she needed to make. And even when she had finally told Greg that she wanted a divorce, he had been furious and aghast that she did not love him enough to know that she was everything to him. Megan had questioned whether or not this was the case, vacillating between being upset at herself for leaving a man who loved her so much and applauding herself for it, until the day Greg took Daniel.

That was the day she understood without a shadow of a doubt that Greg's version of love was only about suffocating control. She had been his puppet to manipulate, and when she'd failed to perform as expected, he'd had to find another way to wrench back his power. That realization, over everything else, was the one thing that had made her the most fearful of all for Daniel because she'd understood that her son would now have to be the one to dance when his strings were pulled. How much of what Greg felt for his son was actual love, and how much was something else entirely? For six years she had uttered the same mantra every night. *He took him because he loved him. He took him because he loved him. He won't hurt him. He won't hurt him. Please, God, let him not hurt him.*

She stands up straight as she recovers her equilibrium. It has taken her years to learn how to state what she wants without leaving any room for discussion, and she banishes thoughts of Greg from her mind.

"I think you should shower first and then I need to change those bandages and clean up your feet," she says.

"Fine," he says lightly. He turns and walks away.

He returns twenty minutes later with a clean body, dressed in the same clothes with his hair still dirty and tangled.

"I think we'll get a haircut first thing this morning," she says. "Actually, we need to stop at the hospital. They want a DNA sample from you."

"Why?"

Megan debates with herself for a moment, deciding how much to tell him. She could say it's just to confirm that he is her son, but that sounds ridiculous. She knows he's her son. She doesn't want to bring up Greg again but after a moment realizes she has no choice. She would rather Daniel hear it from her than from anyone else.

"It's to help identify the... remains they found."

"They won't find anything. It was a bad fire. Fire destroys everything. There'll be nothing left."

"But, Daniel, do you remember what Officer Mara said yesterday? There's always something left."

"Not always. I know about fire. There's not always something left."

Megan searches for the right words. Daniel looks at the floor, scratching through his tangled hair.

"Sweetie, they have found something. They have found... bones."

Daniel's head shoots up, his face white.

"I know, sweetheart. I know how hard it is, and it's okay to cry or yell or get angry. It's okay, whatever you feel it's okay." She lifts her arm to reach out to him but lets her hand drop onto the counter. He doesn't want to be touched.

His face twists and he slams his hand down on the counter right next to hers. Then he points his finger at her, so close he is almost touching her face. "This wouldn't have happened if it wasn't for you. He would be here now and we would be a real family!"

Megan resists the urge to step back.

"Oh, sweetie, I'm so sorry. I'm sorry that you have to go through this. We can leave it, Daniel. We don't have to get the DNA swab done today. We can leave this whole day and you can just have some quiet time to think about Dad, to remember him, take some time to think about him—and it's okay to cry, it's always okay to cry."

Daniel stares at her, meeting her eyes for a moment, and then he simply shrugs, drops his arm, and steps away from her. He looks at the food she has laid out for him and then he goes to sit down on a stool by the kitchen counter. "He said only pussies cry. Sometimes you need to man up." His voice has gone back to neutral.

Megan notes that he has not called Greg "Dad," only "he," and she wonders at this, at how callous it sounds. She finds herself battling surreal confusion and wonders if his outburst even happened at all. *When did he start using words like "pussies," words I always told him were "ugly words"?*

"That's not true at all, Daniel. It's okay to miss your father, it's okay to cry."

"Stop telling me how to feel," he says, and she realizes it's time to back off. There is so much more to say, so many things to discuss, but her son's eyes tell her he has shut down. He is protecting himself, she assumes. It's easier not to feel anything at all.

"Okay, hospital then a haircut," Megan says, irritating herself with her desperate cheerfulness.

Daniel reaches up and touches his hair. "Whatever will make you happy," he says.

"Well, it's not really for me. There's no way you'll be allowed to have hair that long at school."

He shrugs again as he surveys the kitchen counter.

She has laid out a bowl of cereal and some chopped-up fruit, which had been his standard breakfast at six years old. But unsure of what he eats now, she has added two slices of toast and a packaged waffle, along with a row of toppings for him to choose from.

He eats everything, sometimes holding the next pieces of food in each hand as he chews, including the toast and the waffle, which he smears with butter and jam.

"Are you still hungry?" she asks when he's done.

Daniel looks up from his empty plate and meets her eyes but then his gaze shifts to a spot just behind her. She watches him carefully, ignoring the urge to give him a shake and say, "Just answer me like my son, like the boy you used to be."

It takes him a minute to answer and she doesn't take her eyes off him. His face twitches once or twice but his eyes stay focused on the spot behind her. She can see evidence of something going on inside him. He opens his mouth to reply, and Megan knows that it was going to be, "Whatever will make you happy," but then he closes his mouth again and Megan witnesses the battle going on inside him—between what he thinks he should say and what he wants to say.

What did he do to you? she thinks, and a sharp pain spears her chest at what her little boy would have suffered at the hands of a man like Greg, a man who she had taken years to see was a true sociopath, incapable of feeling anything for anyone except himself. What might he have done to her son as a means of punishing her? What levels of anger and frustration at his loss of control would he have taken out on a defenseless little boy? Greg had managed to take a confident young woman, sure of her place in the world, and turn her into someone who struggled to choose a dish off a restaurant menu. What might he have done to a child?

"All you have to do is tell me what you want, Daniel," she whispers. "Don't be afraid—you can tell me exactly what you want."

He locks eyes with her for another brief moment and she reads the panic there. Then he looks down at his hands. "I want two more pieces of toast," he says as though he were asking for something impossible.

"Then that's what you'll have," she says, and her reward is the smallest and quickest of smiles. Megan wants to sing with joy. *There you are, Daniel, I can see you now, there you are.*

Even if he's dead, he will still be in Daniel's head, she reminds herself, knowing how long it took her to get Greg's sneering, belittling tone out of her own head.

She leaves him eating his second serving of toast to go and get Evie changed. In Evie's room she puts her daughter on the floor, where she goes back to practicing her crawling, and Megan sinks down into the rocking chair. She is completely exhausted and she calculates that she has only spent half an hour with her son. They used to sit on the couch together on a Saturday night, legs tangled, sharing a bowl of popcorn, watching a movie together. Once, when speaking to Olivia, she had jokingly referred to him as the best kind of date. "We laugh at the same stuff, can share a pizza because we both like it the same way, and he goes to bed early—what more could I want?"

He had been her son but also an entertaining and sweet and interesting person, and she had loved the time she spent with him. She cannot quite believe that she has just left the same boy in the kitchen. She cannot quite believe what has happened to him, and she is afraid, very afraid, that what she's seen of him so far is only the beginning.

CHAPTER ELEVEN

Megan has to stop twice to ask a nurse if she is heading in the right direction at the hospital. The large building is filled with ramps and corridors leading to radiology and oncology and maternity and the pediatric wing, and Megan finds it difficult to navigate. All around her people are walking with purpose, completely sure of where they have to go. The slightly chemical smell of hospital hangs in the air, drawing Megan back to when she was in labor with Daniel. His heart rate had slowed toward the end of her labor, worrying the nurse, who had called her doctor. In an instant Megan's room had been filled with people, and Greg—who had been holding her hand and breathing with her through each contraction—had been pushed to one side.

"This baby needs to come out immediately," Dr. Sakasky had told her, "but I'm here and everything is going to be fine." Megan can recall nodding at the doctor, certain that she was safe in her competent hands. Daniel had been helped out with a suction cup but was absolutely fine and Megan can remember her deep gratitude to the hospital staff.

Finally, she and Daniel stop outside the door of an office where DNA samples are taken. Megan breathes deeply. The smell of antiseptic is stronger here. "We'll get this done and have a lovely day," she says to Daniel, who stares at her but doesn't reply.

"Hi, we're here to..." she says to the nurse behind the desk but then she simply hands her the sheaf of papers from the police station.

Daniel stands behind her, silent in his dirty clothes and a pair of Megan's purple flip-flops. She wants to explain to the nurse that she is taking her son shopping for new clothes, that she would never normally allow her child to dress like this, but realizes the futility of trying to explain her situation.

The nurse nods as she reads through the papers. "Right, just come through here, Daniel," she says, indicating a door that leads to a small room stocked with what Megan assumes are DNA kits.

"Can I stay with him?" she asks.

"Of course," says the young nurse, with freckles across her nose and her hair pulled back into a high ponytail. "Sit here, Daniel," she says. "This will just take a minute. I'm going to swab your cheek with this, see?" she says as she shows him what looks like a long cotton swab.

He looks up at the nurse and then he looks at Megan and slowly raises his hand a little. It takes Megan a moment to realize that he wants her to hold it, which she does, feeling relieved and grateful at this display of his need for her.

"It won't hurt at all," says the nurse, registering the panic in his eyes.

He nods slowly but doesn't say anything. With his other hand he takes his cell phone out of his pocket. He doesn't turn it on but begins stroking the dark screen, his thumb moving back and forth, smudges building up until the screen is a mess. Megan resists the urge to tell him to stop.

The phone is beginning to bother Megan. Although she knows there is no reason it should, it's almost disturbing in its innocuousness. He had held it in his hand all the way home from the police station, stroking it, like a pet.

"Open up," the nurse instructs as she opens her own mouth. Megan feels her own lips part, the same way they do when she spoons food into Evie's mouth. The nurse swabs the inside of his cheek and then it's done.

The nurse repeats the process with Megan as Daniel watches, his hand still tightly gripping hers.

"Right, sign here, please," she says to Megan. Megan tries to get Daniel to release her hand but he's holding on tightly, squeezing her fingers together. She uses the pen the nurse has given her and scrawls an approximation of her signature with her left hand.

"All done. That wasn't so bad, was it?" she says.

Daniel is silent. He stands up, still holding Megan's hand, and together they walk awkwardly out of the back room and into the office. She feels like her fingers might be going numb because he's squeezing so hard.

At the door of the office he yanks his hand away from hers so fast she stumbles on her feet.

"I'm sorry you had to go through that," she says as they make their way back to the car.

He shrugs.

Megan tries not to sigh as she pulls her car out of the parking lot. "I called Erin, my hairdresser, before we left the house and she says she'll fit you in if we drop by, so let's do that first."

"Whatever will make you happy." His eyes are fixed firmly on the road ahead so he doesn't see Megan shudder at his words.

At the hairdresser's he sits in stony silence while Megan and Erin discuss what to do.

"What do you want to do, Daniel?" Erin asks. "Any ideas on a style?"

He doesn't reply.

"I think just cut it so it's acceptable for school," says Megan.

"Okay, no problem," replies Erin, raising her sculpted eyebrows.

Megan doesn't have the energy to explain more than what she told her on the phone: "My son Daniel is... is home from overseas and he needs a haircut, but he's a bit sensitive so I'm not sure how he's going to react."

"Why don't you sit down and read a magazine and I'll sort this young man out with a wash first," says Erin, sweeping back her own long, blond hair and clipping it on top of her head.

Megan lowers herself into the chair next to Daniel, pretending to read the magazine in her hands but watching her son, the angles of his face becoming more pronounced as the hairdresser works. He remains focused on his own reflection in the mirror, barely moving throughout the haircut. Only his thumb moves on the screen of the mobile phone that he has placed on his lap. At one point it gets covered with hair and Megan opens her mouth to tell him to put it away, but something about the way he is stroking it stops her. He is soothing himself as his hair disappears and a different face appears. She cannot ask him to stop.

"All done," Erin finally says.

"Wow," says Megan, "you look so grown up. It really looks good, Daniel, what do you think?"

"It doesn't look like me."

"You'll get used to it," says Erin jovially.

"It doesn't look like me," he repeats, and Megan's heart sinks.

As they leave the hairdresser's, Megan gestures to the coffee shop next door. "How about something to drink?" she asks, desperate to turn the day around. Daniel doesn't reply but he follows her into the small café, where the barista raises his hand in greeting as he sees her. The smell of coffee hangs in the air and the whooshing sound of steaming milk drowns out the conversations between other customers.

She grabs a table at the back, wanting a quiet spot.

"What can I get you?" asks the waitress, who has followed them over from her spot behind the counter.

"I'll have a peppermint tea and a chocolate chip muffin, and he'll have a chocolate milkshake," she says without thinking. Daniel's favorite treat was always a chocolate milkshake.

"I don't want that," he says.

"Oh," says Megan, flustered as the waitress stares down at them. "What do you want?"

"Coffee."

"Coffee?"

"Yeah, coffee."

"You drink coffee?" she asks when the waitress leaves.

"I like it."

"You never used to like it. I mean, you were too young for it but you once asked for a sip of mine and hated it. Nana used to joke that she'd never seen a child as dedicated to chocolate milkshakes as you were."

"I'm not that child."

"You're still Daniel," Megan replies, her heart racing.

"Maybe I'm not Daniel," he says, meeting her gaze.

Megan feels a prickle of anxiety and then he smiles at her. *It was a joke, just a joke.*

"And Dad... Dad didn't mind you drinking it?" she asks.

"No, he didn't care."

"I'm sure he cared."

"No, not really," he says. "He didn't care about much. He let me do what I wanted as long as I followed a few rules."

"What were his rules?"

He shrugs, looks around the coffee shop, and then rubs his hand over his hair.

"You know it's going to be different now that you're home, right?"

"Is this home?" he asks, staring at the table of people next to them.

"It... is, Daniel, of course it's home."

"In your home you like lots of rules," he mutters, meeting Megan's eyes with his flat, hazel gaze.

"I guess I do." Megan laughs uncertainly.

"You like rules and order and you don't like anything to be out of place. You like things to look right even if they aren't right. You like everyone to smile and be nice even when they don't feel happy."

"That's not . . . that's not true," Megan stutters, stung by his unemotional tone. She knows as she hears the words that she is once again hearing her ex-husband, which only serves to make the words hurt more.

Greg had repeated the same things to her. He hated to be criticized in any way. If she asked him to take out the garbage and he didn't, she wasn't allowed to remind him, even if the bag overflowed onto the kitchen floor. One reminder was greeted with a sigh of distaste, and if she did it again, he would stop whatever he was doing, stomp into the kitchen and wrench the bag out of the can, spilling garbage on the floor, shouting and swearing about everything having to be done on her "bloody timeline," about her "absolute lunacy" of needing everything to look in place and about how she "never gave a shit" about what he was trying to do with his time.

"You were playing video games," she had responded to one of these rants and had earned herself a night of cleaning up the garbage after he went tearing out of the house and grabbed the bag from the outside can so he could bring it in again and throw it all over the floor. After that she had taken the garbage out herself. It was easier than getting into an argument with Greg. After nine years together, seven of them as a married couple, just about everything had been easier than getting into an argument with Greg.

"Sweetheart, listen to me," Megan says as she watches her son drink his coffee after adding three teaspoons of sugar. He's clearly not enjoying it, unable to hide the grimace on his face every time he takes a sip. "Your father and I got divorced because we didn't get along, but you need to know that the things he's told you about me are just his opinion. I'm not the person he's described to you."

"Yes, you are," Daniel spits.

"But how, Daniel? How am I that person?" Megan asks, earning herself a look from the people at the next table.

"He said you didn't want to find me and he was right. I had to find you." Daniel strokes his cell phone compulsively as he speaks.

"That's not true," Megan protests at the unfairness of what he is saying. "I looked for you... I looked for you for years, Daniel."

"Yeah," he says, "he said you would say that if I ever saw you again. That's exactly what he said you'd say."

Megan resists the urge to drag him home and show him her blog, the newspaper articles, the television appearances that are still recorded on her computer to prove to him exactly how hard she had looked for him, but she takes a deep breath and says, "We'll shop today, Daniel, and then tonight I'll show you all the things that happened when you were away and I was trying to find you, okay?"

"You weren't—"

"No, I was, I was and you can ask Nana and Pop and Connor and James and even Lucy because we have all spent the last six years looking for you and hoping that you would come back to us. Okay?"

"Okay," he says finally. His fingers move over the black screen of the cell phone over and over again. He has abandoned his coffee but finished the chocolate muffin she ordered—as she suspected he would.

"Do you want to show me some pictures of you and Dad?" she asks.

He shakes his head but then he says, "Do you really want to see?"

"I do."

He turns on the phone. "I'll show you one. Just one."

"Okay."

He scrolls through his gallery of pictures as Megan drinks the rest of her tea. He holds the phone close to him like a poker player with his cards, occasionally glancing up at her to see if she's trying to catch a glimpse. She keeps her eyes on the table and waits. Finally he turns the phone around to show her a photo of him and Greg standing next to the giant Christ the Redeemer statue at the summit of Mount Corcovado in Rio de Janeiro. They are standing at the base of the towering statue, clutching ice-cream cones, both wearing red baseball caps. Crowds of people are visible in the background.

"When were you there?" Megan asks, staring hard at their huge grins. Her son looks older than six but she can't be sure if he was seven or eight. Why were Greg and Daniel not found if they were using their passports? Would Greg have been capable of producing a false passport? *He was brilliant with technology and worked in cyber security—he would have been capable of anything, even changing her son's name to keep him away from her.*

They both look so happy, she can't help a pang of anger from assaulting her. She had been struggling through every day while Greg traveled the world with their son, having all the experiences she had always dreamed of sharing with him.

"When I was seven or eight. I can't really remember. We went to lots of places. And then we had to come back to Australia because we had no more money."

"Where else did you go? And when did you come back to Australia? How old were you?"

"Wouldn't you like to know," he says. Suddenly he stands up from the table. "Bathroom," he says.

"It's right through there." She gestures, shocked at the sting of his words. *I would like to know. I would really like to know. Didn't you miss me? Didn't you ask for me? Didn't you ask to come home when you returned to Australia?*

Megan would like to get hold of the phone and look through all the pictures by herself even though she knows seeing her ex-husband and son so happy together will break her heart even as it makes her angry. So far Daniel hasn't let it out of his sight. Last night when she looked in on him, he was sleeping with it tightly gripped in his hand. It's his new Billy Blanket.

She has seen that "Daniel and Dad" has been scratched into the plastic on the side of the phone. "It's obviously a security object," Michael had said. "We need to let him hold on to it as long as he wants to. It's his last connection to his father, and it's basically his history over the last six years. Everything else was burned in the fire. He will eventually want to share the pictures with you but for now don't push him."

Daniel returns from the bathroom and stands next to the table.

Megan smiles up at him. "How about we take your phone to a store and get a new SIM for it," she says. "I mean, if they still have them for phones like that. It's pretty old. I'm happy to buy a new one for you." She had set out to buy him a phone for his twelfth birthday but, in the store, the terrible thought that she would not be able to call him on it had stopped her from making the purchase. "I think most kids carry them by the time they're twelve and Lucy got one for her last birthday. I know Max has one."

"Max?" he says, and Megan hears an edge of something in his voice, a kind of longing excitement.

"Yes, you remember Max, don't you?"

Daniel nods. "I remember Max."

"Would you like to see him? We can go and see him whenever you want."

"I . . . no," he says and he turns to leave.

Megan gets up and hurriedly pays the bill, following him out onto the street. A cold wind whistles through the air and Megan worries about Daniel's feet in flip-flops. "We need to get you some shoes, but do you want to stop and get a new SIM card first?"

"Who am I going to call?" He smirks. "Ghostbusters?"

Megan starts laughing but then stops when she sees the look on his face. "That's a very old movie. When did you see it?"

"With him, just like I did everything else. With him."

With him, with him, with him. You should have been with me.

CHAPTER TWELVE

Daniel looks overwhelmed as they enter the shopping center. His head swings from the neon signs of one shop to another. A child throwing a screaming tantrum lies on the floor, and Megan sees him wince at the noise. The smell of frying food drifts up from the food court and she sees him lick his lips, even though he's just eaten.

"Let's start with shoes," she says.

Daniel is compliant as the hours wear on. Compliant but silent. Megan finds herself unable to say no to anything he wants even though he doesn't actually ask for anything. Rather than talking, he stares longingly at items in the shops, or strokes them gently.

"Do you like that?" Megan asks as he touches a handheld PlayStation console in the electronics store. "Do you want one?"

She is prepared for a shrug from Daniel but instead he turns to her and says, "More than anything in the whole world." The words come slowly, dredged up from deep inside himself as though painful to utter, and afterward Megan sees his eyes dart sideways, guiltily roaming around the store for watchful judgment from the other customers. He had clearly been taught not to ask for things, not to want them. Perhaps because he and Greg had so little money, so little to survive on.

"Do you understand in your tiny little mind what it takes for me to earn enough money for you to sit on your ass all day?" Greg had berated her when she'd told him she needed more money to cover their household expenses.

"I think the most important thing you can do is stay home and look after our son. Let me worry about the money," he had said the very next week. Megan had lived in a permanent state of unease and confusion.

He holds the bag with the PlayStation in his hands, occasionally peeking inside when she stops to pick up items of clothing she thinks will fit him in a big department store.

"Right, let's go in here," she says, directing him to the changing rooms. She slides a curtain open and steps inside a cubicle, hanging everything on a silver hook. She turns to find him looking at her. It takes her a moment to realize that he wants her to leave him alone in there.

"I'm sorry," she mutters, backing out. "I keep forgetting how big you are."

"But you can see me, can't you?" Daniel sneers.

"I'm sorry." She sighs, shocked by his tone. She risks a quick glance at her watch—it's only two o'clock but it feels like she and Daniel have been shopping for a week. *He's not enjoying this either. His world has been turned upside down and he's just lost his father.* "Take your time," she calls, injecting cheer into her voice. However strange this is for her, it must be doubly so for him. He's barely old enough to process all of this.

She sinks into a chair outside the changing room and slips two headache pills into her mouth. A mother with a toddler throws her a glance of sympathy and she allows herself a wry smile. *If only you knew the truth,* she thinks.

Daniel emerges from the change room in a pair of pants and a top, and she stands up and reaches out to him, slipping her fingers between the waistband of the pants and his skin. He recoils as though burned as she touches him.

"Sorry, I'm sorry," she says, lifting her hands up as though he's pointing a gun at her. "They look fine, do they feel all right?" she asks.

"They're fine," he says.

While she waits for him to change outfits, she remembers that at six years old Daniel spent more time draped over her or holding her hand or hugging her than anything else. He didn't even balk at sitting on her lap despite being too big for it. She realizes that such a physically close relationship must fade as a child grows, but she has missed the slow raising of boundaries that she is sure happens in every family. Instead she has lost an affectionate little boy and found a skittish, rigid adolescent in his place. Swallowing down another gulp of water, Megan hates Greg with a new fierceness. She hopes he is in hell where he belongs. She shakes her head, instantly guilty at the thought. Her ex-husband had been burned to death. Daniel has just lost his father, and even though he is showing very little emotion, Megan knows that his strange behavior is probably his way of protecting himself from feeling his grief. She admonishes herself to be patient.

By the time they collect Evie and return home, Megan is on the verge of tears.

"Do you want something to eat?" she asks Daniel because she knows that despite lunch and the snacks he's had throughout the day, this is the one thing he will say yes to.

Megan flicks on the television, needing something mindless to watch for a few minutes; the news channel is on.

"...a number of house fires in the region including in the towns of Heddon Greta, Kotara, and Cardiff. Police suspect a serial arsonist," she hears and she immediately presses the button on the remote, her heart racing.

"He likes fires," Daniel mutters.

"Pardon?" says Megan.

Daniel looks at her. "I didn't say anything."

"You did, Daniel, you just said, 'He likes fires.' Who likes fires? Dad? Did Dad like fires?"

"I-didn't-say-anything," Daniel replies, his jaw clenching; and then he leaves the room, leaving her bewildered.

*

"You went a little nuts, Megs," Michael says when he checks the credit card that night.

"I know, I know, I'm sorry, I was trying to... God, I have no idea what I was trying to do."

"I get it, it's okay. You wanted to give him everything, to make up for the years he had nothing."

Megan allows herself a dry laugh. "I would buy him a car if he would just speak to me."

"That bad?"

"Worse than you can imagine."

Michael shuts down the computer and goes to the kitchen, returning with a bottle of wine and two glasses. It's after ten and Megan knows that both of them need to get to bed, but Evie had taken ages to get to sleep and Daniel had only turned off his light after nine thirty. He had been lying in bed playing his new PlayStation, and even though Megan knew it was the wrong thing to allow him to do and that she should start off with him as she meant to go on—instituting rules and boundaries—she didn't have the heart to tell him to stop. He had been playing the PlayStation since they returned home. She had thought about showing him her blog and everything else she had collected but he hadn't seemed interested in anything but the new device and she was exhausted from the day. "Tomorrow," she comforted herself. "I will show him tomorrow."

"Did he say anything to you about what it was like with Greg?" Michael asks after they've both taken a gulp of the deep-red wine.

"Not much. He barely says anything, although every now and again Greg's voice comes straight out of his mouth."

"I imagine it would. He probably didn't have much contact with other people over the last six years."

"They traveled all over the world. He showed me one picture on the phone of him and Greg in Rio. I don't know why they weren't caught."

"Fake passports are easier to obtain than you might think."

"He doesn't feel like my child," she confesses, concentrating on staring at her wine so she can't see the look on his face.

"He's very... very... he's not how you described him."

"I know." Megan sighs, unable to stop tears from falling. "I don't know who he is now. I don't know how to speak to him. He won't even let me touch him."

"That must be... just awful," says Michael. "I wish I knew how to help."

"I think I need help from a professional. Do you think you can ask around at work?"

"Absolutely, Linda deals with kids all the time," he says, referring to another detective at his station. "She'll know who we should contact."

Megan closes her eyes and leans her head onto the top of the soft leather couch. "It feels like he hasn't come home yet; it feels like Daniel isn't home."

"Oh, sweetheart, it will get better. I'm sure it will get better." He raises his glass and drains it. "I think a good night's sleep will help. You can start again in the morning." He stands up and holds out his hand to her.

"I might just sit here for a minute before coming to bed."

"Sure, I'll have a quick shower, but try not to be too late. Evie might not sleep through the night and I don't want you to be too exhausted."

"I'm sure she won't." Megan smiles, experiencing a slight surge of hope that her daughter will wake up in the night. She feels the need for close physical contact with one of her children, and a nighttime feed with Evie will bring her pleasure rather than frustration at missed sleep.

When she hears the shower turn on upstairs, she grabs her laptop and sinks back into the couch with it on her lap. She opens her Facebook page, wanting to tell Tom and Sandi how the day has gone. Since Daniel has come home, she hasn't had the chance to talk to them beyond letting them know her news.

"So incredibly happy for you!!!" Sandi had responded.

"What a wonderful thing," Tom had written. *"Do you know what made him decide to send him back to you?"*

"Greg died. I can't really get into the specifics but he died."

"That's horrible. Poor kid. But at least you got him back."

"This is not how I wanted it to happen."

Megan finds herself being more careful with Tom than she is with Sandi. Her relationship with Tom has become more complicated as the years have passed.

When Daniel had been gone for nearly four years and only a few months before she agreed to go on a date with Michael—Tom had told her he would be visiting Australia and he wanted to meet up.

"How wonderful," Megan had typed. *"I would so love to meet you so we could talk about this all face-to-face. It's strange to think that I feel so close to you but I don't even know what you look like."*

"Jemima is prettier than I am (ha ha). I feel close to you too, Megan. I feel like we've known each other forever, and even though we met in the saddest of circumstances, I am grateful that we met."

"If you tell me when you'll be here, we could get together for dinner or lunch, anything that fits in with your schedule."

"I have a better idea. I'll be staying at the Winslow Hotel in Sydney. Apparently, it has nice views of the city. After I check in, I'll let you know my room number. I'll leave a key for you at the desk. All you need to do is come upstairs and I'll be waiting."

Megan had read his message and laughed. He was obviously joking. He was joking, wasn't he? She felt close to Tom as they suffered through their heartbreak, supporting each other, but she had never really thought they would meet, let alone have any sort of romantic relationship. He lived in Far North Queensland and they were bonded only by their shared experience of having their children taken from them. It was not enough to build a relationship on. She decided to assume he was joking.

"Ha ha, but seriously. I would really like to have lunch with you or something."

"I'm not joking, Megan. We've been talking for years and I feel like we have a really strong connection. Don't you want to be with me as much as I want to be with you?"

Megan had read his words in shock. She had waited for thirty minutes before replying, fretting and chewing a fingernail as she composed a message that wouldn't upset him too much.

"I'm sorry, Tom. I didn't think that our relationship was like that. I don't think I'm ready for any kind of relationship at all, to be honest. I can't see myself ever having a man in my life while my son is missing. It feels wrong. I don't believe I will ever have a relationship like that again."

"I thought we had something special," Tom had written.

"We did, we do," she had replied. *"But I feel like I have something special with Sandi as well. It's not an attraction, it's a meeting of broken hearts, I guess. I don't know if I will ever feel ready for anything more than friendship. Please, can you just be my friend?"*

"Okay, I understand," had been his short reply. Tom had withdrawn and stayed offline for weeks until one day she received a new message from him.

"My trip was canceled, so don't worry about meeting me."

"I would have loved to have met you, Tom. I'm sorry if I hurt your feelings."

"Don't worry about me. I guess I thought there was more between us than there was. I came on too strong. I'm sorry."

"It's okay. You and Sandi have helped me get through these last years. I don't know what I would have done without you."

"Let's just forget it, shall we? I'm happy to have you as a friend."

Megan had imagined that whatever had happened in Tom's head was over, until, less than a year later, she'd told him and Sandi that she was getting married.

"How wonderful," Sandi had written. *"He's a lucky man. I am so glad you've managed to move on and find some happiness. I don't know if I'll ever be able to be with anyone again when I carry my lost children with me all the time, but I am so pleased that you've managed to find a way."*

"Not really move on," Megan had replied. *"I could never really move on, but it's nice to have someone in my life again."*

"I agree, you can never really move on."

"Who is he?" Tom had asked. The abruptness of the question had worried Megan but she wanted to keep Tom as a friend after everything they had been through.

"His name is Michael and he's actually the first detective who ever interviewed me about Daniel. He has called me once a year on the anniversary of Daniel's disappearance and this year he asked me out to dinner."

"So, you've only been going out with him for what, like... eight months? That's quick, isn't it?"

"Maybe," Megan had agreed, *"but it doesn't feel quick. It just feels right. Please don't be angry with me, Tom. I hadn't intended for any of this to happen but I have to admit that it feels good to have something in my life other than just my hopes that Daniel will be found. I hope that one day you find someone as well."*

"I don't think I will ever move on. Even though what my wife did was terrible, I don't think I will ever be able to stop loving her. But maybe that's the difference between men and women. I think once a man loves you, he loves you forever."

"Come on, Tom," Sandi had interjected, *"you know we don't do this to each other. We are parents whose children have been taken from them. We don't argue about whose behavior is worse. Megan deserves a little bit of happiness. You want that for her, just like I do."*

"I'm not saying she doesn't deserve to be happy, of course she does. I want you to be happy, Megan, I really do. I guess I'm just feeling a little lost today. I saw a little girl who was the same age Jemima

was when she was taken. I couldn't stop staring at her and I think eventually her mother got a little worried. I'm sorry if I've upset you, Megan. You do deserve to be happy. I shouldn't have said anything and I won't from now on."

Tom had, true to his word, not talked about her getting married again, and they had easily fallen back into speaking only about their children.

But now things have changed for her and she knows how difficult that must be for Tom. First, she moved on with her life and then her son was returned to her. It must seem very unfair to him.

Daniel's reappearance in her life is something both Tom and Sandi long for with their own children. She needs to remember how blessed she is to have her son sleeping in his bedroom right now.

Sandi has left a message asking how her first day with Daniel has gone, and while Megan wants to tell her that it was just wonderful, she knows she doesn't need to lie to her friend.

"It was strange. I wanted us to just click back into how we had been before his father took him, but he's such a completely different person that I felt like I was spending the day with a stranger."

Megan sees the icon indicating Sandi is online and replying. She smiles, feeling relieved that she can talk to her now.

"Keep trying, it will take time. He's been away for a long time," writes Sandi. *"This is exactly what you have dreamed of for years, and even if it's a little hard, you need to remember that. I would give anything... anything to have my girls back. Nothing is ever simple or easy, not children, not marriage, not life. Don't give up too easily on him. Let him know that you are willing to do whatever it takes to make him feel at home and happy again."*

Megan nods as she reads Sandi's words. There is also a message from Tom asking how things are going.

"A bit difficult," she writes now, reluctant to go into detail.

She puts the computer on the coffee table and goes to empty her nearly full glass of wine into the sink. She won't drink if Evie might need a feed, and she's a little unsettled right now, so it's possible she will.

When she sits down again, Tom has replied.

"It will be, I guess. He lost you six years ago and now he feels like he's lost the only parent he's had for six years. I guess the only advice I could give you is to let him know he can talk to you about his grief. You know, just let him mourn. Let him mourn his father. Even if you are angry with your ex-husband, it's important to let him talk about him."

"I'm not sure I can feel anything toward Greg except anger right now," replies Megan.

"You have him back and your ex is gone. You must have loved him once and I know how much you love your son. Put aside your anger and let him talk about how he's feeling. Boys tend to bottle things up. I know I did when I was younger."

Megan yawns as she reads Tom's words. The day has caught up with her and she needs to go to sleep.

"I will try. Thanks, Tom," she writes, and then she closes down her computer. It's good to have Tom's perspective and she reminds herself to hold back on her complaints with him. She doesn't want to seem ungrateful that her son is home. She has to admit that if Tom's or Sandi's daughters had been the ones to return home, she would struggle to listen to them complain that things weren't perfect. Perfection is an illusion. She makes up her mind to try harder with Daniel in the morning.

Getting up, Megan heads upstairs, where two bedrooms are filled with her children, something she had not imagined was possible a few days ago.

She looks in on both of them. Evie is sprawled across her crib, rosy-cheeked and dark-haired, and Daniel is lying on his side, curled up in his car bed, one hand clutching the cell phone and the other, she is pleased to see, holding his Billy Blanket.

CHAPTER THIRTEEN

Seven days since Daniel's return

"How is it going?" Olivia asks on the phone. "Is he settling in?"

Megan sighs. "I have no idea how to answer that, really." She looks behind her in case Daniel has wandered into the living room. She runs through what she can tell Olivia, debating with herself about what to say. Should she tell her that he has a habit of suddenly being in a room, right next to her, without announcing himself? That he moves soundlessly through the house, wanting but not asking for anything? That he barely speaks to her, and when he does it's apparent he's taken time to rehearse what he's going to say?

"He sleeps through the night and he eats whatever I put in front of him but it feels like he's somewhere else, like his mind is somewhere else," Megan says.

"He has just lost his father."

"He has just lost the monster who was taking care of him."

"Poor Daniel, poor baby," murmurs Olivia.

"I just want him to be able to put this all behind him, but realistically it will be ages until we can have a funeral for Greg. I had to contact our old dentist to send over some dental records to the police and we've sent a swab of Daniel's DNA up there as well. It's so frustrating—there's so much red tape."

"It will be easier for Daniel when he has some real closure and a grave he can go and visit."

"I know, but even with Michael's help it's going to take a long time. I'm just trying to figure out how to . . . to be with him, you know?"

"He's still Daniel, Megs, just older."

"Not really, I don't know how to explain it, but not really. Everything that has happened has changed him so much that who he was at six seems to have completely disappeared. I have no idea what kind of life he was living. I don't know anything about him. He answers my questions with one word and he doesn't speak unless I ask him a direct question. There's no emotion, no joy. I don't know what to say to him or how to talk to him. It's like he's a complete stranger."

Megan covers her mouth with her hand. The words have come out in a rush, startling her. She hadn't meant to say this much. She knows that the only feeling she should be experiencing is one of gratitude that her child is back home with her, where he belongs, and she doesn't want to tell Olivia that he doesn't feel like her child. She cannot bear to say the words.

"Hang in there," says Olivia. "I'm here if you need me."

What she doesn't say to Olivia, what scares her, is that she can feel herself falling back into the same habits she had adopted when she was married to Greg. She talks constantly to cover Daniel's silences and she watches him all the time, looking for a sign that she has made him smile or laugh, or in case she has upset him in some way. It makes her angry with herself because Daniel is not a threat like his father was, but his silent, watchful presence unnerves her and she has no idea when or if things will ever go back to what she thought of as normal.

After saying goodbye to Olivia, Megan goes downstairs, stopping at the door to Michael's office. "They'll be here soon," she says.

"Great, anything you want me to do?"

"No, I'm basically done . . . I just wish I could calm down a little."

"I know, I imagine you're struggling, but it'll be fine. I'm sure it will be."

Megan hears a sound from Evie's room through the monitor she has set up in the kitchen, but her daughter is still fast asleep when she looks in. Daniel has, at least, shown some interest in Evie. He watches her a lot and she has seen him pat her on the head, as though she is a pet, once or twice.

"Hello, Evie," he says to her, and Evie responds with, "Gaah."

In the kitchen she finishes icing the cake she has made for today. Her imaginary scenarios of how everything would play out once Daniel had returned home have been crushed one after the other.

She hopes, fervently hopes, that today goes well. She hasn't yet told Daniel about everyone in the family coming to tea, and they will be here soon. She wipes her hands and takes a deep breath.

As she starts up the stairs, she sees him standing in the doorway of Evie's room.

"Daniel?" she says.

He whirls around and then flings himself back into his room and onto his bed. Megan ascends the stairs quickly and checks on Evie, who is lying peacefully sprawled across her crib.

Daniel has left his door slightly open. He is on his bed, lost in his game, as though he hasn't moved all afternoon.

"What were you doing in Evie's room?"

"I thought," he says, his eyes fixed on the small screen, "that I heard her crying."

"Oh, really? I didn't hear her on the monitor downstairs."

"Why do you always have that thing with you?"

"So I can hear her if she wakes up."

"I thought I heard her."

"I just checked and she's still asleep." She inhales deeply. "Nana and Pop are coming over, and Connor and James and they're bringing Lucy. Do you remember Lucy?" she asks.

He doesn't lift his eyes from his game. "Sure," he says.

You said you didn't remember her in the car on the way home.

"Lucy was so little when you... left, but she's eight years old now. Do you remember how excited you were when Connor and James brought her home from Vietnam?"

Daniel shrugs.

How do you feel about being back home? Why won't you look at me? Please tell me what you're thinking. Let me help you, Daniel. I can help you. Megan swallows all the things she wants to say and simply says, "Okay, well, I'll see you downstairs soon." She returns to the kitchen to get some more cups for the dining room table. She places the cake in the center of the table, the chocolate and vanilla layer cake that is exactly like the one Daniel had asked her to make for his sixth birthday.

The toll of the bell startles her. Megan finds herself nervous, a little sweaty. She has not told her mother how she is feeling about her son's return, hoping it is just her and Daniel readjusting to each other.

She takes a deep breath and opens the front door.

"Darling," says her mother when she sees her and then, "Hello, Daniel."

Megan turns quickly. She had not known that he was standing behind her. "Nana," he says and she hears the tears locked in his throat. He throws himself into his grandmother's arms. "I missed you so much," he says, his voice muffled against the fabric of the gray jumper she's wearing.

"Oh, Daniel darling, I missed you too. You have no idea how much. I thought about you every day."

He has to bend his knees to hug his grandmother. He is taller than she is by almost a whole head. Megan watches the embrace, remembering him holding her mother's hand, looking up at her and telling her a "knock, knock" joke.

"Knock, knock, Nana."

"Who's there, Daniel?"

"Interrupting cow."

"Interrupting cow wh—"

"Moo."

Megan's father puts his hand on Daniel's shoulder and gives it a squeeze, just letting him know he's there. Without letting go of his grandmother, Daniel turns his head. "Can we play chess again, Pop? Can we?"

"Of course," rumbles her father. "I brought the set for you. I left it in the car because I wasn't sure you'd want to play." Packing up the chess game he and Daniel had been playing was one of the most difficult things her father had had to do when they'd sold their house. On the last day they'd lived there, activity had whirled around him as Connor, James, Megan, her mother, and the movers had packed up the last few boxes; but he had been still, sitting at the small table, staring at the chessboard until it was time to go and he no longer had a choice.

"I do," Daniel says, laughing. "I'll come get it with you."

On the way to the car with his grandfather, Daniel stops to greet Connor and James. He doesn't hug either of them, but simply nods and glances quickly at Lucy before looking away.

Megan is at once baffled and upset. He has shown his grandparents more emotion in five minutes than he has shown her in a whole week. He has also basically ignored Connor, James, and Lucy. Megan knows that he had adored Lucy since the day he met her. It had been, according to him when she had tucked him in that night, "the best day of my life."

The day Connor and James had brought Lucy home, Megan, Daniel, and her parents had gone to the airport to pick them up.

At the time, Greg had said, "You'd think they'd managed to have the kid themselves, the way you people are going on and on about it."

"Maybe you shouldn't come to the airport," she had replied.

"Like I care what you think. I wouldn't have come even if you wanted me to."

Megan had by then been waiting for the right moment to tell Greg that she wanted a divorce. She was fearful of his reaction, unsure if the news would be greeted with aggression and violence or weeping and self-pity.

On the way to the airport she had gone through the explanation about adoption again for Daniel.

"But where is Lucy's mum?" he had asked.

"She lives in Vietnam but she couldn't take care of Lucy so she asked Uncle Connor and Uncle James to do it for her."

"But will she visit her? Will Lucy see her mum?" he had asked, and Megan had sensed some panic in his voice.

"Don't worry, darling. I'm not going to ask anyone else to look after you. I will always be here."

"Forever and ever?"

"Forever and ever. But Lucy now has two daddies who will be there for her forever and ever."

"And me," he had said proudly. "I'm going to be the big cousin and it's a big responsibility because I have to help her and play with her and be nice to her."

"Exactly," Megan had said.

She had been a little worried about how he would react to Lucy because she knew that he wasn't meeting her as a baby. At eighteen months old, Lucy would already be a little person in her own right and she wanted them to get along. She wanted him to have another child in the family to play with, even if they were so vastly different in age. She had wanted, had planned, had always imagined that she would have another child, but Greg had said, "I don't want to go back to the broken nights again," even though he was never the one to get up. "You become so involved with the baby it's like I don't even exist and you gained so much weight last time. You know how uncomfortable you were and how you hated the nausea," he had said. And so, months and years passed and Megan had watched her dream of another child fade, convincing herself that Greg was right, that it would be too difficult for her and for their marriage.

She hadn't needed to worry about Daniel and Lucy getting along. From the moment they met, they adored each other.

"I play with Legos, Lucy," Daniel had told her seriously as he sat with her on the floor of Connor's living room, "but you're too little for that. I can build a tower for you and you can knock it down. Mum says babies like to knock stuff down." He'd piled one wooden block on top of another until the tower had begun to wobble. "Knock it down, Lucy, knock it down and it will go bang."

Lucy had stared at the tower for a minute and then swiped her hand at it, sending the blocks tumbling down.

"Yay, Lucy," he'd shouted, clapping his hands. "You made it go bang. Bang, bang, all gone."

"Bang," Lucy had said quietly, and then the adults had had to leave the room for a moment because there were too many tears to explain to Daniel.

Lucy had been two and a half when Greg had picked up Daniel from school and disappeared. Megan knows that at eight, nearly nine, Lucy looks nothing like she did as a chubby baby. She is tall and thin with thick black hair that hangs past her waist. Megan had seen her smile shyly at Daniel and receive nothing in return. Her heart breaks for her niece who has been waiting for her idolized cousin to return. She wants to take her aside and explain that she shouldn't be upset by his behavior, but she herself is upset so she worries she won't sound convincing to the little girl.

As the afternoon wears on Daniel grows increasingly withdrawn. He plays one game of chess with his grandfather and then refuses a piece of cake even though Megan sees him looking over at it every now and again.

He rebuffs any attempts Lucy makes at conversation, communicating in shrugs and monosyllables. He is actively rude to Connor and James, curling his lip and almost sneering whenever either one of them says anything. Megan sees Connor and James exchanging looks and feels the urge to apologize for her son's bad behavior.

"Are you still into science?" Connor asks.

"How can anyone be into science?" His eyes narrow as though the question has offended him.

"Daniel!" exclaims Megan.

"Oh, you'd be surprised by the number of people who are into science. You used to be one of those people when you were little. Do you remember coming to visit me in the lab?"

"No."

"You loved it. You looked through the microscope at the cells dividing and told me you were going to be a scientist when you grew up, just like me."

"Wouldn't want to be like you anymore."

"Daniel, how can you say that to your uncle?" Megan yells, instantly ashamed at herself for raising her voice.

"I can say what I like," he shouts back, startling everyone at the table. "Who cares what job you have or if you took me to your lab? You're a horrible liar, all of you are horrible liars who only care about yourselves." He spits the words, his face and ears growing red and his fists clenched. He stands up before anyone can say anything and continues his tirade. "You never cared about me or my dad. All you did was hurt him and make her divorce him." He points an accusing finger in Megan's direction. "She hurt—"

"That's enough, Daniel, go to your room," Michael says, raising his voice just enough to silence Daniel, who is panting with rage. He opens his mouth to speak again and Michael stands up. Megan watches Daniel's shoulders drop, his eyes widening as he looks up at Michael. "I said go to your room," he repeats quietly.

Daniel lets out a sharp sound of distress and then he spins around and runs to his room, slamming the door so hard the sound reverberates around the house.

A brittle silence descends. "Oh God." Megan sinks her head into her hands. "I'm so sorry, Con, oh God, I'm so sorry."

"Megs, it's okay, it's okay, just relax. He's just blowing off some steam. This must be so weird for him," comforts Connor.

"All twelve-year-old boys are assholes," says James. "I know because I was one."

Everyone at the table laughs, the tension broken.

"Dad, you said a swear-jar word," Lucy says.

"I did, baby," laughs James. "But I think everyone can forgive everyone for any bad behavior today."

"Danny hates us," says Lucy quietly as she picks up cake crumbs with her fingers.

"No, he doesn't, Luce," protests Megan. "He just has to get used to everyone again. I promise you that soon you two will be the best of friends." Megan hopes that the words sound more convincing to eight-year-old Lucy than they do to her.

"I think it's time for us to go," says her mother, and everyone stands up at once. "He will be fine," she says, planting a kiss on Megan's forehead. "I promise he'll be fine."

Megan nods her head, blinking quickly to stop any tears falling. "Fine" feels like the last thing Daniel is going to be.

CHAPTER FOURTEEN

As she cleans up Megan remembers Daniel at five at a family dinner, making jokes and asking questions, interested in everything and everyone. He had been the first and only grandchild for years and had basked in the attention he received at family gatherings.

The level of vitriol hurled at Connor, at all of them, was disturbing. He had never had a temper, had never been the kind of child who sought confrontation. Megan knows that the things he had said were straight out of Greg's mouth, and as she wipes the kitchen counter she despairs at the lies he would have been fed by his father, at how much effort Greg would have put into discrediting them.

The onslaught must have been continuous for the little boy as his father sought to turn him against the people he loved. In the end all she can feel is pity for him. She knows that he is suffering and confused, with no idea what to believe.

"I might go for a run," Michael says, coming into the kitchen.

"I wish I could join you," she says.

"You could—we can put Evie in her carriage. She'll enjoy getting out in the fresh air."

"Maybe you could take her with you. I don't think I should leave him alone and I could use a little time with him. I need to explain about going to the school tomorrow."

"Absolutely." He puts his arms around her, holds her tightly, and she drops her head onto his chest.

"What are we going to do?"

"We're going to take it one day at a time. We're going to get him some help and just take it one day at a time."

Megan nods. Michael releases her, and five minutes later he and Evie are gone, Evie strapped tightly into the carriage, tucked up under a blanket against the late-afternoon chill.

She finds Daniel sitting in his bedroom on his new wooden bed. The room is now overfilled with stuff, after he unwrapped all of his presents from the last six years with an almost amused detachment.

"So much stuff," he'd said when he was done, seemingly unable to take in the piles of books and art supplies, toys and games.

"It is but you don't have to keep it all. You can give it away to someone younger or to charity," Megan had told him.

"No, no!" he'd said. "They're mine, it's mine."

"It's yours," Megan had repeated, reassuring him, her heart breaking for him. *How long since he's had something that's just his except for the useless cell phone and the homemade knife we took away?*

She doesn't like to think about the knife. "He was living fairly rough," Michael has said. "It's the kind of thing boys would have done years ago. We had to take it away but I don't think it's that big a deal."

His eyes are fixed on the screen of his PlayStation, thumbs moving furiously. She can see the cell phone wedged into the pocket of his jeans.

She thinks about how to address what has just happened but finds herself struggling for a way to begin. She doesn't want to upset him any more than he already has been. He seems calm now and she would like him to remain that way.

"Hey, sweetheart," she says softly. He doesn't look at her. "I want to talk to you about what's going to happen tomorrow when we go to school," she continues.

"Okay," he says but he doesn't look away from his game.

"Can you put that down, please?"

He ignores her.

"I mean it, Daniel. Put it down and look at me or I'll take it away." She hates that her tone has changed, that she has had to raise her voice at him.

He throws the game onto his bed. "Fuck, fine."

Greg's words again. Greg's expression.

"I don't want to hear that word again," she says and then she sighs. She needs to be patient with him. "Tomorrow we'll be going to your new school. You're not going to do anything there except take some tests so they can see what year you belong in, and I'll be with you the whole time."

He pulls the phone out of his pocket, stroking the screen with his thumb. He's nervous about tomorrow. The stroking of the phone is the clearest indication of how he's feeling.

She remembers him at three when they talked about him starting his first day of preschool. He had used Billy Blanket to comfort himself, winding and unwinding the blanket around his hand.

"But how long will I go there?" he'd asked at the time.

"Just a few hours, Daniel, but it'll be fun. Mrs. Desmond is going to take care of you, and you like her—you had such fun when you went there last week to play."

"But when can I come home again?"

"I will fetch you at two o'clock. I will fetch you every day at two o'clock until you're happy to stay until three o'clock."

"And what will I eat?"

"I will pack you your lunch—all your favorite things in your Thomas the Tank Engine lunch box that we bought."

Round and round his hand the Billy Blanket went.

Back and forth across the screen of the cell phone his thumb now goes.

You're still my boy. Still the same sensitive little boy.

"So, sweetheart—are you okay with that?" she asks softly.

"Does it matter how I feel?" He stares at the black screen of his phone and Megan resists the urge to grab it away from him.

"Of course it matters, Daniel. You need to go to school, that's the law, but if you don't like the school maybe we can look at another one. We could wait if you don't feel ready."

"You won't wait and you won't care if I hate the stupid school you've picked." His voice is low, menacing, and he still doesn't look at her.

"I've just said I would."

"He said you always did that, said you would do something and then backed away. He said you told him you would have another baby but then you didn't want to and that you said you loved him but then you didn't. He said you told him you wanted to save your marriage but then you just filed for divorce."

How do I answer this?

"Daniel, what happens between two people when they're married is something only they understand. I did want another baby but..." *It was him who didn't want another child, and why would he have told you this anyway? What was he trying to accomplish?* She sighs. "I know that the divorce upset your dad but it was the best thing for both of us."

"It wasn't the best thing for me."

"I know, baby, I know, but I didn't know he was going to take you. I didn't know what would happen."

He shoves the phone back into his pocket.

Look at me. Please just look at me.

"I didn't know, Daniel, I just didn't know he was going to take you from me, and I have spent the last six years blaming myself."

"Of course you knew." The words are spat at Megan and finally he looks directly at her, locking eyes with her, holding her gaze.

"How could I have known, Daniel?"

"You knew because you told him."

"Told him what?"

"You told him to take me."

Later she will wish she had reacted calmly, that she had swallowed her fury and explained that this was not the truth, but the afternoon had worn her down. Her face heats up and she explodes, her voice escalating in decibels with each thing she says. "Why would I have said that, Daniel? Why would I ever have said something so awful and stupid? Who says something like that? How could you have ever believed that of me?"

"He told me you asked him to take me away because you were tired of taking care of me, because I made a mess and I didn't listen, because you stopped loving me like you stopped loving him!" he screams back, and then shockingly, horrifyingly, he leaps off the bed and shoves her backward, making her stumble. She steps backward out of his bedroom.

"I hate you," he growls. "I hate you, I hate you, I hate you."

"D-Daniel," she stutters, too astonished to do anything else.

He steps forward and slams his bedroom door so hard it trembles in its frame.

When Michael returns with Evie, Megan is sitting on the sofa, shredding a damp tissue to pieces.

"What happened, what happened?" he asks, panic in his voice.

Megan sobs her way through an explanation and Michael sits down next to her and grabs her hand. "It's okay, it's going to be okay. It was a difficult afternoon. I think we should just leave him alone for a bit. He doesn't know how or what to feel. He shouldn't have shoved you, and we will talk to him about that, but don't confront him now. Let him cool off."

"It felt…it felt just like it used to feel when Greg got angry. I don't know what to do, Michael. It's like he isn't even my son."

Michael sighs, "I got an email while I was out. It's the results of the DNA test you did."

"The results of the DNA test? Oh yes of course," says Megan.

"Do you want to know... I mean we know... you know but..."

Megan drops her head into her hands. *Do I want to know? What if? What if?* She looks up at Michael, "What does it say?"

Michael opens up the email, scans the information quickly. "You're a match," he says softly.

"We're a match," she says. She had known this would be the case because of course he's her son. She nods her head, accepting this wonderful news. She doesn't even want to think about the small part of her, the very small part of her that expected a different result.

"Just give him some space. I think he needs a little quiet time. I'm sure he's upset about what he's done. I say we get on with dinner and I will speak to him in the morning."

"Okay... but, Michael, it was so scary, he was so scary. I'm afraid of him. I think I'm afraid of my own son." *My own son, my son.*

At two o'clock in the morning Megan gives up on sleep, deciding to make herself a cup of herbal tea.

As she makes her way down the stairs, she hears a sound coming from the kitchen, a soft grunting noise. She stops and turns to look back to her bedroom, wanting to dash upstairs and wake Michael. The sound of something running across the roof makes her jump. *Just a possum, calm down.*

In the kitchen, Daniel is sitting at the counter. He has the leftover cake from afternoon tea in front of him and he is tearing into it with both hands, grunting as he eats, making him seem more animal than boy.

"Daniel," she gasps. He immediately stops and stares blankly at her. Megan freezes. "Um... if you wanted cake... you can eat it... you just should have used a plate."

"Sorry," he says, his hands curled into claws, bits of cake dropping onto the counter.

"I think it's time to go back to bed now," she says and Daniel nods at her. She grabs a cloth and wipes his hands while he stares at her.

"When I was six, you made me a birthday cake. It was chocolate and white and it had superheroes on top of it. I like superheroes." A smile plays on his lips and she can't help smiling back at the obvious happiness the memory brings him.

She finishes cleaning his hands. "I know you like superheroes, darling. Spiderman was your favorite because he could climb walls."

"And swing from webs," he says, his voice soft.

"And swing from webs," she agrees. "But now it's time for sleep. Can you go back to your bedroom and go to sleep?"

"Back to sleep," he says and he leaves the kitchen.

Back in bed, too shaken to think about making herself some tea, she curls herself around Michael, trying to get some comfort from his warmth and bulk. She watches the alarm clock on his bedside table as the numbers turn over and the night fades into day.

The terrible thought that Greg may have used food as a punishment or a reward with Daniel keeps her anxious and awake. He is thin but not overly so, and yet he treats every mealtime as though it might be his last.

"What kind of things did you eat when you lived with... with Dad?" she had asked him a few days after he arrived home.

"Whatever we could afford, sometimes nothing," he had replied.

It floors Megan that Greg's hatred of her ran so deep that he would make not only his son suffer but himself as well.

Finally, as dawn breaks, she drifts into a light doze, only to hear Evie's cries twenty minutes later. She stumbles out of bed, exhausted and despairing.

It shouldn't be this hard. Surely it shouldn't be this hard.

CHAPTER FIFTEEN

Eight days since Daniel's return

At the local primary school Megan watches anxiously from the back of a classroom as Daniel works his way through English questions and a reading worksheet. The teacher sitting with him is the special needs teacher. Megan has opted to place Daniel in the final year of primary school. Sending him to high school feels like it might be too much for him. She wants a warmer, more nurturing environment.

"Not that we think he has special needs," the principal, Mr. Gordon, has assured her, "it's just that Mel is best placed to determine which class he should go into so we can start him in the next few days."

The primary school closest to Megan's house is a sprawling campus of low buildings surrounding a large playground filled with climbing frames and swings and slides. It's a large school and Megan had debated with herself over whether or not to send Daniel here or to try and manage the fees at one of the smaller private schools where he might get more attention and understanding.

"It's not a problem, we can make it work," Michael had assured her, "but maybe start with the local primary school and we'll go private for high school." Megan had heard the word "we," feeling the grateful relief once again that she had a partner to navigate her life with.

"What if he's really unhappy?"

"Then we'll deal with that then, Megs. He's not exactly jumping for joy now, is he?"

"No," she'd agreed, "no, he's not." And then because she couldn't help herself, she had allowed herself a rueful laugh.

Mr. Gordon had immediately put her mind at rest when she had called to make an appointment.

"We have an excellent on-site psychologist, and his teachers will be fully briefed as to the situation."

"I don't want it to be discussed too much," Megan had said. "I want him to be able to get back to normal life as soon as possible."

"Of course you do. It will only be discussed in the context of alerting his teachers to give him a little extra attention if he needs it. I don't think there is any need to have the whole story traveling around the school community. I don't want you to concern yourself at all, Mrs. Kade. We are very adept at dealing with children from difficult family situations."

Megan had thought that Mr. Gordon probably had little idea of how difficult a situation this was. Even as Daniel's mother, she cannot quite believe what has happened.

Mel, the special needs teacher, is an overweight woman who has to sit back frequently to take a deep breath before she continues to speak again. In the hour that Megan has been sitting at the back of the classroom, Daniel has looked directly at the woman just twice. He has instead concentrated on looking just behind her, on looking at the paper in front of her, and on staring at his cell phone.

"Perhaps you can leave that with your mum," Mel had said kindly, gesturing to his phone.

"No," he'd replied. He hadn't explained; he'd simply refused. Megan had lifted her shoulders in a silent shrug at Mel, who'd nodded her head as though she understood.

Megan can hear him sounding out more complicated words. His halting efforts break her heart. In his kindergarten year he was at the top of the class, and when he went into first grade Megan had been called in to talk about allowing him to skip a year. She hadn't thought it was a good idea, and now, as she listens to him struggle, she feels her body constricted by fury. *What on earth had Greg been doing with him? How could he not have sent him to school? What did Daniel do all day while he was at work?* She has so many questions she would like to ask him, but she knows that everything she wants to know will have to wait. He cannot even tell her what he wants for breakfast without being prompted. They have a long way to go.

This morning, when she was changing Evie for the day, she had heard Michael speaking to Daniel in his room. She had taken her time in Evie's room, listening to the conversation.

"Are you sure you want me to be the one to speak to him, Megs? It might make things worse. I'm not his father," Michael had said when she'd asked him to speak to Daniel.

"I know but...I hope that one day...I just don't think he'll listen to me. He's so angry with me, and every time he looks at me, I can see all the trash Greg said about me going around in his head. If he gets upset you can back off, but give it a try, please."

"Not acceptable," she'd heard Michael say, followed by a sullen, "Sorry," from Daniel.

When she'd heard Michael leave the room, she'd taken Evie downstairs quickly, in case Daniel was with him. She hadn't wanted him to think she'd been listening in.

"I've had a chat," Michael had told her when he found her in the kitchen. "He knows he's not allowed to lay hands on you or anyone, not ever. I've asked him to apologize but if he doesn't, maybe just leave it. And why don't you look through those names of psychologists I gave you again? We need to get this sorted out."

It all feels like too much. Megan is hopeful that school will be a steadying influence on Daniel, but as she listens to him read she is not so sure.

She worries that Mel will suggest he move down a year or two. She knows that he will feel humiliated by this. He is too tall to be in the years below. He should be halfway through his first year of high school. He will tower over his classmates, and she knows that he will be an easy target for bullies. He will hate it. What child wouldn't? She drags her mind back to the classroom and watches him nod as Mel speaks quietly to him.

Finally, Mel stands up and gives Daniel a smile. "We're done for now, young man. I can see you're going to do really well in this class."

He looks down at his shoes.

"Say thank you to Mel," says Megan.

He lifts his head and roams his eyes up and down Mel's body. "Thank…you…Mel," he spits. Megan would like to tell the teacher that this is more than she received this morning from her son.

She watches the teacher blush. "Go wait for me outside, Daniel," she says, failing to conceal her irritation.

"I'm sorry about him," she says when he has left. "I don't know why he's…Well, you know the history, I'm sure."

"Oh, yes," says Mel, patting her tight blond curls into place even though her hair hasn't moved an inch. "I'm sure things will improve."

"Yes, thank…thank you for doing this, I mean for being so patient."

"Oh, it's nothing," says Mel, and she picks her things up off the desk and lumbers toward the classroom door. As she goes to open it, she stops and turns around. "He's very clever," she says.

"Really? I mean…he was when he was little, but I was listening to him and I'm sure most of the kids in this year can read better than that. I don't think he's been to school."

"Mrs. Kade, can I tell you something?"

"Yes?"

"Please don't say anything to Principal Gordon because I'm only speaking to you as a mother, and I know he wouldn't want me to say anything to you until we have done a little more assessment, but I feel you should know this…"

"I won't . . . I won't say anything."

"I'm sure that what just happened over the last hour in this classroom wasn't real. He can read, he can comprehend, and his math ability is very high."

"I don't understand."

"It's odd, I know, but I'm assuming it has something to do with how he's been raised by your ex-husband, and something to do with the trauma of losing his father—and, well, I could go on. He's been through a lot but I know he was mostly faking. I watched him read to the end of the passage before he began sounding out words like a much younger child, and he did the math questions correctly before he rubbed them out and put in the wrong answers. He thought I was marking some papers but I wasn't. I was watching him."

Megan feels abashed at having assumed the same thing, at having wondered why Mel was not paying more attention.

"I wasn't trying to be deceptive," explains Mel. "I know what he's been through and I was worried that intense scrutiny would make him freeze up. He's perfectly capable of being in our class, and were it not for everything he's been through, I would suggest sending him on to high school, but perhaps primary school is the best place for him now until he's settled in."

Megan nods, stunned by the revelation.

"Principal Gordon will give you all the necessary forms, and I'm sure that he can start Monday next week."

"Thanks . . . thank you," says Megan.

Once they have returned to the car, Megan turns to Daniel, who is stroking the face of his mobile phone. "Was that hard for you?" she asks gently.

He shrugs his shoulders and then flicks his eyes at her.

At home Evie is taking her midday nap, watched over by her grandmother. Daniel gives his grandmother a short, tight hug before disappearing to his room. Megan knows she would be beyond grateful for a hug of any sort from him right now, for even the slightest amount of physical affection.

"How did it go?" asks Susanna.

"They're going to put him in the school year that's just below where he should be. There's only six months of the school year left so it's better to let him finish the year at primary school."

"Well, that's good news, Megan—why do you look so unhappy?"

"Oh, I'm not." Megan sighs. Explaining it all would take too much energy and she's not sure she wouldn't sound a little paranoid. "It will be fine." She smiles instead as her mother picks up her knitting and gets ready to leave.

"You'll call me if you need me?"

"I will, thanks, Mum," says Megan and she walks her mother to the front door.

In the kitchen she makes herself a strong cup of coffee. She wants to talk to Daniel about what happened when he was away—and for that, she needs caffeine. She wants to show him the blog and the Facebook page and the newspaper articles she has kept. She goes to her room and grabs the large box on the top shelf of her wardrobe. It's a box that used to contain a pair of long boots. At first, she had just used it to keep everything in one place, but as the years went by, she began to decorate it. It's covered in pictures of Daniel at every age and she has shellacked over the top of it, giving it strength and sheen. Decorating the box had helped her find a way back into her own art again, and most of her paintings over the last few years have been of Daniel. She has even painted pictures of him based on the age progression pictures. They look nothing like he does now. The features are similar but the curious wonder at life in his eyes is gone, which somehow changes his whole face.

She takes two giant sips of her coffee and then she takes the box to his room.

As she goes to open the door, she hears Daniel's voice. At first, she thinks he must be humming some tune to himself, and she feels a spark of joy that he feels happy and safe enough to do so. *Maybe we'll be okay.* She presses her ear to the door and listens, wanting to preserve the moment, but he is not singing—he is speaking.

His slightly muffled voice sounds like it is pleading with someone.

"This is not my bed and this is not my house and this is not my family," he whispers, his voice tinged with despair. "Not my bed and not my house and not my family."

Megan feels shock ripple through her and she opens the door quickly to see Daniel lying on the floor. His cell phone is next to him, and on its screen is a picture of Greg wearing a cap and sunglasses, his face tan with a huge grin. Daniel is looking up at the ceiling, tears running down his face.

"Daniel," she says, and he turns quickly to look at her, fear evident in the way his body stiffens and his eyes lock onto hers. He swipes quickly at his face.

"Who were you speaking to?" asks Megan.

"Dad," he says, as if it should have been obvious. He sits up and picks up the phone, staring at the picture for a moment before turning it off.

"Oh, Daniel," she says, "oh, sweetheart." What an enormous loss this is for a child.

She puts the box on the floor in front of him and sits down next to him on the carpet. She would like to wrap her arms around him but she knows that he will flinch at her touch.

"That's okay, you can talk to him... to a picture of him. I'm sure you can still feel him with you even though he's not here anymore."

"I know he's dead," states Daniel flatly.

"Yes," agrees Megan. "Do you want to talk about the fire, about how it happened? Do you want to talk about Dad, about anything? You can talk to me about anything, anything at all."

He looks at her.

"Anything at all, sweetheart, I promise," she says.

He nods and looks down at the cell phone; his thumb begins its convulsive movement across the screen.

"He told me we were going on a vacation," he says, his fingers making sweaty marks on the black face of his cell phone.

"A vacation? You mean when he picked you up from school when you were six?"

"A vacation to visit Granny Audrey and Grandpa William in England," he says.

"And did you... did you visit them? Did you have your vacation?"

"I liked the airplane but I wished you were there. Dad said you didn't want to come. He said you hated Granny Audrey and Grandpa William."

"That's not true," protests Megan. "I liked them very much. I didn't know your dad was taking you to England that day. He shouldn't have done that without telling me."

"I know you were tired of taking care of me."

"No, I wasn't," she says softly. "I was never tired of taking care of you. I could never be tired of taking care of you. It was the one thing I loved more than anything in the whole world because I loved you more than anything in the whole world."

"Now you have her," spits Daniel.

"Now I love you both more than anything in the whole world."

"Just leave me alone." He gets up off the floor and climbs onto his new bed, turning toward the wall.

Megan feels utterly helpless. She wants to go to him, to hold and comfort him, but she knows he does not want her there. His words have cut deep inside her. She hasn't even managed to show him what she has collected in the box. He hasn't even looked at it.

Wounded, she steps out of his room, closes his door and makes her way to the kitchen, finding the names of psychologists that Michael has collected for her. She and Daniel can no longer do this alone. They obviously need a great deal of help.

CHAPTER SIXTEEN

Wednesday, May 20, 2015

Two years since Daniel was taken

Megan wakes from a dream about three-year-old Daniel in his favorite park, his little legs determinedly climbing the steps for the slide, his tongue poking out as he concentrates.

He has been gone for two years already. Two years in which she has felt the passing of every minute, every hour without him.

She slides out of bed and finds clean running gear. She runs a lot now. Mostly early in the morning before work but sometimes she runs at night if she can't sleep. The movement and the physical pain keep her centered in the here and now. On the nights when she finds herself in bed, going over all her failures that led to her son being taken from her, she hauls herself out into the cold or the rain and she runs. The burn in her legs is the first thing that distracts her from her circular punishing thoughts, and then the burning in her lungs forces her to concentrate on her breathing. She listens to her feet, loud in the silent night, and she feels her mind empty.

"Why must you do it at night?" her mother had asked, anguished at what she considered reckless behavior.

"Sometimes I have to," had been the only thing she could think to reply. She had never been the kind of person to take refuge in exercise, not until now. She had begun with walking and then progressed to a few minutes of running. Exercise was the last of her options, she thinks. She had tried drowning her despair and she had tried talking about it with a therapist.

"I don't know when you're going to see him again," her therapist had said. "I don't even know if you will. All I can do is try to help you find a way to cope with this situation."

"That's not enough," she had said through tears that never seemed to stop returning, and then she had paid her final bill and walked out.

In the autumn morning, Megan breathes the cold in, panting until she settles into her stride. Her body is strong and lean now. She feels more powerful, more in control.

She crests a hill, feels the pain in her legs increase, pushes herself to run faster as the image of the new age progression photograph sent to her from the Department of Missing Persons appears before her. Daniel's front teeth have been filled, changing his face completely. The picture makes her flinch each time she sees it. Her son's little-boy years have faded from his face, and so her six-year-old son seems to have truly disappeared. She has put the photograph on the fridge next to the one from last year. The two images sit below a row of six fridge magnets, each with a photo celebrating a year in Daniel's life. She knows that, one day, those that are computer generated may eclipse the number she has of him from babyhood to six. It's an agonizing thought.

Megan listens to the thump of her feet on the ground. "Don't think, don't think, don't think," she mouths in time to her steps.

The sun rises higher in the sky as she runs, illuminating gardens as she passes by. She does this route often and by now knows which houses to avoid looking at. *Don't look at number fifty-four, they have a swing set in the front. Don't look at number sixty-two, they leave their toys and bikes in the garden.*

Back at home she showers quickly and makes herself breakfast. She is watching something on cable television. She doesn't watch the news, can't watch the news. There are missing children, hurt children, abused children everywhere. How can the police possibly save them all?

As she sips her coffee, she opens Facebook.

There is a message from Sandi, who is now living overseas in Italy studying art.

"Hey, darling. Thinking of you today. I hope you get through it thinking of your little boy's smile and his laugh and all the other wonderful things you remember about him."

When Sandi had told Megan about her decision to move a month ago, she'd explained, *"I may as well live my life. It's been five years already. I need to do something while I wait for them to come back into my life. People keep telling me that this is the way forward but I'm not sure. What if I move forward and lose them forever?"*

Megan had known that Sandi's decision would have come with so much heartbreak it was best not to delve into it. *"Good for you. I am sure it will be wonderful and you'll learn and experience so much,"* she had replied, because what else was there to say?

She could never leave Australia. What if Daniel tried to find her and she was gone? The thought terrifies her.

She and Sandi spend a lot of time discussing things other than their missing children, like their shared interest in the surrealist art movement, comparing and contrasting their favorite painters and decorating ideas for dream houses neither of them will ever own.

"I wish we could meet and sit down together over lunch or dinner. I feel like we would never run out of things to say," Megan has told her.

"We will one day, darling, when the time is right. Everything happens for a reason and I know that one day we will be in the same place at the same time and then there will be a lot of wine consumed and a lot of laughing for two women who've been through the worst."

"Thanks, sweetie. Hope all is going well and you are on your way to becoming a master artist. xx."

Today there is also a message from Tom.

"Hi Megan. I hope that today is a peaceful day for you."

"Thank you," she writes.

"I know it doesn't help much," is his immediate reply, *"but what else can you say?"*

"Nothing helps much, does it? I know that in a few minutes my phone will ring and it will be my mother, and then my brother will call and I'll have to reassure everyone that I'm fine, and then I'll go to work and reassure everyone there that I'm fine, and by the end of the day I'll just be exhausted from lying," she replies.

"We can never really be fine, can we?" Tom types. *"Not without our kids. I've been thinking a lot about Leah lately and how I could have managed the whole thing better."*

"I know it's hard to do but you have to stop blaming yourself. I know the blame rests with Greg. I know he's the one who took my child. I am trying... really trying to let go of the other stuff, the stuff that I could have done. It's the same thing with Leah. You couldn't have watched her all day, every day. She was always going to find a way to take her."

"I know, Megan. I've heard that from so many people, but I keep trying to reimagine the situation, and this time I'm kinder to Leah, and instead of taking Jem she and I manage to work it out. Whatever anyone says there is a reason that the saying 'It takes two to tango' exists. I have to acknowledge my part in the dance. She wanted another chance."

"I don't think Greg wanted to work anything out with me. I think he just wanted to control me."

"If he walked back into your life right now, what would you say to him?"

Megan thinks about this question. Her first instinct is to write that she would do everything she could to physically annihilate Greg, but when she really considers it, she realizes that's not the truth.

"I've been so angry at him for so long, but funnily enough, I think the first thing I would say to him would be, 'Thank you.' I would just be grateful to him for bringing my son back."

"Yeah, that's how I would feel too. Look, I have to go. We'll speak soon, okay?"

"Okay. Bye, Tom, and thanks."

Tom signs off his usual way: *"Xx."*

Her phone rings and she takes a deep breath, readying herself to speak to her mother.

She answers without looking at the screen. "Hi, Mum."

"Megan?"

"Oh, sorry, I was expecting my mother."

"It's Michael Kade, Detective Michael Kade, I'm just calling to see how you are." The words come out in a rush as though he has to say them fast enough to prevent Megan from getting her hopes up. Megan remembers the way she screamed last year when he called, and she feels herself grow hot with shame. She had never called to apologize.

"Hello, Detective Kade. I'm sorry... sorry about last year."

"Please, no need to apologize. It was a tough day, just like today is a tough day. I wanted to call and let you know that we are still looking. We won't close the case until we find him."

"Thanks... thank you, that's good to know. I assume if there were any new leads or anything you would have..."

"No question, even if it's the smallest thing we will call you about it."

"Good. Do you call everyone on the anniversary of the disappearance?"

"I, uh... I do tend to call the families with missing kids."

Megan would like to end the call, craving the solace of silence, but doesn't want to sound too abrupt. "So how long have you been working with missing persons?" she asks instead, trying to picture Detective Kade. Muscular arms and broad shoulders are all she can visualize.

"It's been four years now."

"And do you like it?"

"I guess... I guess I do. I mean I hate it when we fail, when we can't find the person we're looking for, but when we succeed, it's pretty amazing."

"How often do you succeed?"

"Not as much as we would like."

"Oh." She wishes she hadn't asked the question, wishes she hadn't heard that answer. She needs to be able to hold on to hope, and her body floods with despair at the words. *Not as much as we would like.*

"Are you still teaching art?" he asks.

"Yes, still in the same place. It's strange to think that I now have classes filled with people who just assume I'm a single woman without children."

"It must be, but you like the work?"

"It's very peaceful, even on the worst days. I have older people during the day and teenagers and kids in the afternoons after school. The classes with kids who are Daniel's age are hard but wonderful at the same time. I feel like I can connect with him a little even though he's not here."

In the background someone speaks to Detective Kade, and she hears the hush as he places his hand over the speaker on his phone.

"I'm sorry, Megan, I have to go," he says. "If you'd like to talk a bit more, maybe we could meet for a coffee?"

"Oh," says Megan, "that's very nice of you, but I'm fine, I mean I'm okay, thanks, but thanks for calling, it was very kind of you." She doesn't think she can meet up with the man responsible for finding her son, doesn't think she would be able to sit across the table from him without the day he disappeared consuming her thoughts.

"Not at all, take care of yourself."

"You too."

Megan hangs up the phone and finds herself thinking about the detective's voice. On impulse she googles him and finds a picture of him in an article on some charity work being done by the police of New South Wales. He has thick dark hair and brown eyes and she can see she had been right about his arms.

The phone rings again.

"Hi, Mum," she answers, and before her mother can ask, she says, "I'm doing okay."

CHAPTER SEVENTEEN

Daniel—eight years old

This is a shitty flat. That's what Dad calls it: "shitty."

"I'm sorry it's such a shitty flat, Daniel, but I don't have the money for a better one. We have to keep moving so that the police don't find us and try to send you to a terrible foster home, where bad things will happen to you."

"Maybe the police will take me back to Mum," Daniel had said, but Dad didn't think that would happen.

"I'm sure she's told them she doesn't want you. She probably moved away by now so she can get on with her life without us. She doesn't know how to love, Daniel; she doesn't love me and she doesn't love you."

"Maybe I could stay with Nana and Pop?"

"I don't think your mother would let them take care of you—she's a really selfish woman, trust me, I know. Even if they really wanted you, she wouldn't let them have you."

"Maybe I could go to Uncle Connor and Uncle James, then?" he had asked his dad, and he had been embarrassed because his nose was running and his cheeks got wet with his tears but he couldn't help it.

"They have Lucy, they wouldn't want another kid."

He hates being in the flat alone all day but Dad is looking for work where people will pay him cash. They need cash so they can eat. He hasn't had any breakfast, and if Dad doesn't come back soon, he won't have any lunch.

Dad had told him to drink water, but he's tired of water.

The flat smells funny because the person who used to live in it was very old and they've left all their stuff here and it all smells like wet dog even though there wasn't a dog who lived here.

They've been in this flat for one month now, ever since they came back to Australia. Dad won't tell him the name of the town they're in but he says it's for his protection. There is a phone in the flat but when Daniel had lifted it up to see if it was working, Dad had ripped it away from him and pulled the cord out. "Don't you understand what will happen if the police find us?" he had shouted.

"I just wanted to see if it worked," Daniel had told him but then he had to bite his lip because that wasn't really true. He was going to call Mum. Mum taught him his phone number when he was five. They used to sing it in the car on the way to school. He was going to call Mum from the phone and ask her if he could come back and live with her. Maybe if she heard his voice, she would love him again.

"If the police find us, they will throw me in jail, Daniel," Dad had said. "Do you want me to go to jail? Do you want to be left all alone with no one to love you?"

Dad says the same things all the time. Daniel is tired of hearing it. He is tired of only being with Dad, of not going to school, of not having friends or being allowed to play games on the computer. It's not fun with Dad anymore but he has to accept it because no one else will take care of him. He wishes he was big and strong so he could take care of himself and then he would find Mum and shout at her for not loving him. He would shout and shout. He never used to want to shout so much but now it feels like there's a volcano inside him, bubbling away, just waiting to erupt.

Dad was mad at him this morning because he cried in his sleep but he couldn't help it. He didn't know he was crying. He was dreaming about being home. He misses Mum and Billy Blanket and Nana and Pop. He misses his bed and his room even though sometimes it's hard to remember what everything looked like. Sometimes when Dad tells him that Mum doesn't love him, he wonders if that's really the truth. She used to kiss him and cuddle him and call him her "beautiful boy." So why did she stop loving him?

The door opens and Dad comes in carrying food. Daniel feels a jumping happiness inside him because he can smell a burger and fries and he loves fries more than anything in the world. Dad knows that because Dad loves him and he will never stop loving him. He's promised that he will never be like Mum. He will never stop loving him and taking care of him.

CHAPTER EIGHTEEN

Ten days since Daniel's return

Megan is not sure what wakes her but suddenly she is wide awake, her heart racing. She strains to hear the sound that has driven her from sleep. She looks over at the baby monitor but on the screen, Evie is peacefully sprawled across her crib. She knows that her daughter will be up soon enough and that she should just turn over and go back to sleep, but a sense of unease prickles at her and she finds herself sliding out of bed and tiptoeing down the hallway. She walks past Evie's room, silent but for the little snuffling sounds Evie makes in her sleep, and continues down the hallway to Daniel's room, where she can hear a faint murmuring.

Talking in his sleep, she thinks, meaning to go in, stroke his head, and rearrange his covers as she had always done when he was little and found himself whimpering in the middle of a dream. She knows that now Daniel will never let her touch him like this when he is awake, but she thinks she may be able to get away with it if he is dreaming, a thought that forces her to swallow quickly, chasing away her despair.

When she gets to his door she stops for a moment and listens, hoping that he may say something that will give her some insight into her child.

His first session with Eliza, the therapist, has left her no closer to understanding her son. While he was with the therapist, Megan sat in the waiting room, alternately paging restlessly through old magazines and checking Facebook on her phone. Every now and again Eliza's pretty young receptionist would offer her a cup of tea, but Megan wasn't able to stomach the idea. When the hour was up Daniel had slouched out of the office and thrown himself down into the chair next to hers. "Can we go now?" he'd demanded.

"How was it?" she'd asked and had been answered with him rolling his eyes at her. Megan had tried to suppress a smile at this typical reaction from a preteen boy.

"Megan—can I have a minute?" Eliza had said, and Megan had felt herself flush at Daniel's rudeness. She hadn't realized that Eliza was standing in the doorway. "Will you be okay?" she'd asked as she stood up.

"Fine," had come the reply through clenched teeth.

In the therapist's office, Megan had clasped her hands together in her lap and looked at the older woman, whose hair was gray and styled in a perfect bob. "How is he?"

"I know that we've had a general chat about everything that has happened to Daniel but I always try to have a chat with the parents of the children I am seeing after every session. I will, at all times, try to respect his privacy because I need to build up a level of trust between the two of us, so I won't tell you everything he says and I have assured him of that, but I will try to give you a general idea of where I feel he is at after each session. Does that sound fair?"

"Ah, yes, sure," Megan had replied, a little cowed by the upright posture of the therapist and her somewhat brittle tone. Michael had heard from colleagues at the station who dealt with child abuse cases that Eliza was one of the best therapists for traumatized adolescents, but sitting in front of the woman, Megan began to question her decision.

"I can tell you that he was very reluctant to speak to me at first. He's very angry."

"Yes..."

"I think he's a very intelligent young man, exceptional even, although he does seem to be trying to almost hide that as though he doesn't want anyone to know. That may just be because he is unsure of his place right now and is keeping himself safe. He didn't really want to discuss his feelings about being home just yet but I am confident that will come with time. The only thing I am really concerned about is the fact that he seems to have little or no emotion when it comes to speaking about his father's death."

"Yes, I've noticed that as well."

"My opinion is that he's subverting his feelings to protect you and himself, and he may feel that discussing your ex-husband with you will not be well received."

"I've asked him about Greg. I've even tried to encourage him to talk about him and remember him."

"I'm sure you're doing the best you can," Eliza had said, leaning forward in her chair.

Megan had read her expression as sincere but she'd still felt judged.

"This is not something that has just happened to Daniel," Eliza had carried on. "This is something that turned both your lives upside down six years ago and is doing the same thing again now. It's something you both have to get through together. I know you are doing everything you can think of, and over the next few weeks and months I will give you strategies to try, but for now all I want to encourage you to do is to begin speaking about Greg again, maybe even talk about some happy memories you might have so that he feels he can let himself mourn his father."

"Okay... okay," Megan had muttered.

After the therapy session, she had called her mother to check on Evie before taking Daniel to a café nearby.

"Do you want a coffee?" she'd asked when they sat down.

"Milkshake," Daniel had said.

"What flavor?" she'd asked as the waitress came over to their table. She had gotten it wrong again, but then it's all she seemed to do with Daniel: get it wrong.

"Chocolate," he'd said, staring at a couple sitting at the table behind them. *Had ordering coffee the last time just been a test? Was he trying, even on his first day home, to see where the boundary was?*

"Please," Megan had said, and Daniel had moved his gaze to her face.

"Please," he had repeated.

"I'll get a green tea, thanks," Megan had told the waitress.

She knows that this infuriating behavior is part of adolescence but she can't help being furious at Greg because she never got to have her sweet seven-year-old and eight-year-old and all the years after that. She knows there are mothers who have lamented that their lovely children turned into monsters overnight, and she has found herself pissed off at those women because they have no real idea what it means to have a beautiful little boy one day and then nothing but emptiness and hope until a wary, distant adolescent turns up.

Now, standing outside his bedroom door in the middle of the night, Megan pushes her ear against the wood, trying to make out his words.

"Please, please," she hears him say and then there is silence. She touches her hand to her heart and holds her breath—she has no idea who he is begging in his sleep. He sounds so young, so incredibly sad.

"Please, please," he says again and then, "I want to go home. Let me go home."

Megan pushes the door open slowly. He is clearly in the middle of a nightmare and she doesn't want to startle him, but she cannot leave him adrift in his subconscious when he is so obviously suffering. In his voice she can hear her six-year-old son pleading with his father to let him return to her. She wants to put her arms around him and soothe him with the truth that he is home now and always will be.

She looks at his bed first, trying to make out his form in the subtle glow of the night-light in the hallway, but he is not in his bed. Her eyes quickly sweep the room and she sees him sitting next to his desk on the floor. He has his cell phone in his hand, his thumb moving over the screen.

"Daniel? Are you okay? What are you doing?" she asks.

Daniel turns to look at her.

"Look, it's Dad," he says and then he giggles. Not a sound she has heard from him in the time he has been home. Not a sound she has heard since he was taken six years ago. She feels goose bumps rise along her arms. *Who are you and where has my son gone?*

Megan walks into the room and crouches down next to him. He holds the phone out to her. On it is a picture of him and Greg standing outside Audrey and William's house in England. *He was there, he was there, they lied!* Six-year-old Daniel is holding a fluffy dog in his arms and he is laughing at the person taking the picture. Greg looks delighted with himself. Daniel giggles again. Megan wonders if he is in the middle of a dream even though he is sitting on the floor. She knows that sleepwalking is a sign of extreme stress.

"I can see it's Dad," she says softly.

"I want to speak to him."

"Oh, baby, oh, sweetheart, I know you do. You can speak to him. I'm sure he can hear you."

"No, no, I want to speak to him," he whispers and he begins pushing down on the keypad.

She gently covers his hand with hers. "You can't call him, Daniel, not really call him, but you can speak to him. It's okay to speak to someone who's gone—lots of people do it and it's okay."

"He gave me this phone so I could call him. He said..."

"I know, sweetheart, but..."

He looks directly at her and she can see that he's not asleep at all. "Dad was in the fire. He got burned, all burned. Dad died," he says. He rubs his hands up and down his arms and then swipes at his face where tears have appeared.

"You can still speak to him. I'm sure he's still looking after you, still watching you and taking care of you."

"He said he would love me no matter where he was, even if he was in heaven, and he said he would always hear me talk to him, always."

Megan is momentarily grateful to Greg for giving his son this idea that she knows will be giving him comfort.

"That's true and it's okay to talk to him and to talk about him."

"He loved you, even after everything you did, he still loved you," says Daniel with a smile.

Megan cannot think of what to say or do so she simply nods.

He gets up off the floor and climbs back into his bed, still clutching the cell phone.

"Should I tuck you in?" asks Megan, even as her hands begin to do just that.

"Yes, yes please," he replies, and in his voice, Megan hears again the six-year-old child she had known and loved.

She smooths the blankets over him and gives his shoulder a squeeze. "Sleep tight," she says.

"Sleep loose," he replies and then he giggles again. Once again, the sound is shocking and uncharacteristic of the boy he is now. She wants to reply but can see that he is almost immediately asleep.

Megan tries not to cry. He has remembered their usual bedtime words.

"Sleep tight," she would say after tucking him in and putting his Billy Blanket against his cheek.

"Sleep loose," he would reply and then he would laugh, knowing that they would go back and forth with "loose," "tight," "loose," "tight" until finally she would say, "You win, sleep loose," and the game would be over.

"Sleep tight," she says again but there is silence from Daniel.

Back in bed she breathes in and out slowly, willing her body back to sleep.

Since their last therapy session, she has been trying to bring up Greg, to speak about him in a more positive manner. Yesterday she had been helping Daniel with a school project on Egypt he'd been given to do at home before he started school. She'd been pleasantly surprised by his eagerness to build a pyramid. She had been sitting with him, the kitchen table covered in popsicle sticks, small pieces of wood and miniature jars of paint, and without even thinking she had said, "Your dad would know how to do this. He was always good at this kind of thing."

"He built lots of stuff for me when we lived together," he had replied. "He built a bookcase out of old wood and he sanded it until it was smooth and then we painted it together." His smile had been wide and his pleasure in the memory evident.

"It's good for you to talk about your dad. I want you to talk about him, to remember him."

"I didn't think you would want that. You hated him so much." Daniel's smile had disappeared and his face had assumed the blank composure she was getting used to.

"I don't mind you talking about him at all. He was your father. You should be able to talk about him."

He had picked up the glue and spread it onto a stick of wood. Megan had searched for something to keep the conversation going, watching her son open and close his mouth a few times.

"Do you still hate him, even though he's... he's..."

"Even though he's dead?" Megan had finished for him, aware that even though he was not looking at her but at the pieces of wood he was gluing together, he was desperate for an answer to this tentatively asked question. She could feel Eliza in the room warning her to be careful of what she said. "Hate is not the right word. I was angry with him for a long time but he was your father and I will always love that he helped me create you."

He had sat back in the chair and looked directly at her. "Then why didn't you just stay with him, just stay married to him?"

"It's complicated, sweetheart. Marriage is complicated and—"

"Whatever," he had said, cutting her off, shutting himself down. She'd felt like someone who had inadvertently flicked a light switch, plunging a room into darkness without meaning to.

Megan turns on her side, listens to Michael's breathing. She had lied to Daniel about how she feels. Her hate for Greg is constant, a stone lodged inside her, but her son doesn't need to bear the burden of that. He is struggling enough. She knows that they will be able to have a funeral once the autopsy and the investigation have been completed, and that will hopefully bring Daniel closure. She is once again furious with Greg for putting his child through this. He doesn't deserve anything from her except her loathing. Even as she thinks this, she feels guilty. Greg burned to death in a fire and she can conceive of no more awful death than that.

CHAPTER NINETEEN

Eleven days since Daniel's return

Detective Wardell is obviously pregnant. Her brown hair is pulled back into a tight ponytail but curls seem to have escaped from everywhere as though the elastic around her hair cannot contain them. Her rosy cheeks glow with good health and Megan cannot help but smile when she opens the door and sees her. All morning she has been troubled by an uneasy feeling about this interview, about what Daniel might reveal about his life with Greg and about himself.

"How far along are you?" she asks after they've exchanged handshakes.

"Nearly six months now, so not long to go."

"No," murmurs Megan, drawn back to her pregnancy with Daniel and the bursting energy she'd felt when she was in her second trimester. It was so different from her pregnancy with Evie, where she was fearful all the time, consumed with guilt about having another child, and worried about being an older mother.

Megan directs the detective into the living room where Daniel is waiting on the sofa. "Michael will be right in," she says, grateful that he has taken the day off. Daniel is stroking the face of his phone. "It will be fine," she'd told him over breakfast this morning. "Just tell her whatever you can remember." He had not acknowledged what she'd said.

Megan dithers for a moment, debating where to sit. She settles for next to Daniel on the sofa, but not right next to him. Detective

Wardell takes an armchair, lowering herself into it with a little huff of breath.

"Sorry about that," says Michael as he comes in from his office, "just finishing up on the phone. Hello, how are you, Detective?"

"Very well, thank you, sir."

Michael sits down right next to Daniel on the sofa and Megan is amazed to see Daniel shoot Michael a look of gratitude. She looks down at her lap and smiles, hopeful that Michael is beginning to break down his defenses.

"Hi, Daniel, how are you doing?" begins the detective. She hits the record button on her phone.

"Fine," he replies, his thumb moving over the screen of his phone.

"Now I just want to talk to you about the fire. Is that okay?"

Daniel looks at Michael, who gives him a small nod.

"Yeah, okay."

"Do you know how the fire started?"

"The hotplate, in the kitchen. It was old but we didn't have anything else to cook on."

"How do you know it was the hotplate? Did you see the fire start?"

"We were asleep."

"So how do you know it was the hotplate?"

"I'm not sure, I just think it was. It was old and the cord was frayed and he said, 'That thing will start a fire one day,' but we could never afford to buy a new one, so I think it was the hotplate. We had beans on toast for dinner. He heated the beans up in a pot so maybe he didn't turn it off or something like that."

"When you say 'he,' you mean your dad, right?" asks the detective.

"Who else would I mean?"

"Did you and Dad eat beans on toast often?" Megan asks, interrupting the interview without thinking.

"A lot," Daniel replies. "We never had much money and it's cheap. He would have gotten a job if..."

"If?" Megan says.

"Nothing," he says, looking down at the black screen.

"Okay, if we could just get back to the fire please, Daniel. Do you remember what happened exactly? For example, were you asleep and woke up when you smelled smoke or felt the heat?"

"I was asleep and he...Dad was asleep and then I...I started to cough. I coughed and coughed and that woke me up. I took a deep breath in and then I knew my room was filled with smoke. I shouted, 'Dad, Dad,' because I couldn't stop coughing..." He pauses.

Megan looks at her son. "You can tell the detective whatever you remember, Daniel. It's fine."

"I know," he says, his jaw tight, his body rigid.

"Don't worry," the detective says. "Whatever you can remember is fine. I'm sure a lot of the details are a bit hazy. It was a hard thing to have to go through. What happened after you called your dad?"

"He...he didn't answer and so I got out of bed and I kind of crouched over and went to his room. He was in his bed but when I went over to him, he was sleeping. I tried to get him to wake up. I shook him and I...I even hit him but he wouldn't wake up and then I thought I should try to get him out of the house so I dragged him out of his bed..." Daniel stops speaking and focuses on the wall behind the detective.

Megan covers her mouth with her hand. She is unable to stop her tears. *This poor child. My poor baby.*

"I tried to drag him out of the house but he was too heavy. He was too heavy...so I couldn't. I didn't know he was so heavy. I tried but I couldn't get him out, I couldn't save him." Daniel stops speaking. He looks up from his phone, his eyes bright with unshed tears.

The three adults in the room wait. Megan wants to grab her son and hold him tight, tell him it wasn't his fault. She lifts her hands to reach over but then she catches a look from Michael. He gives his head a quick shake and she lowers her arms, knowing that Daniel will only retract from her touch.

Daniel takes a deep, shuddering breath and looks at the detective. "And then I could feel the fire coming to get me and I had to get out of the house so I ran out and I tried to turn on the hose outside but the water in the tank was too low and none came out and then I just...just sat and watched the house burn."

"That must have been really difficult for you," says Detective Wardell. "Did you think about calling anyone?"

"I left Dad's phone in the house. All I had was this old cell phone and I didn't have anyone else's number."

Why wouldn't he have dialed triple zero? Panic? Fear?

"Okay." Detective Wardell struggles to keep her face neutral. "How about telling a neighbor? Did you think about that?"

"I didn't know the neighbor. I wasn't allowed to talk to any of our neighbors—no matter where we lived—but when we lived there, we couldn't even see the neighbors. Sometimes we drove past another house but I didn't know how to get there from our house."

"So, you had a car?"

"He had a car."

"Can you describe the car?"

"Um, blue and a station wagon. A Toyota station wagon."

"Do you remember the plate number?"

"No," Daniel answers. He slides his phone into the pocket of his pants and then folds his arms.

"Not at all? A few letters or numbers maybe?"

"I never looked at it; he bought it from some guy."

"Some guy—do you remember anything about him?"

"No."

"Surely the car was there," interrupts Megan, but Detective Wardell shakes her head.

"Maybe someone stole it?" attempts Daniel.

"Maybe," agrees the detective.

"So how long did you watch the house burn for, Daniel?"

"How is he supposed to remember that?" Megan says.

"Mrs. Kade, there is no right or wrong answer. I'm trying to figure out what happened."

"Maybe you could get us something to drink, Megs," says Michael quietly, and Megan knows she is being asked to control herself.

"Would you like something to drink?" she asks ungraciously, wanting the woman out of her house and away from her son. Any kinship she felt with her because of the shared experience of pregnancy has disappeared. It is horrifying to watch Daniel recount this experience, horrifying.

"I'm fine, thank you. Do you know how long it was, Daniel?" the detective repeats, angering Megan with her relentlessness.

"No, I don't... but it was a long time. And then the rain came and I started walking."

"You didn't have shoes when you got to the police station and your clothes were dry."

Megan cannot fathom what this statement is meant to prove. She starts to say something but then she looks at Michael, who shakes his head again. She bites down on her lip, irritated that she is being told how to behave.

"I had shoes for a long time, just flip-flops, but then I lost them in... in some mud. That's when my feet got cut. I stood on a sharp stone but I got it out."

"Fair enough. And how did you manage to keep yourself dry?"

"There was a kind of overhang of rock and I sat under there for a bit until the rain wasn't so bad. Then my clothes dried in the sun."

"Okay, I can see that," says the detective. "And did you go to school in Heddon Greta? Before... before the fire?"

"No, I wasn't allowed. I got books from the library. He got them for me. I had to keep hidden and secret."

"Why did you have to keep hidden and secret?"

Megan feels Michael's hand on her shoulder before she even gets a chance to say anything. She doesn't want Daniel to have to explain. Surely Detective Wardell is aware of the situation.

He doesn't reply to the question. The phone comes out of his pocket again, and his thumb resumes its compulsive movement across the screen.

"Why did you have to keep hidden, Daniel?" she asks again, and her tone has changed a little. She no longer sounds gentle to Megan, but rather as though she is questioning a suspect. Megan feels acid in her throat. She wants to stand up and order the detective out of her house but the constant pressure of Michael's hand on her shoulder keeps her sitting and quiet.

"So she couldn't find us," says Daniel softly.

"She?" inquires the detective, and as she says this, she raises her hands to fend off Megan's protests because this time Megan can actually feel herself rising from the sofa.

"Mum," sneers Daniel. "She wanted to take me away from Dad. She wanted to keep me from ever seeing him again but only to punish him because she didn't want me in her life anymore. She was going to take me away and give me to a foster family who would hurt me."

"That's enough!" shouts Megan. "Detective, I'm sure you have all the information Daniel can give you."

Daniel stands up. "Can I go now?"

"Well, I would—" begins the detective.

"You can go now," says Michael firmly. "I think it's enough for today."

Megan watches the detective color. Michael is the more senior detective of the pair, and even though this is not his investigation, hierarchy comes first.

She feels a flash of sympathy for the woman and searches her mind for something to ask or say that will return her some dignity.

"Do you have many other cases to deal with now?" she asks gently.

"Well, we're always busy," replies the detective, and then she looks at Michael, one cop to another. "We're looking for a missing backpacker and we're investigating a series of fires in the region. The two seem to have . . . coincided."

Michael nods as though they've had a conversation only the two of them have been privy to.

"I heard about those fires," Megan says. "You don't think that it has anything to do with . . . ? What's his name, the backpacker? It's sad that you haven't found him yet."

"Steven Hindley. We'll find him soon, I'm sure."

"Steven, Steven, Steven," Daniel whispers, making Megan jump. She had assumed he had left the room but he is standing by the door, his face white.

Detective Wardell pushes the record button on her phone again. "Yes," she says softly, "Steven Hindley. He was in Newcastle but no one has heard from him in weeks. His parents are here now. They miss him very much."

Daniel nods at her words, his lower lip trembling a little. Megan wants to shut the conversation down but she doesn't know exactly what she's hearing.

"Did you know him, Daniel, the backpacker?" the detective asks. "Did you know Steven?" Her tone is gentle again, as though she is trying to get him to step back from a ledge.

"Was he in Heddon Greta?" Michael asks before Daniel has a chance to answer.

"He was there for a few days but the landlord at the pub thinks he was making his way to Sydney. Did you know him, Daniel?" the detective prompts again.

Megan looks at Michael, who shrugs his shoulders.

"No," says Daniel, shaking his head slowly as though the movement is painful. "I didn't *know* him."

"But you met him," states the detective. "You met Steven, didn't you, Daniel?"

Daniel nods, shocking Megan.

"He likes fires," Daniel said when we were watching television. Is Steven the one who likes fires? Is that who Daniel was talking about even though he denied saying anything? Had the words just slipped out?

"Where did you meet him?"

"I...can't say."

"You can't say or you're not allowed to say?"

"Not allowed to say," he says, a smile touching at the corners of his mouth.

"Why are you not allowed to say?"

He swallows twice but remains silent.

"Did Steven Hindley hurt you, Daniel? Did he do something to hurt you? Did he hurt your dad?" Detective Wardell asks quickly.

"No," he answers, shaking his head, and then as though he is testing out the concept of the word, he says it again: "No." His eyes dart around the room.

"When did you last see him?"

"I don't..." he begins and then he looks directly at the detective. His face colors right to his ears. "I don't know, I can't remember!" he yells. "I don't remember anymore. I don't know. I don't know."

He tears out of the room and rushes up the stairs to his bedroom, where he slams the door so hard Megan is afraid it has come off its hinges.

"What was that about?" asks Michael, his tone sharp with rebuke.

"I'm sorry, sir, I shouldn't have pushed. I just thought he wanted to tell me something. I don't know why he would have met Steven Hindley. He seemed almost afraid of him."

"Heddon Greta is, as you know, a small town, Detective, and if he passed through there, they could have come across each other. Maybe he was just surprised to hear the name of someone he'd met once. You're taking three separate cases and trying to link them together—be careful of finding connections where there may be none."

"But, sir, Daniel has said that he kept hidden. No one in Heddon Greta knew of his existence, so how would he have come across Steven if he was always hiding?"

"He's twelve, Detective Wardell. He's been through a horribly traumatic experience and a hideously stressful six years. I think we can forgive him for not exactly remembering everything perfectly. It's possible that he did get out of the house once or twice—anything is possible."

"You're right, I'm sorry. Perhaps we can talk to him again when he's feeling a bit more settled."

"I'll let you know," Michael says, standing up.

He hustles the detective out of the house. Megan finds herself paralyzed on the sofa.

Daniel's words repeat in her head. *She wanted to take me away from Dad. She didn't want me in her life anymore. She was going to take me away and give me to a foster family who would hurt me. She, she, she.* That's who she is to her son; that's who Greg has made her into. Not "Mum" but "she." She is the reason for every bad day her son experienced over the last six years. Megan leans forward and buries her face in her hands. *It's never going to get better*, she thinks. *I am never going to get him back.*

CHAPTER TWENTY

Dinner is conducted in front of some game show on television. No one feels like talking.

Daniel inhales his food and then leaves Megan and Michael sitting on the couch.

"I should go and talk to him, but I have no idea what to say."

"I wish I could help, Megs. It may be best to speak to Eliza first, get her take on things."

"Probably."

"They're going to want to interview him again. Detective Wardell would like him to come up to Heddon Greta. They want to take him through what happened at the house and try and trace the route he took when he left."

Megan stands up, holding her dinner plate, where her chicken and salad sit untouched. "No."

"You can't just say no, Megan. It's an investigation."

"No, no, I'm not doing that. He's a child. It's cruel to take him back to the place where he lost his father. I don't care what I have to do to stop it, but it's not happening." She stomps her way to the kitchen and throws her food in the garbage, her stomach twisting with fury. She would not let them drag him back there.

Michael walks into the kitchen and empties his own mostly full plate into the garbage.

"I'm sorry, Megs, I know it's not what you want to hear."

"It's not, Michael, and I can tell you with absolute certainty that I'm not allowing it to happen. I'll get a lawyer if necessary."

"Okay, okay, take it easy, Megs. I'm on your side, remember. I'll talk to her again, let her know that we're against the idea."

Megan feels her shoulders relax at the word "we. "Michael is in this with her, he is.

She hears the shower turn on upstairs.

"What did you say to her, to the detective, when you walked her out? You were gone for a long time."

"I told her how hard it has been. She understood that she perhaps pushed things too far. She was trying to get him to tell her what really happened on the night of the fire."

"What do you mean, what really happened?"

"Yeah, I wanted to speak to her a bit more before I discussed it with you."

"What happened? Discuss it with me now, Michael. He's my son. I shouldn't be left in the dark."

Michael sighs and fills the kettle. "Do you want a cup of tea or something?"

"No, I'm fine, please just tell me what she said."

"It turns out there is a real possibility of a connection with Steven Hindley and with the fires that have been started close by. Detective Wardell explained her theory to me and it is something that's possible."

"Explain it to me, Michael. I don't understand."

"The fire investigators think the fire was deliberately lit. They haven't formally identified the remains they found inside the house but they obviously think it's Greg."

"Deliberately lit?"

"Yeah, but there's more, Megan. Daniel was barefoot when he entered the police station but he only had a couple of scratches on his feet and a few blisters. His feet should have been in much worse shape. He didn't say he lost his shoes until today even though that's what everyone had assumed. If he didn't have shoes and he had actually walked the ten kilometers in the cold with wet clothes, he should have had really messed up feet and be suffering from mild hypothermia. There is no way he should have been in such good physical shape."

"I don't understand. Why are they only saying this now?" Megan asks.

"They've always had questions. They wanted to give him some time to settle in before they spoke to him again. Detective Wardell feels… feels that he may have been given a lift nearly the whole way. She feels that there may be another person involved who may have also helped light the fire."

"Helped who light the fire?"

"Helped Daniel light the fire, Megs."

Megan slumps onto a chair next to the kitchen counter. "Helped Daniel light the fire?" she repeats.

"Yes, they think that it's possible he may have been responsible for the fire but also that he could have had help."

"I just don't…" Megan's arms prickle and she scratches at her skin. *What? What? What? How can Daniel have deliberately lit a fire that killed his father? It's inconceivable.*

"It's hard to hear, I know, and it may just be supposition—that's why I didn't want to say anything, but when Daniel mentioned Steven Hindley, Detective Wardell assumed a connection between the two."

"So maybe Steven lit the fire and stole the car? Maybe he didn't want to hurt a child?"

Daniel can't have done anything to hurt Greg. It isn't who he is. She knows that it would explain why he can't talk about his father's death: he feels guilty because the backpacker let him live. It would explain why he is so guarded and locked inside himself: he is afraid that the truth will be discovered. But even as these thoughts run through her head, there is a niggling, stray idea that who Daniel was is not who he is now. She has no idea of who he is now and therefore no idea of what he's really capable of.

No, no, I'm not going to think like that about my son, not my beautiful boy.

"Detective Wardell also noticed Daniel's tendency to refer to his father as 'he.' It's a distancing technique. It's something people do to prevent themselves from connecting emotionally."

"I noticed it as well but maybe that's just because he's afraid of what might happen if he lets himself really feel this loss. It could be that he's protecting himself. He wouldn't do something like this. It's... impossible."

"There isn't a clear answer here yet, Megs. Detective Wardell hadn't linked Daniel and Steven until today, but she had linked Steven to the fires. Until today she just believed that there was someone else in the house with Daniel and Greg. Today she realized that Daniel and Steven know each other—and according to her, Steven Hindley has a record, a very old charge from when he was a teenager. He's from the UK and the police never would have known about it if he hadn't gone missing."

"What was his record for?"

"It was a long time ago and he was only a kid."

"So, what was it for?"

"Arson."

"Arson." Megan drops her head into her hands. "Daniel could have been killed. He could have died."

"I'm sorry, Megs. I didn't want Detective Wardell to push him any further today but he is going to need to talk to her again. Something happened there. It may even be that..."

"That what?"

"Nothing, I'm just thinking through some ideas."

"That what, Michael?"

"That... that they planned it together. They may have planned this whole thing together."

"Oh God." Megan feels her throat close. She stands up and takes a deep breath. "He wouldn't have done something like that. It had to have been the backpacker's idea. He loved his father. How can they think he lit the fire, that he killed Greg?" She remembers the knife, the crude, homemade knife with designs burned into the handle. *Is it impossible that Daniel could have started a fire?*

"All of this is just supposition. They are right at the beginning of the investigation. Detective Wardell wouldn't have even said anything if I wasn't a detective as well. They may be completely wrong. If he did light the fire, there must have been a reason."

"But how can you think, how can anybody think he could have done such a thing? It's... it's monstrous. He can't be a monster... He's my little boy, he can't be a monster." She walks back and forth, her legs needing to move. Her heart is racing. She shakes her head. She will not accept that this is possible. *No, no, no.*

"Please don't do this to yourself. If he did it—and I do mean *if*—then maybe he felt he had no choice. We don't know anything about his years with Greg. We don't know how bad it got. That's why you've taken him to see Eliza. We'll figure out what happened but we do need to give it some time."

"What if he did actually light the fire? God... it's... it's unthinkable. I can't have raised a child who would do such a thing."

"But you haven't really raised him, Megan, not for the last six years."

Megan flinches at the cruel truth of his words. "I... I guess not, but then what do I do now? What do I do if I feel, if I know that there is something he's not telling us, some secret he's keeping? What do I do?"

"All I can say is what I've said before, and that's one day at a time. I know it's not very helpful but it's the best we can do right now." Michael walks over and plants a soft kiss on her forehead. "It will be okay, Megs. We'll make sure it's all okay."

She leans into him gratefully but she knows that sometimes things cannot be made okay.

CHAPTER TWENTY-ONE

Twelve days since Daniel's return

At seven the next morning, Megan knocks on Daniel's door. In her hands are her computer and the box covered in pictures of him. She opens the door and finds him already up, his eyes on his PlayStation.

"You're up early," she says.

"Yeah, I wanted to level up."

"Okay, but I think that it would be best if you didn't play games before school. I'd rather you sleep, and if you do wake up early, maybe read." She speaks softly but firmly. He needs to know there are boundaries. She had assumed he would be up early, knowing that starting school would cause some anxiety. Yesterday's interview is not something she's going to talk about with him, not until Eliza has spoken to him first. He has enough to deal with today.

"So, I wanted to show you some stuff, some things on my computer and in this box." She wants to show him as much as she can before he starts school, hoping to help him understand how much he is loved so that he can feel the certainty of her support as he navigates a new world. She also hopes that he will understand that the things his father said were not true.

Daniel doesn't look at her. He keeps his eyes on his game and then he shakes his head and grimaces. "Game over," he says.

"Good, now can you look at this with me?"

Daniel sits up straighter in his bed. "Yeah, okay."

She hands him the box first. He runs his hands over the top of it. "They're all pictures of me." A small smile appears on his face, a real smile, a smile she remembers, and her heart tugs at the sight.

"Yep, all pictures of you. It's an old shoebox but I covered it with pictures of you."

"I was an ugly baby."

"No, you weren't," she laughs. "You were beautiful. You didn't like to nap though, not like Evie."

He continues tracing his fingers over the box. "That's me at the birthday party where you hired the animal farm."

"Yes, they made a big mess in the garden."

"You made a farm cake with green icing."

"I did. Nana helped me."

"That's me with Lucy, when she was little."

"It's from the day she came home from the airport."

"When's that from?" he asks, pointing at a picture of the two of them on a beach. Daniel is four years old.

"It's from a vacation we took to the coast. It was only for a few days."

"Who took the picture?"

"Dad did."

"Dad did? You look happy."

"I was."

The smile appears again and Megan cannot help stroking his back, just a quick, light touch. He doesn't pull away and her face splits into a grin at that fact.

"I want to show you what's inside." Megan takes the lid off and pulls out a newspaper article. "This one was in the *Sydney Morning Herald*," she says, handing him the article with the headline: "Police urge the public to be on the lookout for a father and son." Megan watches Daniel read the article.

"The police were looking for us," he says.

"They were."

"Why does it say Detective Michael Kade?"

"Because Michael was the detective in charge of your case."

"And then you married him?"

"Yes, but only just over a year ago."

"So, if I hadn't been taken by Dad, you never would have met him, so me being gone was kind of good for you."

Megan takes a deep breath and then she touches Daniel's chin with just the tip of her finger to be sure she has his attention. Again, he doesn't flinch, and she feels bolstered to carry on. "You being taken was the worst thing that had ever happened in my life, the very worst."

He leans back away from her and drops the article back into the box.

Megan's stomach plummets but she carries on, opening her computer. "This is my 'Find Daniel' blog, and here you can see the Facebook posts I did. Here are all the articles that were written about it, and here—look at this. This is me on television."

Daniel watches as she clicks through screens. "You look really sad," he says, sounding mystified, after watching two television clips.

"I wasn't just sad, Daniel, I was heartbroken. Can you see? Do you understand now?"

"You looked for me," he says slowly.

"We all looked for you. Connor and James and Nana and Pop, we all looked. This box is filled with the stuff we did: see, there's me in a magazine and here are some posters that I put up all around the neighborhood. I hired a private detective and paid him for years and the police also kept looking. No one stopped looking for you until you walked into the police station in Heddon Greta."

"Then why," he says slowly, "didn't you find me?"

"Your dad made sure that I couldn't. You know that."

"He kept me safe. He kept me safe from you," Daniel says, his voice raised. "You didn't want me anyway. You just didn't want him to have me." He shoves the box away from him and moves his legs, forcing Megan to catch her computer before it falls off the bed.

"That's not true, Daniel," she says, trying but failing to keep her voice steady. "I wanted you to have both your parents."

"No, no, no." He shakes his head and moves around her so he can climb off the bed. "I don't want to see this anymore. It's all lies, all of it." He rushes out of the room and she hears the bathroom door slam shut. He leaves her sitting crestfallen on his rumpled blue duvet.

She wants to go after him but cautions herself to wait, to give him time. Instead, she plays a clip of one of her television appearances, pondering if the woman she is seeing could have anticipated what kind of a child would come back to her. *Is the child who has returned the kind of child who would start a fire? Is he the kind of child who would hurt someone?*

"Megs, I have to leave," Michael calls from downstairs, forcing her to leave her old self where she was. After putting the box and the computer in her bedroom, she goes downstairs.

"How did it go?" asks Michael.

"He thinks it's all lies."

Michael shakes his head. "Poor kid, Greg really did a number on him."

Megan nods. "And it feels like he's still doing it."

Mr. Gordon is waiting for them outside the school office. "Daniel's teacher is Mrs. Oxford, and she and the whole class are very excited about meeting Daniel," he says.

He places a hand gently on Daniel's shoulder. "You can say goodbye to Mum here, Daniel."

"Oh," says Megan, holding Evie on her hip and feeling flustered. "I thought I would—"

"Bye," says Daniel, quickly, firmly, leaving her no room to argue.

Mr. Gordon nods at her and she understands she is dismissed.

Back in her car she feels jittery and sad, just as she did on the first day he started kindergarten.

At home, after Evie goes down for a nap, she goes into her studio. Mr. Pietro has told her that she can return to work whenever she feels ready but she's not sure when that will be. She wants to be home with Evie until she's around eight months at least. Her mother would be happy to babysit for her one day a week and, until Daniel returned, she had been considering this idea, but now she's not sure. She doesn't think she will have the capacity to give her students what they need as she struggles to help Daniel adjust and as they settle into life as a family.

She stands in her studio, a small room off the kitchen that used to be one of two offices downstairs. One of the first things she did when they moved in was to install a larger window so she had enough light to work.

She stands looking at the painting she was working on two weeks ago. It's of Evie, asleep, sprawled across her crib, her black curls framing her face. After a few minutes of standing on the spot, staring, she knows she will not be able to work. Instead she gets her computer.

In the living room she opens it up and sends Tom and Sandi a message. She thinks about explaining everything that has happened but decides against mentioning the interview and the police and their terrible suspicions. Instead she tries to put into words what she is feeling.

"I think Daniel is struggling with his father's death. He seems to be distancing himself from feeling anything at all, and I think that because he's doing that, he's not connecting with me either. Two nights ago, I heard him pleading with someone and I thought he was asleep but I don't think he was. He told me he wanted to talk to his father and he started pressing buttons on the phone he carries around to try and call him. I don't know what to do to help him. The therapist doesn't seem to be getting anywhere."

Only Tom is online, although she knows that he may have just left Facebook open. But after a few minutes, he replies to her message.

"Did he actually think he could call his father?"

"No, I don't think so. I think he was just desperate and maybe kind of half asleep. I'm not sure he knew what he was doing. The phone doesn't have a SIM card."

"That must have freaked you out a little."

"It did. He had a photo of Greg up on the phone and he was talking to that."

"I guess it's something people do sometimes. My father used to speak to a picture of my mother after she died."

"It could mean nothing but I'm worried that even though he knows his father is dead, he's still trying to deny it. It feels like that may be the one thing standing in the way of him settling back into his life with me."

She supposes both she and Daniel are struggling to accept things in their own ways. *Did Daniel light the fire? Did someone help him light it? Was he involved in some elaborate plot to kill his father? No, no, not possible.*

She waits for Tom to reply, wishing it was Sandi instead. Sandi is easier to talk to.

"I'm not sure how to help here, Megan. Of course it's hard for him to accept his father's death. He's a kid."

"I know. I want him to just be a kid, to be like he was before he was taken."

"But that can never happen, Megan. Can you imagine how hard it is for him to be there and to see you with a new husband and a new child? He must feel like you moved on with your life and forgot about him."

"But you know that's not what happened. We've been speaking for six years and you know how long it took for me to even contemplate dating someone."

"I know that, but Daniel doesn't. He's only young and he's hurt, remember. Maybe he never considered the idea of you marrying again. I know I could never marry again."

"It's not something I expected either."

"Yeah, but you have even though you said you wouldn't, and now there's another child in the picture. He didn't have a sister and now he does. I'm sure it's confusing. Try to see it from his side."

Megan looks at the words on the screen and considers shutting down her computer.

She can't help feeling that his anger over her marriage to Michael is still there, regardless of what he's said. She wonders if she should not have simply unfriended him on Facebook and taken down her blog so he couldn't find her even though she knows she would have found that near impossible to do. There is something about talking to someone who has experienced the same awful thing she has that keeps her coming back. No one else can really understand how difficult this is for her. But all her conversations with Tom are starting to feel the same, as though he feels she betrayed him and Daniel's return is just a reason for him to keep reminding her that she told him she would never marry again. She is tired of having to defend herself to a man she's never even met.

After a few minutes of silence, she writes, *"Tom, I can't explain to you why I married again, and in any case, I don't think I owe anyone an explanation. I never missed a day of worrying about, thinking about, and missing Daniel. You know that, you've been there through it all with me. I know this may be hard for you because he is home and Jemima is not, and I am so sorry for that, you know how sorry I am, but I was looking for some help from a friend. That's all."*

"Okay," Tom replies. *"I apologize. I'm sorry if I came across wrong. I was just saying that you need to see it from your son's point of view. He loved his dad and now he's gone, and as far as he can see you've created a whole new life without him. That may be why things are difficult."*

"Look, I think it's best if we don't speak for a while, with everything that's going on. I'm sorry but perhaps this is too much for both of us. I wish you all the best and I truly hope that your little girl comes home soon. Maybe we can speak one day in the future."

Megan browses the net for another twenty minutes, waiting for Tom to reply; she can see he's online, but she doesn't hear from him again.

She allows a thought to form that she has never considered before about Tom. Could it be possible that his ex-wife took his daughter and disappeared for a very good reason? There are women who have to run from their husbands, who have no choice but to hide so that they can keep themselves and their children safe. What if Tom's wife was only trying to keep her daughter safe? The things he has told Megan are only from his perspective, only one side of the story.

As she thinks about her new theory, she realizes that Tom's love for his wife borders on the obsessive, even after she supposedly took his daughter and disappeared. She feels guilty for thinking this, but she cannot help but remember how her heart used to pound when the doorbell would ring and she knew it was Greg picking up Daniel for an access visit.

"I'll do anything to get you back, Megan, anything," Greg had said on the last Saturday before he'd taken Daniel and disappeared.

"There's nothing you can do," Megan had replied. "Our marriage is over and we both need to move on. I really hope that we can just find a way to be friends so that we can raise Daniel together without any drama."

"You're the one choosing the drama, Megan," Greg had said. "Remember that. This was all your choice. Yours and not mine."

She has replayed those words in her head over and over again, knowing afterward that Greg had been warning her of what was to come, berating herself for not having listened more closely.

She goes to Tom's page, where she studies his profile picture of Jemima, his beautiful daughter frozen forever at four years old. Her cursor hovers over the "Friends" button for a moment. It's better this way. She clicks, unfriends him, and Tom is out of her life after six years.

CHAPTER TWENTY-TWO

After dropping Evie off at her mother's, Megan parks in a side road and then strides into school, just as the final bell tolls. She walks to the classroom and waits outside. The door bursts open and the boys and girls file out. Megan pastes a smile on her face, trying to cover the gut-churning anxiety she has been dealing with all day, and waits for Daniel. "Where is he? Where is he? Where is he?" she thinks, even as she knows that he is safely in his classroom being watched by his teacher, but she cannot calm down. That hideous day, six years ago, comes back to her and her heart races just as it did then.

When she sees him, she opens her mouth to greet him but he glances quickly at her and she sees him clench a fist. He grabs his bag from its place against the wall and walks off without her.

Megan stands in stunned silence as the other students give her curious glances, and then she turns and follows Daniel out of the school gates. Only when they are a few feet away from everyone does he stop walking and allow her to catch up.

Megan had looked around her as she exited the school and realized her error. She was the only mother inside the school. Even the youngest children walked out alone to greet their parents.

Daniel is too old to have her stand outside his classroom, yet she assumed that he would be feeling a little lost and would welcome her presence. *Another mistake I've made*, she thinks guiltily.

"I keep getting it wrong with him, Mum. I don't know how to treat him at all," she had told her mother.

"You have to get used to having a twelve-year-old, Megan. You haven't had the six years of learning in between. It will come, just relax."

"My car is the other way," she says quietly to Daniel when she catches up with him. She turns around and begins walking to her car while he follows her, far enough behind her so that no one can be certain they are together.

"I'm sorry," she says when they are both in the car and she has pulled out into traffic. "I shouldn't have come to the classroom."

"No, you shouldn't," he says, and then he bursts into noisy tears that are so surprising Megan has to turn down a side street and pull over so she can comfort him.

Once she has stopped driving, she tentatively holds out her arms, expecting him to shy away, but to her sheer relief he falls into her embrace and cries hot tears for at least five minutes. Though her son is crying and that kills her, she can't help but revel in the feeling of being able to hold him, of being needed by him, and at this normal display of intense emotion. When he's done, she hands him a tissue from her bag. "Was it that bad?" she asks.

"No, it was fine. It wasn't... wasn't like, like I expected it to be. They were nice. They were all so nice and some boys asked me to play basketball at lunch, and when I missed, they didn't yell or anything, they were just cool about it."

"I don't understand, it sounds like a great first day. Why are you so upset?"

"I'm not upset, I'm just... You wouldn't understand."

"Try me."

"He said that school was filled with assholes and that's why I had to learn at home. He said they would all give me shit because my mum didn't want me and that no one would understand why I had to keep where I lived a secret because everyone would ask questions and then tease me because even my mother couldn't love me. He said that everyone would keep at me until I told them the truth and then the teachers would call the social workers and I would get sent away to foster care. And that's what happened the last time I went. I told them something and the principal called and...we had to run away. I was so scared that would happen again. But today it wasn't like that at all."

"When were you in school? I thought you hadn't been to school in six years?"

"I was for a few weeks when I was like, ten."

"And you had to leave?"

"I broke the rules. I had to follow the rules so he would take care of me and want me. You didn't want me."

"I always wanted you, Daniel," Megan whispers, hatred for all of Greg's lies simmering inside her. "I showed you the newspaper articles and the blog and the posts on Facebook, didn't I?"

"You can't believe everything you see on the internet," he states, staring out of the car window. He sits up and moves as far away from her as he can.

Megan wants to howl with frustration. Every time she thinks she's taken a step forward with her son, he pushes her two steps backward. "That stuff I showed you was true, Daniel. It was true and I lived it every day and I never stopped looking for you or loving you."

"You could have made all of that up when you knew I was coming home. He said you would."

Megan rubs her head where a tight band has begun to form. "But I didn't make it up, darling. How can you think that? I missed you, I looked for you, I love you so, so much. Maybe you need to start thinking about some of the things Dad told you. He said school was filled with assholes and it wasn't, was it?"

"No."

"He said they would ask you lots of questions about where you lived, but did that happen?"

"No."

"So, do you think it's possible that some of the other stuff he told you may not have been the truth?"

"I...I don't know. I don't know," he says, staring out of the window at an old man walking his dog.

"I did want you, Daniel, I did, and I never stopped hoping you would come home."

"And then you got married again and had another kid."

Once Daniel's tears have ceased and his rare show of emotion is over, he is back to speaking in his flat, unemotional tone. She thinks about how Tom had been right about how Daniel feels. *I need to do better*. Her heart aches as she feels the distance grow between her and her son, right there in the car.

"That's not...that's not how it happened."

"That's exactly how it happened. You forgot about me. When I was gone you went and made yourself a whole new life."

Megan wonders what she could say to convince her son, trying to find the right words to counter his argument. But she knows that it will take a long time for Daniel to understand that the things Greg told him were his own twisted version of events. It will take her a long time to undo Greg's damage.

Eliza had said, "The foundation for Greg taking Daniel was most probably laid in the months before he took him, when he had his access visits. I am sure that your ex-husband began his campaign then to separate your son from you using tactics that come under the heading of parental alienation. It's a systematic breaking down of a child's relationship with one parent by the other parent."

Megan had sighed on hearing this. It was what Greg had been doing since the day she'd asked him for a divorce.

"Why did you steal all Daddy's money?" five-year-old Daniel had asked her after returning from spending his first Saturday night with his father.

"Why would you ask me that, Daniel? How could I have stolen Dad's money?"

"You stole it all and now he has to live in a yucky room and I have to sleep on the couch." Megan had been shocked at the words. She had looked at her son, whose eyes were blazing with anger as he stood with folded arms: a mini Greg with his defiant, square chin.

"Daniel, I didn't steal Daddy's money," she'd finally said. "Daddy gives me money so I can take care of you."

"Why have you stopped loving Daddy?"

"I explained this, darling. Sometimes people who are married just don't get along anymore. It had nothing to do with you. Daddy and I were fighting too much and now that we aren't living together it's much better for everyone."

That day, those words had been enough of an explanation for Daniel, but every week he had come back angry at her, defensive of his "sad" father, and full of questions about how much she really loved him and if she would eventually stop loving him like she had stopped loving his daddy. She should have seen the signs, of course she should have seen the signs, but what difference would it have made? She is pretty sure that if she'd called her lawyer and said, "Greg is telling Daniel that I stopped loving him," the answer would have been, "Isn't that exactly what happened?"

"Mothers can't stop loving their children, Daniel," she'd said once.

"Wives can stop loving their husbands?" he'd inquired, cocking his head to the side, genuinely trying to work it out.

"Yes."

"Will Nana stop loving Pop?"

"No."

"Why? Why can you stop loving Daddy and Nana not stop loving Pop?"

"It's... because... Do you want to go out for ice cream?" she'd asked brightly, too tired to find the right way to explain things to her five-year-old.

"Ooh, mint chocolate chip, mint chocolate chip." He had clapped and jumped and Megan hadn't had to find a way to explain things that day.

"I know how difficult this is for you, Daniel," she says to him now. "I understand how hard it must be to come home and find that you have a new baby sister and I have a new husband," she says as she pulls away from the curb. She doesn't look at him. She concentrates on the traffic as she speaks, hoping that if she is not looking directly at him, he will feel more comfortable about continuing to talk to her.

"Whatever," he says and then he slumps down in his seat and closes his eyes.

That evening Michael doesn't come home for dinner because he's working late, and at nearly midnight, Megan is still sitting on the couch in the living room. She has the television volume on low and only a lamp on the side table turned on. She finds it peaceful to sit in the dark, staring at but not connecting with the images on television.

"What are you doing?" is said in a harsh whisper, making Megan startle and yelp.

"Daniel! What are you doing up?"

"What are you doing up?" he retorts.

"I couldn't... I couldn't sleep."

"Dad couldn't sleep either," he says.

"Did he always have trouble sleeping?"

"Not always, only sometimes. When he thought about you, he couldn't sleep."

How much did he still think about me? How much anger was he holding on to? What do I say to this? What is the right thing to say? "Oh…that's…did that worry you? When Dad couldn't sleep?"

"I told him he should stop thinking about you. I told him and told him but he was really mad that you didn't love him anymore. Really mad."

"You can't be mad at someone if they don't love you, Daniel. You can't force someone to love you."

"Sometimes…sometimes you can," he says, and in the low light Megan sees a half smile on his face. "Do you want to see a picture of me?" he asks, and Megan sees that he has his phone clutched in his hand.

"Yes, I'd love to." Megan shifts along the sofa, making room for him to join her, but he doesn't sit down. He looks through the phone and walks over to her, holding it so she can see the picture he's found. Only when he is right next to her can she make out what she's looking at. It is Daniel at maybe ten or eleven years old. He is staring at whoever is taking the photo with a look on his face that is both sullen and broken. His hair is down to his shoulders, tangled with curls. He has a black eye and a puffed-up lip.

Megan gasps. "Who…who did that to you?"

"That's what happens when you break the rules," he says and then he smiles at her.

Megan shakes her head. "I'm so sorry, baby, I'm so sorry, I didn't know."

"You let him take me," he growls, "you wanted him to take me."

"No, I didn't, I didn't." Megan is shaking her head, tears streaming down her cheeks. "I didn't, I promise I didn't."

"I'm going back to bed now," he says calmly as though they have been discussing the weather. Then he leaves her alone, the photo imprinted in her brain, haunting her.

Megan covers her mouth with her hand. She wants to scream but she doesn't want to wake Evie. *I knew it, I knew it, I knew it.*

In the six years he had been apart from her, she had prayed that his father was keeping him safe, but she had also hoped with everything she had that her son would remain docile and sweet, that he would not anger Greg, that he would not—as she had done once, twice, three times, or more during her marriage—"push Greg's buttons."

Emotional manipulation was Greg's weapon of choice but he didn't like it if she fought back, if she bested him in an argument. On the rare occasions that she had managed to do so, he had lashed out. She had been shoved against a wall so hard the breath had been knocked out of her, punched on the shoulder, and had a door slammed against her foot. No one had ever seen the bruises and Greg had always apologized, while still stating that it had been an accident, with flowers and long love letters about how much she meant to him, about how he would simply die without her, about all the wonderful things they would do together. Letters that she had destroyed a long time ago.

She will have to tell Eliza about the picture of Daniel on his phone. She needs to tell Michael and Detective Wardell. If Daniel is the one who lit the fire, it will explain why. Maybe it was his only choice, his only way out. Maybe that's why he was running from his father: he was finally old enough *to* run.

She needs to say something to him. She needs to find the words to help him, to tell him she understands, to let him know she is there for him. She gets up and goes to his room, her legs shaking with shock. He is lying in bed with his eyes closed but she knows he hasn't gone back to sleep. "Daniel, darling, you need to tell Eliza about what happened, about that picture. You need to tell her that Dad... Dad hit you."

His eyelids spring open and he stares right at her, his eyes round and dark in the dim light. "Dad didn't hit me. Why would he hit me?" he whispers.

"You... you just showed me the picture, you told me it's what happened when you broke the rules. Give me the phone, and I'll find it."

CHAPTER TWENTY-THREE

Friday, May 20, 2016

Three years since Daniel was taken

Megan is awake before dawn, dressed in her running gear, waiting for time to pass so that she can run along with the sunrise.

When she sees the first sliver of light appear, she is out the door and listening to her pounding feet. Today she will run and then she will meet her mother for breakfast and then she'll go to work. She'll meet Olivia for lunch and then she will watch a month's worth of recorded movies and then it will be midnight and three whole years will have gone by since she's seen her son. He is nine years old by now.

She would like to know if he still likes peanut butter, if he eats his vegetables without complaint, if he even gets vegetables. Does he still sleep on his side, curled up in the fetal position? What size sweater does he wear? Does he like reading? Who is his best friend?

This is supposed to get easier. But it only gets worse. Sometimes a terrible, stray thought makes itself known: "if he had died." If he had died, there would be no chance of him coming back. She would not do a double take every time she saw a little boy with brown curly hair. She would not google her ex-husband's name and her son's name every day. She would not still be posting updates on her blog and Facebook. She would have to have found a way to move forward or die. If he had died, she is sure she would have had no choice except to die too, but he is still alive, still somewhere out in the world growing up without her. So she's stuck here in this horrific limbo.

On Wednesday afternoons, she has an art class filled with teenage girls. Last week they were working on a portrait of a family member, and one girl was drawing her little brother. "He's beautiful," Megan had told her when she'd looked at the picture of him. He had fine blond hair and bright blue eyes.

"He looks cute but he's a complete pain in the ass. You wouldn't believe how difficult a nine-year-old can be," the girl had replied.

Megan had opened her mouth to tell her that her own son was nine years old, and then she had realized that the girl had no idea Megan had a child. And even worse than this routinely stunning revelation that floored her each time she had it was the fact that she had no experience with a nine-year-old boy at all.

Megan feels the sun on her face as she runs. She can smell the fruity, soft fragrance of honeysuckle everywhere she runs. It's the warmest autumn ever recorded and Megan is enjoying the fact that the early mornings aren't too cold yet.

She is getting tired now, but not tired enough. She needs to force her body to feel so depleted that all she can think about is a hot shower and some rest, sending her into oblivion. She looks left as she runs past a house where she can hear a baby crying. *I will never hold my baby again*, she thinks.

Don't think, don't think, don't think.

Today she has her class from the retirement village. Right now, they're working on landscapes, and in class last week, Megan had stood behind a woman named Jean, who was painting a little boy just off to the side of the picture. "Perhaps save the little boy for when we do portraits," Megan had said.

"Oh no, my dear," Jean had replied. "That's my little Raymond. He died when he was five years old and he's in every picture I ever do," and then she'd smiled at Megan.

"I'm so sorry," she'd said, and she could feel the tears coming. *How are you still here? How are you able to get up every day and continue living?*

"Now don't you worry yourself, love," Jean had said, touching her arm. "It was many, many years ago. I miss him still but time has made it easier to bear."

Megan doesn't know if this will ever be possible for her. She had bitten down on her lip to stop herself from telling Jean about Daniel. She prefers the art studio to be a place where she is just Megan the teacher, not Megan the mother whose ex-husband stole her son. There is an expression her mother has worn for the last three years. It is pity and concern and love all mixed together, and sometimes Megan wants to yell at Susanna to stop looking at her like that. She wants Connor and James to stop looking at her like that as well. She would like to have just one conversation where they don't ask her how she is in the anxious tone they have all taken to using with her. It's not going to happen. She is never going to be fine.

Megan feels her legs burn as she pushes herself up a hill. At the top she turns around. It is time to go home. Tomorrow she will spend the day with Lucy, who at five is tall and beautiful. Spending the day with her five-year-old niece makes Megan feel like a mother again.

"You're still a mother," Susanna had said when Megan had told her this.

"Are you still a mother if you have no child?"

"He is somewhere in the world, Megan, and once you've had a child, you're a mother forever. That cannot be taken from you."

Megan pushes herself into a final sprint to her building. The streets are filling up with traffic, other runners, and cyclists. The day has begun.

In her flat Megan returns her missed calls. She had felt her phone buzz over and over as she ran, despite the early hour.

She thanks her brother and James for thinking of her but ends the call quickly.

She calls her mother and confirms where they will meet for breakfast.

"How are you?" asks Susanna.

Megan laughs. "I'll see you in a bit, Mum."

The truth is she has no idea how she is. She is functioning so she must be relatively okay, but that is only because she is creating an ever-increasing emotional distance between herself and the world. She runs instead of shedding tears or getting angry.

As she is getting ready to leave for breakfast, her phone rings again. "Hello," she says, impatient to be out the door.

"Hi, Megan, it's Detective Michael Kade, just checking in, no actual news from our side."

Megan laughs. Despite the day, she laughs. "I like the way you get that said so quickly I don't even have time to ask the question."

"Yeah, I, well... I didn't want to let you down but I did want to see how you were doing."

"I'm going to breakfast with my mother and lunch with my friend Olivia, and then after work, I'm going to watch television and try with all my might to pretend that today is not today."

"That sounds like a good way to get through. Whatever works for you is a good way to get through the day. The case is still active, just so you know."

"I know," Megan says and then there is silence. They listen to each other breathe, and even though Megan opens her mouth to say goodbye and thank you, those aren't the words that come out. Instead she asks something she has wanted to ask someone for months: "Every night I go into his bedroom and I say goodnight to him. Is that weird?"

"No, it's not weird."

"Last week I went in there to clean and I noticed a poster had fallen off the wall. It was a poster of Cookie Monster and I went to put it back up, and then I thought that a nine-year-old boy probably wouldn't have a poster of Cookie Monster on his wall. I think I cried for an hour after that, and I'd managed to not cry for months." The words have tripped out without Megan thinking. She has not wanted to share this with anyone in her family, but she has wanted to tell someone. Michael Kade will have to do.

"I'm so sorry, Megan. I'm so deeply sorry that we have not managed to find your son for you."

"Do you have kids?"

"No, I was married for a few years but she didn't want children and I did. In the end it was easier to go our separate ways."

Megan feels like they have stumbled into a real conversation, and she is not sure how she feels about it. "I have to go," she mumbles. "I'm going to be late for breakfast."

"Okay, I hope the day is peaceful."

"Thanks..."

"Oh, Megan..."

"Yes?"

"What are you going to watch on television?"

They speak for another ten minutes, discussing television programs they like and books they've enjoyed reading.

"Can we maybe meet for coffee?" he finally asks.

"I... no... no, I don't think so."

"Okay, that's okay..."

"But, Detective Kade—"

"Michael, please."

"Michael..."

"Yes?"

"Thanks so much for calling."

"My pleasure, Megan, my pleasure."

CHAPTER TWENTY-FOUR

Daniel—nine years old

Daniel watches his father sand back the old piece of timber that he says he's going to use to make a new bookcase for his room.

"Feel this," he says, and Daniel runs his hand along the patch he's just finished.

"Feels good," he says.

"What's up, mate? You're a bit quiet today?" his father says.

Daniel shakes his head a little. His dad shrugs his shoulders and goes back to sanding the wood.

Daniel would like to tell him what's wrong but he knows that his dad doesn't want to hear that anything is wrong. He never does. He gets angry if Daniel says something is wrong. He yells and yells about how ungrateful Daniel is and how he's given up everything for him, to save him. And once, once he shoved Daniel because he got so mad. He said sorry afterward, he said sorry a lot. He doesn't mean to get so angry; he can't help it because he loves Daniel so much and he wants to keep him safe.

Daniel doesn't like his new bedroom. It smells weird and even though this house is better than the shitty flat they were in before, he doesn't know why they have to keep moving. He understands about Mum wanting to find him and give him to a foster family, although sometimes he wonders why, if she doesn't want him, she cares if he's with Dad at all.

"She just wants to punish me, Daniel," Dad says when he asks this question. "It's all about hurting me and I don't like to say it but hurting you as well."

Daniel sometimes finds it hard to understand this about Mum. She had never acted like she didn't like him; sometimes she got angry, sometimes she shouted, but she always told him she loved him, she told him all the time.

He tries not to think about Mum and about Nana and Pop and Connor and James and Lucy. He wonders what Lucy looks like now that she's bigger. Sometimes he forgets a little bit what his mum looks like and that makes him want to cry because even if she doesn't love him, he can't stop loving her, and he's really trying to stop.

Daniel goes back to his small, musty bedroom and lies on the bed with the weird pink sheets. This town is called Balnarring and it's in Victoria. It's an hour away from Melbourne, and Melbourne is a twelve-hour drive to Sydney. It's much shorter by airplane. He wonders how long it would take to walk to Sydney. If he left today, how long would it take?

He turns over on his bed and looks at the wall. If Mum and the police really wanted him back—even to just put him into foster care—she would have looked for him, wouldn't she? There would have been something on the news or on the computer. He's allowed to use the computer now, but only when Dad is watching him and only for a short time at night to do research; that's how he knows how far away from Sydney he is. He had looked that up when Dad went to the bathroom. He also tried to look up his name, but all the results about him were blocked. He's not sure what that means, but maybe it means that there are no results about him because no one cares where he is?

Dad takes the computer with him when he leaves the house. He sleeps with it next to him as well. Daniel knows that his mum has Facebook. If he could get onto the computer without Dad watching him, maybe he could find her Facebook page. If he could find his mother on the internet, he would ask her why she didn't want him, just ask.

"Daniel, what are you doing in there?" his dad calls.

"Nothing," he says. Dad is always checking on him, always asking him what he's doing. Dad never leaves him alone.

CHAPTER TWENTY-FIVE

Sixteen days since Daniel's return

Megan opens her eyes to Evie babbling in her crib. It's 6 a.m. and the house is cold. She stretches, wondering how long her daughter will be happy in her crib. She looks over at the monitor. Evie is sitting up, holding her arm through the bars. Daniel is on the floor next to her, showing her his old cell phone. Megan sits up quickly and grabs the monitor. It's still dark in Evie's room so she can't see exactly what Daniel is showing her but it can only be pictures of him and Greg. She watches for a minute as he pushes buttons on the phone and then turns the screen around to show Evie, who keeps trying to reach for it.

"Da, da, da, da!" Evie finally shouts, frustrated.

Megan puts the monitor down to go and get her. She pushes her feet into slippers and wraps herself in her warm gown, thinking that she will compliment Daniel on his attempts to bond with his sister. As she goes to leave the room, she hears him speak over the monitor. "That's why some people shouldn't be parents, Evie," he says.

She shakes her head. *He didn't just say that, did he?* When she gets to her daughter's room he's not there. She looks into his room to see him curled up in bed, his eyes closed as though he has yet to wake up.

She opens her mouth to say something, to tell him that she knows he's awake, but then she simply closes the door quietly. Maybe she misheard? She's starting to feel a little crazy.

*

That afternoon she stands anxiously at the school gates and waits for Daniel to come out. She stands alone. He's only been at school for a week and Megan has been too consumed with how he is doing to relax enough to even smile at another mother. She watches students stream past her, identifying the ones she thinks may also be in Daniel's year. She finds herself holding her breath as she waits for Daniel to appear, unable to stop a creeping fear from eating away at her. She cannot prevent the flashbacks that haunt her every afternoon, to the day he disappeared, to how she stood calm and blithely unconcerned when he failed to appear. Each time he appears, she feels herself let go of the breath she is holding. Greg may be gone but she wonders if the idea that her son will not be there will ever leave her. He has a new cell phone now with a location app that she's told him he always has to keep turned on, but he leaves it at home most days. Only the old phone goes everywhere with him, as though he is taking Greg along with him, keeping his images and memories close.

She finally spots him on his way out of the school. His head is down and his hands are jammed in his pockets, and Megan experiences a twinge of unease at the idea that he may have had a bad day. A boy who looks about his age runs past him and slaps him on the back, making Megan flinch, but then he calls, "Bye, Daniel—friend me on Skype so we can talk."

Daniel's head shoots up and he grins back. "See you, Amit, I will." The smile remains on his face until he catches sight of Megan, and then his head drops again and his hands slide back into his pockets.

So, it's only me who makes him unhappy, thinks Megan, and she feels self-pitying tears threaten to fall. She swipes quickly at her face.

She has not brought up the picture on his phone with him again or his denial that it even existed. She has not asked him about being in Evie's room either, and every now and again it occurs to her that she is avoiding asking him questions she doesn't want the answers to. *Did Dad hit you, Daniel? What are you saying to Evie? Did you light a fire? Did someone who likes fires help you?* She is waiting until his appointment with Eliza, hoping that the therapist will have some insight, that she will be able to find the answers to all these questions.

In the meantime, she watches her son all the time, waiting for him to relinquish his phone for even a minute so she can look through the pictures, but so far, he takes it with him everywhere, even into the bathroom. She knows that she and Michael can force him to give it to them, but she fears that any strides they are making with him would be set back.

"Do you have any homework?" she asks once they are in the car.

He doesn't reply.

"Daniel, do you have any homework?" she repeats, thinking with agony that if this had been six years ago, she would have said, "Earth to Daniel, can you hear me, Daniel?" and he would have responded, "Daniel to Mum, reading you loud and clear."

"Yes," he finally says. "I have to do a project on my family. I have to trace my relatives back to when they first arrived in Australia. I have to talk about the immigrant or the convict experience. I have to speak to Nana and Pop and then I have to call Granny Audrey and Grandpa William. Do you have their number in England?"

Megan feels her voice catch in her throat. Such a simple question and yet she has a feeling her answer will determine how the rest of today or this week will play out with her son.

"I think I have their number," she says to him, "but I don't know if you should contact them. I am sure they are very, very sad about Dad."

"Why?" asks Daniel.

She sighs. It's such a strange question, as though he cannot understand his grandparents' grief over the death of their son.

Eliza has told her, "We all grieve in our own ways, Megan. You cannot assume that what is or would be right for you is right for him. He's processing his grief. It will take time. He is protecting himself by not allowing himself to feel the full force of this loss. He will eventually have to deal with it but it will have to be on his own terms."

Megan is sick of being told that everything will take time. She waited for six years' worth of time to have her son back. And she worries, she worries all the time since his interview with Detective Wardell that his inability to fully express how he feels is because he's concealing something more terrible than she can imagine. Something else she will discuss with Eliza; something else that the psychologist may dismiss. At least, she hopes this will be the case.

"I think Granny Audrey and Grandpa William would be sad because they can never see Dad again because he died in the fire," she says gently.

"I know that," spits Daniel.

"So, then you understand why they would be sad."

"I don't think they feel sad. I think they're angry," says Daniel.

"Angry?"

"Yeah, I think they must be really mad at you."

"At me? Why?" Megan turns to look at Daniel while she waits for the garage door to open.

Daniel smiles at her. "Because if it hadn't been for you, Dad wouldn't have burned in the fire. This all happened because of you. Just like the divorce, just like him having to take me to keep me safe, just like us running out of money. It's all your fault."

Megan shakes her head and pulls into the garage.

"And do you know what?" he asks.

"What?" she replies, feeling her skin grow cold.

"People who hurt other people need to pay for what they've done."

She looks over at him, at her son. In the dim light of the garage, his eyes are dark, his gaze flat.

"Is that what happened to Dad, Daniel?" she whispers. "Did he pay for hurting you?"

A wide smile crawls across his face and Megan feels herself stiffen.

"Dad got burned in a fire," he says, and then the smile disappears and he drops his head into his hands.

"It's okay," she whispers. She reaches over to touch him but he opens the car door and darts upstairs.

He didn't just say that. He didn't just smile and say that, Megan thinks as she hears him call "hello" to his grandmother.

Megan listens to her own voice tell her mother, "Thanks for babysitting," but after she has closed the front door, she watches her hands shake as she fills the kettle. Why had he smiled? What was he thinking? She watches Evie chewing on a toy, babbling and dribbling; a smile appears whenever she catches sight of her mother.

"Hello, sweetheart," she says, getting down onto the floor and kissing her daughter's soft, dark hair.

"Mmm, mmm, mum, mum," says Evie.

I cannot do this anymore. I cannot take it anymore. "I wish he had never come home," she whispers, just loud enough for her own ears. But as soon as she says the words, guilt slams into her. She shakes her head, wishing the words away, tears rolling down her face.

You're a terrible mother, an ungrateful bitch. You don't deserve to have children.

There he is again, in the room, dead but not dead. Greg will never go away, never stop tormenting her.

Megan stands up and returns to the kitchen. She throws her newly poured cup of tea in the sink and instead pulls a bottle of vodka out of the freezer. She has two quick mouthfuls, savoring the acidic burn before she puts it away again. She closes her eyes and takes a deep breath.

"Stop it now. Enough," she says loudly enough to make Evie stop playing with her toy. Her daughter crawls over to the kitchen, searching for something else to do.

She is being ridiculous. She needs to deal with things one day at a time. She does not want Daniel to contact Audrey and William. She knows that, in their grief, they will not hesitate to blame her. She knows, without a doubt, that they will take an innocuous conversation about their family tree and find a way to discuss her, to denigrate her. She is struggling enough, trying to get him to fight through the lies his father has told him; there is no way she is letting his calculating parents speak to her son until she is sure that he is in a more stable place.

She rehearses the conversation she will have to have with him when she tells him he is not allowed to contact his grandparents. Round and round she goes in her head, debating if preventing him from speaking to them is the right thing to do, if she is just being selfish and paranoid or if she has a legitimate reason for saying no.

After ten minutes of standing in the kitchen, mindlessly watching Evie unpack her drawer full of pots and pans, she realizes that she is doing exactly what Greg wants her to do. She is questioning herself, arguing with herself, judging her choices instead of standing by them.

"Screw you, Greg," she whispers. "I'm not letting them speak to him. No way."

The following Monday, she makes a call to the school. She speaks to Mrs. Oxford, explaining the situation with his English grandparents. She talks until she is sure she understands and she tells her so. "I don't want you to worry, Mrs. Kade," she says. "I will sort it out. We have a lot of complicated families in the classroom, and more than one child who doesn't speak to one set of grandparents. I should have thought this through more thoroughly. My apologies."

"Oh, please don't, I'm sorry. I'm sorry for Daniel, for all the kids with—as you say—complicated families. I don't want you to feel you have to change the project for Daniel. I just thought you could have a word with him, maybe explain that he doesn't need to trace both sides of his family."

"Leave it with me, Mrs. Kade. All will be well."

CHAPTER TWENTY-SIX

Twenty-two days since Daniel's return

A few days of relative peace follow. Daniel spends time with his grandparents, looking through old family albums and composing charts and a family tree, after being told he need only trace one side of his family. With each day that goes by without incident, Megan allows herself to take deeper breaths.

He gets more comfortable interacting with Evie in front of her, and she's grateful she didn't mention seeing him in her room as she watches him handing her a toy and showing her how it works. Evie, of course, thinks he's the most wonderful thing she's ever seen.

"No project work today?" Megan asks Daniel as she watches him spread his books over the kitchen counter after school.

"Nah, I've got advanced math to do."

"I didn't know you were in the advanced math class."

"Well, duh, Mum, I'm the best at math in the whole class."

Megan allows herself a small chuckle. "I'm sure you are."

She would like to ask him how he got so good at math if he barely attended school in the last six years, but she knows it's best to keep quiet and let Daniel tell her about his life with his father when he feels like it. It's starting to come out in snippets. Little pieces of information trip off his tongue almost by accident.

"I played that game on Dad's computer," he'd told her when she'd opened up a reading game on her iPad that introduced letters to babies.

"It goes all the way to high school," he'd explained when she'd looked at him questioningly.

"I learned to make my own scrambled eggs with Dad," he'd told her when she'd found him in the kitchen on Sunday morning cooking himself breakfast.

"I went there with Dad," he'd said when they were watching a program on Venice and its canals.

If Megan ever pushes, asks more questions, he simply shuts down. Sometimes it feels as though he would like to tell her more but something is stopping him, something is holding him back.

Megan opens the fridge and then she curses quietly under her breath.

"What's wrong?" asks Daniel.

Megan had assumed that Daniel was engrossed in his math problems and not paying any attention to her at all, but she is starting to realize that whatever her son is doing he is always paying attention to everything.

He watches her feed Evie even though he seems to be staring at the television. When Michael comes home from work and kisses her on the lips, Megan invariably catches sight of Daniel out of the corner of her eye, standing stock-still, staring at them. Michael has told her to ignore it, but sometimes when Daniel watches her it doesn't seem to be because he's interested; it's something stranger.

Stop being ridiculous, she tells herself, chasing any unpleasant thoughts away. *This is a good afternoon*, she reminds herself. *Everything is fine.*

"I've run out of milk and Michael is working late tonight," she says.

"You can get some more," he says.

"I can but I don't want to wake Evie from her nap—she'll be so cranky. I'm just being lazy, I suppose. I'll go and get her."

"I can watch her," he says quietly.

"Oh...oh, no, that's okay, you've never really watched her before and she can be...difficult."

"She's asleep. Every afternoon she sleeps for forty minutes exactly. That's what you told Michael. She shouldn't be asleep now because she's usually awake by now but she didn't sleep this morning; that's what you told Nana when we came home from school. She's been asleep for twenty minutes so you have twenty minutes to get milk from that store we go past every day on the way to school."

Megan laughs and then she stops when she sees that he is not smiling at all. Instead he is looking at her without expression. He has not made a joke. He has simply conveyed some information.

"I…I suppose I could duck out quickly, but what would you do if she wakes up?"

"I would pick her up and sit on the rocking chair in her room until you came home. That's what you do with her. She likes the rocking chair."

"But you've never picked her up before. I know she's not a tiny baby but you have to know how to hold a baby."

"Okay, then I'll just talk to her until you come home. I can show her some toys she likes. She likes the ball that lights up and makes all those sounds. I know she likes that toy."

Megan begins to shake her head to say no to Daniel's idea, but something stops her. He has been home for nearly a month already and he has never offered to do anything at all to help her. He makes his bed and puts his dishes in the dishwasher if she asks him to, but he never takes the initiative to do anything beyond get himself dressed in the morning and make himself some food if he's hungry. Even that feels like an achievement because the first time she'd found him in the kitchen with the fridge open, he had started, "Sorry, I was just…"

"Don't worry, Daniel. It's fine to get something from the fridge if you want to. It's your house, your home."

"It's *his* home," he had said, closing the fridge.

"No," she had answered him firmly, "it's our home. Mine and Michael's and Evie's and yours as well."

He had looked at her and then opened his mouth to argue. She had watched him go through the same process she had seen him go through many times before. He wanted to say something but he felt another way. There was a correct way for him to respond but he didn't want to do that.

"Okay," he had finally said.

Despite this small step forward it still feels like he is treating her and Michael as benevolent hosts rather than as his mother and stepfather. But right now, he is trying to take a step forward, to take a proper step forward into being a big brother. She should encourage him.

Megan takes a deep breath, interrupting her churning mind, and says, "That would be good, or you could read her a book or something."

"Okay," he says and then he goes back to doing his homework while Megan runs through the idea in her mind. The store is a two-minute drive away and she knows that there is usually parking outside. She could be there and back in ten minutes.

"Right," she says, grabbing her purse. "I have my cell phone so you can call me. The number is right here on the fridge. I'll be so quick you won't even notice I'm gone."

He smiles at her and she takes a deep breath. Maybe giving him a little responsibility will help. He has not yet bonded completely with Evie, and Megan knows that is something that will take time. So far, she hasn't left them alone together for even a moment. She wants him to learn to love his little sister, to treat her with the kindness and patience he used to treat Lucy with.

On the way out, she stops her car in front of the mailbox and grabs the letters that have been delivered that morning. At the first and only traffic light, she glances through what she had quickly dumped on the front passenger seat. She gasps aloud at the sight of a familiar blue envelope with her old address written on the front. She has been redirecting her mail from her old apartment for the last year and a half in case Daniel somehow found a way to contact her. She recognizes Audrey's handwriting instantly. Neat, cursive script with each letter perfectly formed. The last line of her address wavers a little as though her hand has begun to shake with the effort of keeping the letters precise. Megan cannot help a slight twinge of sympathy for her. Age is catching up to Audrey.

She rubs her arm, cold in the afternoon sun. It feels like the woman is watching her, listening to her. Why has she written after all this time? Why has she written just days after Daniel mentioned wanting to get in touch with his grandparents?

Parked outside the store, she opens her car door to go inside but closes it again and opens the letter. It is short, only half a page. Vicious, spiteful words leap into the air. Her hands may have begun to shake, but she is still the same judgmental, aggrieved woman she has been for her whole life.

Dear Megan,

I never wanted to write this. I never wanted to contact you again. You do not deserve to hear from William and me, but you have finally had your wish granted. My son is gone. He is gone and you have Daniel back with you. I will never recover from hearing how my darling son lost his life. I cannot believe I had to give them a sample of my DNA because my child's body is so damaged, so broken that they cannot identify him. Do you know what it feels like for a mother to hear how her child suffered in death? My heart is broken. It can never be repaired. William told me not to contact you but I have decided to appeal to the smallest shred of love you may still have for your ex-father-in-law and myself. Daniel is my only grandchild. I am eighty years old and don't imagine I will live much longer, so I am asking you to allow us to see him. We will send money and plane tickets for both of you, or we will come to Australia. I am not asking for much, but I may be asking for a miracle. Look into your heart as a mother and consider allowing us to see him one last time.

Thank you,
Audrey

Megan gets out of her car, holding the letter, her hands trembling, and then she stands outside the store in front of a garbage can and rips it into tiny little pieces. She watches them float down and land in a pool of pink liquid oozing out of a paper cup.

When she is done, she glances at her watch and runs into the store and down the right aisle to get the milk.

In front of her house, she checks her watch again. She had been gone just over ten minutes but it feels like forever. *Everything is just fine*, she thinks as she pushes the button to open her garage door.

As soon as she gets out of the car, she hears Evie screaming.

CHAPTER TWENTY-SEVEN

Megan leaves the milk and her bag in the car and rushes up the steps from the garage to Evie's room. Her daughter is sitting up in her crib, her face is beetroot-red, and tears are streaming down her face.

Daniel is crouched in the corner of Evie's room with his fingers in his ears. As he sees her, he takes them out of his ears and grabs his cell phone from the floor in front of him. His thumb automatically begins its compulsive rubbing of the screen and his body rocks back and forth, back and forth.

Megan grabs Evie out of the crib and holds her close, shushing her and bouncing her, checking that she isn't hurt in any way. She doesn't say anything to Daniel, aware of her rapid heartbeat and the adrenaline rushing around inside her. She looks Evie over, touching her arms and legs, checking for marks or bruises.

Finally, Evie settles and Megan carries her into her bedroom, where there is a bouncy chair in front of the television for her. She seats her and turns on a short video that entrances her, giving her a baby teether to chew on from a stash in her bedside table. Evie stares at the television. Whatever had bothered her is long forgotten.

In Evie's room Daniel is still crouched in the corner. Megan fears the pressure of his thumb on the phone screen will force cracks into the glass. Shock makes his face pale.

She fights the urge to shake what happened out of him and instead sits down on the floor next to him. "What happened?" she asks.

"She woke up," is his wooden reply.

"Okay, so she woke up, but she usually wakes up happy. Why was she screaming?"

"I tried to pick her up, but I didn't know how heavy she was going to be or that she wouldn't want me to touch her, and she squirmed around and I kind of dropped her back into the crib and then she started screaming. She just kept screaming. Her voice is so loud. It's so loud." He sounds completely bewildered.

"But we talked about this. I told you to just talk to her. Why did you try to pick her up?"

"I wanted to see if I could do it."

"Why?"

"In case I needed to."

"But you won't need to pick her up until you know how to do it. I'll teach you if you want, but I told you not to pick her up."

"I think she hates me," he says.

"No," she protests. "She doesn't hate you, she just doesn't know you yet. I think she can sense that you're her big brother. The more time you spend with her, the more you'll get to know each other."

"Half-brother," he says.

"Yes," agrees Megan, "you are her half-brother but you are her brother. I know that me being married again and having another child is hard, but this is how things are now, Daniel. I'm your mother too and I love you the same way I love Evie. Lots of families have more than one child. A mother can love as many children as she has. You have no idea how happy I am to have you home again. I have missed you so much."

"Why didn't you call me when I lived with Dad, then?"

"How could I have called you? I had no idea where you were."

"He said he told you. When we were on the plane to go on vacation and visit Granny and Grandpa, he said he told you and you wanted me to go with him. He said that he told you to call me every day but you never called."

"Believe me, darling, I would have called if I'd known where you were."

"Yeah," says Daniel, standing up. "He told me you would say that."

Megan wants to scream in frustration. Daniel walks out of Evie's room and then she hears his bedroom door slam.

"I can't win, Greg," she mutters, "and I'm sure that's exactly what you wanted, you bastard."

She goes back downstairs to the garage and picks up the milk and her bag, taking Evie with her, trying not think about why she doesn't want to leave her daughter alone for even a minute.

In the kitchen she begins preparing for dinner when a thought stuns her into stillness. She runs upstairs and knocks quickly on Daniel's bedroom door, opening it without waiting for him to invite her in.

"When we talk about Dad, Daniel, why do you keep telling me that he said I would say that? Did he tell you he was going to send you home?"

Megan sees him swallow hard. Pain flits across his face but his eyes don't leave the screen of his PlayStation. "Sometimes he would tell me he would send me back to you when he was mad at me. Then he would tell me about all the things you would say, all the lies you would tell, and all the things that would happen to me."

"And then you would behave so he wouldn't send you home?"

"My home was with him."

"But before that your home was with me, and you must have missed me sometimes, you must have asked to come home sometimes?"

"He didn't like it if I did that."

"And what did he do when he didn't like what you did?" Megan asks quietly, not wanting to break the spell of his words. She feels goose bumps rise along her arms. *I don't want to hear it. I don't want to know.*

"What?" he says. "What are you talking about? Why are you in here?"

"Daniel, look at me."

He drops the handheld device onto his chest and does as she says.

"What are you not telling me about Dad? Is there something you're not telling me? Because I feel like there's something you want to tell me, something you want to say."

He leaps off the bed and moves toward her, yelling, "I don't want to tell you anything except that I hate it here and I hate you! I wish I could go back to Dad. I hate you!"

"Oh, Daniel," says Megan. "Oh, baby, please calm down. You can't go back to Dad."

Daniel stops and then he slumps onto his bed. "He's dead," he says. "I know he's dead."

When Michael gets home after midnight, Megan is still awake.

"Bad day?" he asks as he lies down next to her.

She sighs. "If I didn't have a DNA match, I wouldn't believe he was my son. There is something wrong, more wrong than him having lost his father and being home with me."

"Megan, listen," says Michael, easing the laptop out of her hands and shutting it down. "He's been away a long time and he's been told that you didn't want him. That screws up any kid. I have a feeling things are going to get a lot more complicated from here on in anyway."

"Why?" Megan experiences a quick, sharp pain across her chest. *What now? What now?*

Michael puts his hands behind his head. "I spoke to Detective Wardell today. She says they're still struggling to get useful DNA from the body, but they've ascertained that the fire started in the kitchen. Gasoline was used."

"So, it wasn't the hotplate?"

"No, not the hotplate."

"So, they think... Do they think Daniel did it?" Her heart sinks. *It is possible? Is it really possible that he did this?* All the things she has been trying to dismiss, the picture on his phone, what she thinks she heard him say to Evie, what he said to her in the car. All these things are pointing toward a child so damaged he may have done this terrible thing. Yet she cannot bring herself to believe it.

"Daniel, or the person who took the car—because they believe someone did take the car. They have a countrywide search on for it."

"It has to have been someone else," she says, fighting to hold on to that truth. "Regardless of how badly Greg treated him, I can't believe that he would do something so heinous. He's scared of someone, someone who threatened him or something. That's why he's been so strange. He's worried whoever hurt Greg is still out there."

"I thought Greg didn't treat him badly?"

"I didn't say anything about this because..."

"Say anything about what?"

She takes a deep breath. "Daniel showed me a picture of himself on the phone. He had a black eye and he told me... he said, 'That's what happens when you break the rules.'"

Michael sits up and looks at her. "How could you not have told me about this?"

Because he's my son, because there is no one to protect him but me, because I signed the forms to let Greg take him, because this is all my fault and I don't want people to think there's something wrong with him even though I do. I do think there's something wrong.

"I'm sorry," she says instead of anything else. "I shouldn't have hidden it from you but a few minutes later when I went to talk to him about it, he denied there was any picture. He told me I was lying."

"If they can somehow tie the fire to him, we will need a way to prove that he was pushed into it."

"It wasn't him, Michael, I know it wasn't him. I know my son." *Do I know my son?*

"I don't need you to protect him from me, Megs. I'm here with you and we'll get through this together. I'm willing to do anything to help but we have to start with the truth."

Michael gets off the bed. He paces back and forth, running his hands through his hair. "I'm not sure we should have him in this house. He may be dealing with a lot more than we understand right now. I don't know what happened, but until we have the whole truth, I'm not sure he should be here."

"Then where is he supposed to go, Michael?"

"Maybe he can stay with your parents."

"No," says Megan in a fierce whisper. "I will not let go of this child again. I will not send him away. He's been through enough. We'll get him more help, we'll see Eliza twice a week until we have the truth. My son would not have done something like this." Megan can feel her body heat up.

"Okay, okay," says Michael, holding up his hands. "But you better not leave him alone with Evie, not ever."

Megan swallows, deciding not to tell him about the milk incident. Only when her husband has left the room does she allow herself to burst into tears. Only then does she accept what she thinks she may have known from the first day he returned: there is something wrong with her child. She is afraid of what is going to happen to her family, to her life.

But mostly, mostly she is afraid of Daniel.

CHAPTER TWENTY-EIGHT

Saturday, May 20, 2017

Four years since Daniel was taken

Megan opens her eyes and stares at her alarm clock, willing it to go off. She can hear the rain outside, and when she pokes a foot out from under the covers, she can feel the chill in the air.

She knows she should just skip her run this morning. She knows it would be stupid to go out in this downpour, but when her alarm beeps she gets up anyway and puts on her running gear with a rain jacket and cap to keep the water off her face.

It's dark outside and the streets are empty. It's difficult in the beginning as she tries to find her stride and watch where she's going. She runs through a puddle and feels cold water soak into her socks.

Finally, her body settles into a rhythm with the music she is listening to and she feels herself relax. It's 5 a.m. She only has to be at work at ten, but she wants to try a different approach to this day this year. She wants to leap into it with her fists up and fight her way through the hours, pushing away feelings of despair.

Daniel is ten years old. She wonders how tall he is. She wonders if his face has lost its little-boy chubbiness. What's his favorite food now? Does he have a computer? What does he like to watch on television? What does he like to read? Does Greg take him to the library like she used to?

She hopes that her son is no longer missing her even though she misses him every single day. She would like him to be happy, and if that means she has become a distant memory to him, then she can accept that.

The rain comes down harder and Megan trips over something in her path, almost but not falling over. A car speeds past her with its headlights on and honks as if to let her know what she is doing is ridiculous. But still she runs.

By the time she gets back home she is soaking and freezing. She stands under the shower until her hot water grows cool, luxuriating in the feeling of no longer being cold.

Once she is dressed, she looks at her phone. It's too early for anyone in her family to call her. She opens her laptop instead and finds a message from Sandi wishing her a good day and one from Tom, who she can see is online.

"I'm thinking of you today, lovely Megan, and I hope you get through it."

Tom has recently taken to calling her "lovely Megan." Megan doesn't love the idea but can't quite see how to get Tom to stop doing it without hurting his feelings. She wants to believe that he has moved past his hurt at her refusal to leap into a relationship with him. When he had contacted her again after not speaking to her for a few weeks, she had felt herself breathe deeply, relief suffusing her body. She hadn't wanted to lose him as a friend. Perhaps allowing him to call her "lovely Megan" is just a small thing she can do for him.

"Thanks, Tom. I've been for my run already so it's just a matter of waiting for work to start so I can get through today."

"I hope it passes quickly for you. Can I ask you a question?"

"Ask away."

"Do you ever think about having another child?"

Megan shivers despite the heated apartment. This thought has crossed her mind once or twice but it is always accompanied by feelings of guilt and defeat, as though another child will negate her love for her son and mean that he is never found.

"Honestly, I don't know if I could. It feels like it would be a betrayal of Daniel, like I was forgetting him, you know? Sometimes I find myself looking at other families and I do miss it, but the thought of starting to date again and having to explain my situation to someone else feels impossible."

Megan has typed her answer carefully, aware that she and Tom might be heading back into dangerous territory.

"Nothing is impossible, Megan. I do know that if I ever managed to date and fall in love with someone again, it would have to be a person who really understood my situation. Do you understand what I'm saying?"

Megan is about to reply when her phone rings, which she is grateful for. She is not going to get into a conversation like this with Tom, knowing where it can lead.

"Got to go, phone is ringing, speak soon. X," she types before answering her phone, hoping that he will accept her non-reply.

She is expecting her mother but instead it is Michael Kade.

"Hi, Megan, I know it's early but I also know you get up early to run, so I thought I would take the chance to just call and check in."

"You're right, I've already been for my run. I'm... I'm okay, I guess... Well, you know how it is."

"I know," he says, and Megan leans her head back against the couch. He has a deep voice, almost as though he was once a smoker but he's told her he never has been. She has spoken to him three times in the last year, just quick casual chats. He had asked her to go for coffee again but she had, once again, refused his offer.

"What a stupid thing to do," James had chastised her when she'd told him about her calls with the detective. "He's gorgeous and will find some un-fucked-up woman to date any minute now."

"If you weren't married to my brother and I didn't love you so much, you wouldn't be allowed to be this rude, you know," Megan had laughed, "and if he finds someone, he finds someone. I don't know when or if I'll ever be ready."

"I wanted to let you know," says Michael now, "that I'm leaving missing persons. I'm moving over to serious crimes. It's a promotion and something I've wanted to do for a while now."

"Oh..." Megan finds herself unable to say the correct thing. She knows she should congratulate him but all she can think is, *Who will look for Daniel now?*

"I'm never going to stop looking for him, Megan," Michael tells her before she can even pose the question. "Even though I won't be directly involved, I will keep reminding my replacement, a really nice woman named Tali, about the case. He will not be forgotten. I promise."

"How can you be sure about that?"

"Because I am. I just made you a promise. You don't know me very well but it's not something I take lightly."

"Okay, I believe you."

"You should. You would if..."

"If?"

"If you got to know me better. I'm giving this one more shot, Megan...will you meet me for dinner?"

"I..." Megan looks around her neat apartment where nothing ever moves unless she moves it. Sometimes she leaves a mess in the kitchen just so she can come back in and sigh and then clean up as though Daniel has been in there, as though someone other than her has been in there. There are times when she realizes that she has not spoken to a single soul all day if she hasn't been at work. In a moment of clarity, she realizes that this idea would make Greg happy. He took Daniel to punish her and make her suffer, and if he knew that she was still alone after all these years, he would congratulate himself on having achieved exactly what he wanted.

"Yes...yes, Detective Kade, I will meet you for dinner," she says, determined.

"Tonight?"

"Not tonight. How about tomorrow?"

Thoughts of her dinner date with Michael juxtapose with thoughts about Daniel all day. Megan feels sad and guilty and excited all at the same time. She doesn't want to feel anything except her loss.

On Sunday night Megan meets Michael at an Italian restaurant. They talk about his music and the jazz band he sometimes plays in. They talk about her work and how she has recently begun painting again. "Mostly pictures of Daniel." They laugh about a common dislike of fish but a love of spaghetti.

When he drops her home, he leans toward her and she feels her heart rate speed up, knowing what's about to happen. When his lips touch hers, they are soft and firm and she sinks into the feeling, reveling in something she hasn't done for years and years.

Afterward, she doesn't mean to cry.

"I'm sorry," he says, "I'm so sorry, I thought..."

"No... no," she shakes her head, "it's not that, it's not that I didn't want it. I did, I did. It's just been so long since I've been kissed. Years actually. It's nice, it's really nice. Please do it again."

She would like to invite him in but she's not ready for that yet. Instead she is the one who leans forward, and this time when he kisses her, he pushes his body against her a little, leaving her breathless. When she closes the door, she looks around her apartment and things feel different, less severe, less spartan.

She browses the net for a little while, and sees that Tom is online.

She wants to tell someone, to talk to someone, but not Tom.

She sees Sandi is also online.

"I had a date tonight, my first in forever," she types.

"A date?" Sandi responds instantly.

"Yep."

"How was it? Did you like him? What does he look like? Why have you decided to date again?"

Megan laughs. Sandi sounds just like her girlfriends used to when they were teenagers.

"I do like him and he's gorgeous. I don't know why I said yes, I just... I just said yes."

"I don't think I could be with another man myself. My ex was the love of my life, really. It's hard when the love of your life betrays you."

"Why would the loves of our lives have done something like this to us?"

"Good question. Are you going to see him again?"

"I think so, yes... yes, I am."

Megan waits a few minutes for Sandi's reply but she is suddenly offline.

She closes down her computer and climbs into bed. As she's drifting off, she thinks about Detective Kade and the way he kissed her. She falls asleep easily for the first time in four years and she dreams of Daniel in his paddling pool. He splashes her and she laughs and he says, "It's okay, Mum. It's okay."

In the morning she knows that she is finally ready to make space in her life for someone else.

CHAPTER TWENTY-NINE

Daniel—ten years old

Daniel sits in the playground alone. He tries to eat his sandwich slowly so that he feels full when he's done. This town is called Herberton and it's in Queensland. When Dad told him they were moving here, Daniel thought it would mean beaches and surfing and other cool stuff, but they live far away from the beach in something called a "granny flat" at the back of someone's house. The people who live in the house are old and cross and whenever they see Daniel, they frown at him, even though he never makes any noise.

Dad hasn't been able to get much work in this town so they don't have much money, but he has let him go to school. He has to use the name Daniel Ross here but he's used to being Daniel Ross now. Dad told them he'd lost all his records and that his mother had died and even though the principal looked at Dad like he was strange, he still said Daniel could come to school. Dad got mad when he saw how much the uniform cost so Daniel tries not to run around at lunch and get it dirty because he only has one pair of pants and one shirt.

Daniel wanted to go to school—even though Dad told him how hard it would be—but now he's scared to talk to anyone in case they ask him about Mum and then they laugh at him because his mum doesn't love him, or even worse, they call the police.

In the afternoons, he walks home and he tries not to watch all the other kids and their mums. He doesn't like to watch hugs being handed out. He doesn't like to smell the sweet flower smell of other mothers who come with treats to give their kids and laugh when they see them. Dad has told him that the best thing to do when you're sad is to put up a wall around your feelings so they can't get to you.

"Just imagine you're building it brick by brick so nothing can make you feel bad."

Daniel is getting really good at building the wall, at not feeling anything at all, but he still doesn't like to look at the mothers.

He finishes chewing his sandwich and looks over at where the other kids are playing soccer. He wishes that he could be allowed in the art classroom during lunch, but his art teacher—Mr. Wood—says no one is allowed. He says Daniel is the best artist in his class. Daniel thinks about Mum when he's doing art and then he has to build his wall and make sure it's strong so none of his feelings can hurt him. Sometimes he thinks he really hates his mother. She hated him so he may as well hate her.

He gets up and goes to the library because the library is open during lunch and at least there are books and books are the best because he doesn't have to think about anything when he's reading them. Some of the kids from his class hang out in the library so it's okay. It's warm and quiet in there and Daniel spots Victoria as soon as he walks in. He likes Victoria: she's kind and she seems to want to be his friend. She smells like strawberry bubble gum even though she's not allowed gum at school. He grabs a book about the history of computers and goes to sit down next to her, remembering all the things Dad has told him so he doesn't say the wrong thing: *Your name is Daniel Ross. Your mother is dead. You used to live in Melbourne but you can't remember where. Your name is Daniel Ross. Your mother is dead. Your mother is dead. Your mother is dead.*

"Nerd," says Victoria when she sees the book he has, but she smiles when she says it so Daniel knows it's just a joke.

Victoria is reading the first Harry Potter book again.

"How many times can you read that?" he asks.

"Until I get into Hogwarts." She smiles. "Anyway, I'm not really reading it, I'm looking at my phone."

Daniel looks down at her lap, where her fingers scroll through Instagram images. "You're not allowed to have your phone on you at school," he says. "And you're too young to have Instagram." There is a rule at this school that all children hand in their phones to the office when they arrive for the day.

"The secretary wasn't watching this morning, so I acted like I handed it in, but I didn't," she whispers and then she giggles. "And everyone has Insta, Daniel."

He can't help laughing along with her. The librarian looks up and lifts her eyebrows and they both stifle their laughter.

"Can I look at it?" mouths Daniel.

Victoria hands over the phone and he feels the thrill of holding something he's not allowed to have. Once, before she handed it in to the school secretary, Victoria showed him how her phone works so he knows what to do. He closes down her Instagram as Victoria's eyes are drawn back to the page she is supposedly reading. He finds her Facebook app and then he looks at Victoria again, but she's not watching him; instead she is absorbed in her book.

He quickly types "Megan Stanthorpe," and as soon as the results come up, he spots the page that belongs to his mother because the profile picture is of the two of them when Daniel was four or five.

"What exactly are you doing over there?" the librarian says, standing up and walking over to where he and Victoria are sitting.

He jumps and the phone lands on the floor.

The librarian looks at it and then she holds out her hand. "Yours, I presume," she says to Victoria because the phone is covered by a pink case with butterfly decals.

"Yes, miss," says Victoria, her face flushing.

"I'll just take it to the office, shall I?" says the librarian.

Victoria nods.

"Don't do it again," she says with a small smile. "Now off you go, both of you, lunch is nearly over."

"Sorry," whispers Daniel as they leave the library together.

Victoria shrugs. "No big deal. What were you looking up, anyway?"

"Nothing," says Daniel, and he feels a heavy sadness inside—his mother still has a picture of him. Maybe she only liked him when he was small? He clenches his fists, building his wall. "Nothing," he says as the bell rings and lunch is over.

CHAPTER THIRTY

One month since Daniel's return

Megan watches Daniel work his way through eggs and toast. She waits until he's finished his last mouthful before speaking, hyper-aware that she needs to sound casual.

"Have you heard of a computer game called *League of Legends*?" she asks.

Daniel's head shoots up. "Yeah, everyone has, it's this like game and all of the characters have this lore behind them and they have power and they fight and..."

You're still a little boy, just a little boy. How can anyone think you could start a fire that killed someone?

"Is anyone playing it at school?"

"Everyone, I mean mainly the boys, but some girls too."

Megan nods her head. She has heard about the game from Olivia.

At first Megan had assumed that Max would be one of the most important people for Daniel to spend time with, but any time over the past couple of weeks when she has suggested inviting Max over, Daniel has refused. "We don't have anything in common anymore. We don't go to the same school. What would we say to each other?"

"You were best friends, you can talk about all the things you used to do together and I'm sure that you'll have lots of things in common."

"We're not old men. We don't want to talk about things we remember."

Megan has let it go but has quizzed Olivia on the games Max is playing, the books he is reading, the television he is watching. She assumed that a computer game would be a good place to start. She hadn't even heard of the game until Olivia told her about it. She has a lot to catch up on.

"It sounds like a fun game," she says to Daniel.

"Everyone says it is. I mean, they talk about it..."

"What is it, Daniel?"

"I...Nothing. I don't want to talk to you about it."

Megan wants to push, to ask why, but she has learned not to do this. There have been times over the weeks since he came home when Daniel has simply talked to her, as though he has always been with her, and then fallen silent when he realizes what he's doing. It's as though he needs to keep remembering that he must not allow himself to connect with her.

"How about," she says as though the idea has just occurred to her, "you download the game and we get one of the gift cards so you can level up or whatever you need to do."

"Really?" asks Daniel, incredulous.

"Yes, I don't see a problem with it."

"But you know it's an online game?"

"Yes, and I also know that you've had the cyber-safety talk at school so you understand that you don't give out personal details and you come and get me if someone gets a little weird."

"Yeah, but..."

"But what?"

"If the game is online anyone can find me."

"Who's looking for you, Daniel?"

Megan watches her son's face change. The excitement disappears and the wariness returns.

"No one, but Dad said they could find me if I played online."

Megan stiffens. "They?"

"The police, you, and the people who wanted to take me away."

"Darling, you're with me and no one is looking for you because we've found you and it's okay for you to be online."

"He said if the police found me..."

"If the police had found you, you would have come home, just like you have," Megan says, not wanting to hear Greg's poison again.

Megan can see Daniel fighting to stay distant from her, to maintain his anger even in the face of the wonderful development of being able to download the game.

"He loved me more than anything, you know. Once, he said that if I left him, he would kill himself. He said he couldn't live without me and one day when I didn't answer him when he called because I was out in the bush at the back, he went like... like crazy."

"He went crazy," Megan repeats, understanding that he is not really speaking to her so much as speaking his thoughts. If she asks a question, he will shut down again.

"I heard him screaming my name, just screaming over and over again... Daniel, Daniel, Daniel, and then I came running and he was standing by the shack with a knife in his hand, a big kitchen knife. 'I thought I'd lost you, I thought they had found you and taken you,' he said and he was crying and then he took the knife and held it to his neck and pushed it against his skin and some blood came out. 'If I ever lose you, I'll kill myself, I will kill myself,' he screamed and then I tried to grab the knife from him and cut my hand." Daniel's voice is low as he attempts to keep emotion out but Megan can hear the panic, the fear, the certainty that he was in the wrong for worrying his father.

Megan picks up a cloth and keeps her hands busy cleaning up drops of spilled milk and toast crumbs. A terrible feeling of déjà vu settles inside her. She had been at the end of Greg's threats to kill himself many times in the few months leading to their separation.

Daniel watches her, silent for a moment. "He just didn't want to lose me," he says quietly. "He didn't mean a lot of the stuff he did."

"I...I understand," Megan croaks because she does, because she lived it.

How could I have married this man and allowed him to father a child? she thinks, wondering, not for the first time, if Greg had not just been a "difficult man" but rather a man suffering from some form of mental illness.

"Do you really want me to download the game?" he asks.

"I do," she says and the spell is broken, the conversation over, and he bounds up the stairs to his computer.

On the way to school Evie listens as Daniel explains the game to Megan, occasionally saying, "Gaah," seemingly in support of his new and instant obsession.

Daniel laughs. "See, Mum, she wants to play too. You're too little, Evie."

Megan cannot prevent a bubble of joy rising up inside her. When she stops the car outside school she says, "I'm sure Olivia mentioned that Max plays that game as well. Strange that you both like it."

"Not strange...everyone is playing it."

"Oh, well, maybe..."

"Maybe Max can help me level up," he says excitedly.

"I guess I could ask them over this afternoon; he may have time to help you get started."

"Yeah, yeah, that would be good. Bye, Mum," he calls as he climbs out of the car.

Megan watches him slouch into school. She has told him a lie, a small lie. She has already invited Olivia over for this afternoon, but if he had said no or not suggested it himself, she would have canceled.

"So far, so good," she says to Evie.

*

While Evie naps Megan stands in her studio, cleaning brushes, hoping that just being in the space will inspire her to begin working again. Her phone is in her pocket but she keeps checking it, ever vigilant for a call from the school about Daniel.

"He's doing fine," Mr. Gordon had told her. "He's a polite and enthusiastic student."

"And what about friends?" she had asked. "Does he have any friends?"

"I believe he spends a lot of time in the library at the moment. I think he's very comfortable there."

She is hoping that after a little time he will find his way out of the library and into the playground.

Her phone rings, causing her to panic. Has something happened to Daniel? Her heart rate settles when she sees it's Michael.

"Hey," says Michael. "I wanted to call you right away to tell you that they've found Greg's car."

"Where?" She wipes at the same spot on the paintbrush handle again and again.

"Melbourne. Someone had set it on fire near a large landfill."

"How do they know it was Greg's car?"

"It took a bit of work to find out. According to the officer in charge, Greg had never registered the car because, well, obviously he wouldn't have if he was keeping a low profile, but they managed to trace it back to the previous owner. He told them he'd sold the car to a man named Greg Ross for cash."

"So how did they connect Greg with that Greg?"

"Well, the basics about the car are in the database. The car wasn't so damaged they couldn't see that it was blue and that it was a Toyota station wagon. It took them a few days but they finally put it together, and the previous owner identified Greg from a picture we have of him."

"But why was it in Melbourne?"

"No one knows," he says, "but whoever took the car must have been involved. There's no other explanation."

"So, they don't think Daniel lit the fire anymore?"

"They are not ruling anything out, Megs, but they are looking for someone else. It is starting to look like the more likely scenario."

Megan breathes a sigh of relief, feeling her heart lighten.

"Steven Hindley?" she asks.

"It seems to fit with his history of arson, but nothing is being ruled out as yet."

Her muscles relax. She comforts herself with the fact that the car was found in Melbourne. The person who set the fire, who possibly killed Greg and forced Daniel to flee, is far away from them. Until she is told otherwise, she has decided to presume that this is exactly what has happened. This theory brings with it a whole host of new concerns. What did Daniel witness? How does a child recover from seeing his father possibly killed? Why had Steven been allowed into their home if Greg was trying to keep a low profile?

"It does bring up a lot of other questions if it is the case," says Michael as though he has read her mind.

"I know but at least..."

"At least?"

"At least we can be sure that it wasn't Daniel, that he's not responsible for hurting anyone."

She cannot, will not, believe he could be responsible. She keeps forcing herself to remember Daniel as a baby and a toddler and a young child, to remember his innate kindness and his deep sensitivity. Daniel could never hurt anyone, which is exactly what Eliza has said: "Deliberately lighting a fire is the behavior of a psychopath. Your son is not a psychopath. I am absolutely certain of that."

"I hope that's the case, Megs," says Michael, "I really do. I'll see you later."

Megan picks up another paintbrush and rubs at it with her rag.

Detective Wardell will be back in a couple of weeks to try and interview Daniel again. Megan hasn't told him yet as she doesn't want him to panic.

She hopes that finding a way to lose herself in her painting will help her deal with everything, but so far, it's not working at all. *If Steven Hindley set the fire, why did he allow Daniel to get out of the house? Was the fire an accident? What is Daniel holding inside? What secrets is he keeping?*

"Enough," she tells herself as Evie's babble comes over the monitor. "It's enough. I'm not going to think about this anymore."

By the time she needs to fetch Daniel from school she's worried she made a mistake asking Olivia to bring Max over. She has no idea how the interaction will go. She's nervous about Olivia seeing Daniel for the first time, wary of any judgment, although she knows Olivia isn't like that.

When she fetches Daniel from school, he's quiet.

"If you don't feel ready to see Max," she says, "I can cancel."

"No, it's fine, it's just…"

"It's just?"

"What if he doesn't like me anymore?"

"I guess he may be feeling the same way, and the two of you will kind of figure it out together. If you don't get along anymore, you don't get along, no big deal."

"Okay," he says and then he looks out of the window and nods as though assuring himself. "Okay," he whispers.

Olivia, Max and, Gemma arrive ten minutes after they get home. Four-year-old Gemma loves playing with Evie, treating her like her own personal doll. Megan and Olivia sip cups of tea in the kitchen, watching but not watching the boys, who are sitting next to each other on the couch, staring at the television as they share a bowl of popcorn and some cookies.

"Should I say something?" whispers Olivia.

Megan shrugs her shoulders. "I don't know."

"Max," she calls, and Max drags his eyes from the television. "What character are you playing on *League* right now?"

"I've told you a million times, Mum—Katarina."

"She's, like, one of the strongest, isn't she?" asks Daniel.

"Yeah, but I also play Lee Sin, the Blind Monk," says Max.

"Amit at school plays him. I haven't even started really."

"I can show you some stuff," drawls Max, and Megan wants to cheer when they both get up, leaving their dirty plates and the television on, and disappear into Daniel's bedroom until Olivia announces it's time to go.

"It felt exactly like a normal afternoon," Megan tells Michael at the end of the day, beaming. "It felt like it was how it was always meant to be."

"That's so great, love, I told you all he needed was some time."

"Baby steps and patience," Megan has begun repeating to herself, making it her own personal mantra. "Baby steps and patience."

CHAPTER THIRTY-ONE

Five weeks since Daniel's return

"What about a picnic?" says Megan to her husband and son.

It's Sunday morning, and the winter sunshine floods in through the large glass sliding doors that lead from the kitchen and living area onto the garden. Evie is crawling around her toy kitchen, occasionally pulling herself up to lean on the plastic stove and then falling back down onto the floor.

Megan feels what she believes is almost an absurd sense of well-being. She is trying to out-think her negative thoughts, to let go of her expectations, and to practice patience. She has been trying, for the past few days, to compliment Daniel whenever she catches him doing something positive.

She is managing to irritate herself as she strives to consistently sound bright and cheerful, but she is following Eliza's advice. Megan has congratulated him for making his bed, for handing Evie a toy, and even for laughing at a joke Michael told at dinner, although he had looked guilty afterward. To her own ears she sounds brittle and desperate but she has found that there are moments in the day when Daniel looks almost relaxed, when he seems to forget that there is some script he should be reading from; and when the child she remembers peeks through, her heart soars.

She is also trying not to think about the fire, about the backpacker, and how Daniel may have been involved.

Michael smiles at her suggestion of a picnic. "I think that would be great. I could use some sun." Daniel has his eyes glued to his PlayStation screen and merely shrugs. He is playing a game Max introduced him to.

"I'll get everything ready while you two pop up to the shops and get pastries for dessert. How does that sound?" Megan says.

"What do you think, mate? Want to come and choose what you'd like?" asks Michael.

Daniel shrugs again but Megan knows this is tantamount to enthusiastic agreement. Michael is always careful to look elsewhere when he makes these kinds of offers, and also always careful to only call him "sport" or "mate," never "son." She didn't think it was possible for her to love Michael more than she already did, but watching his careful efforts confirms for her that she has lucked out. She is pretty sure that most other men would have run a mile if they had to deal with all the complications involving the return of a kidnapped child. Daniel has stopped sneering when Michael speaks, and sometimes Megan will find him sitting as close to him as possible without actually acknowledging him or touching him. She and Michael both know that if he reaches out to her son, he will be rebuffed. Daniel will need to be the one to make the first move with Michael, maybe for months or years or maybe even forever.

For their picnic they choose a park that Megan remembers visiting with her son many times.

As she unfolds the picnic blanket, she watches him roam his eyes over the park. She doesn't say anything to him, waiting and hoping that some memory will be sparked.

"We came here all the time," says Daniel finally. "I broke my wrist when I fell off that climbing frame—remember?"

"I remember," says Megan as the image of four-year-old Daniel cradling his wrist gently while they waited for an X-ray at the hospital comes to her.

"I forgot about this park," he murmurs. "I loved this park."

"You did," agrees Megan. "I think we spent at least two afternoons a week here until you started school."

"I forgot about this park," he says again.

"But you remember now and that's good," she replies with a smile.

"He said you never took me to the park."

"He said...but you knew that wasn't true, didn't you?"

"Sometimes I did...sometimes I thought I dreamed it and he kept telling me I never even went to the park with you because you never wanted to be a mother. He kept telling me and telling me until I just...forgot about this park."

Megan tries to find something to say, something that doesn't express the rage she can feel building up inside her.

"Not true, sweetheart," she finally says, "but you know that now, don't you, because you remember."

"I remember," agrees Daniel, and then he walks over to where Michael is pushing Evie on the baby swing. He stands watching them awkwardly with his hands in his pockets, too big to go on the equipment but somehow looking desperate for the chance to be the little boy he once was when he pumped his legs to get his swing to reach higher and higher until he felt like he was flying.

What happens to a child who has had this experience? wonders Megan. *How does he grow up and get married or become a father? How does he ever learn to be safe inside his own skin, inside his own thoughts?*

She sits down on the blanket and begins unpacking her cooler bag, deciding that today she will not think about this. Today she will enjoy the sunshine with her son and daughter and husband. Today she will just be Megan, who is a wife and a mother, out for the day with her family. Today, she will just be.

CHAPTER THIRTY-TWO

Six weeks since Daniel's return

"How's he doing?" Megan asks Olivia.

"Megs," she says, laughing. "This is the third time you've called and he's only been here a few hours. I told you I would call if I was worried in any way."

"I know, I know," sighs Megan. "It's just…"

"It's just that this is the first time he's been on a sleepover and you can't stop worrying about him. I remember Max's first sleepover—I slept with my phone in my hand and I have nowhere near the reasons to worry like you do, but you have to trust me and you have to trust him. If he even looks like he's getting uncomfortable, I will call you, and Roy is willing to drive him back in the middle of the night if necessary."

"Thanks, Liv, sorry I'm being such a pain. If Michael were here instead of working, I'm sure he would ply me with drink and a bad movie but I just can't seem to relax."

"Go clean something—organizing always relaxes you."

"Okay, and I promise not to call you until tomorrow morning."

"And I promise to call you for the slightest worry I have."

"Deal," laughs Megan.

She checks the time. It's only eight o'clock and Michael will be home at ten after working the late shift. She knows she should just relax and enjoy her free time but she cannot stop worrying about something going wrong. Daniel had greeted the invitation from Max with enthusiasm.

"I never really liked sleepovers when I was your age," Megan had told him, hoping that she could give him an easy way to decline the invitation if he wanted to.

"I've never had one before," he'd said.

"Never? Not with any of your friends when you lived with… with Dad?"

"I didn't really have friends," he had informed her flatly. "Dad didn't like anyone at the house because…because they might report us to the police."

"But you must have had some friends at the school you attended, even if you were only there for a short time?"

"Not…not really," he had replied and then his gaze had gone flat and he had stared past her.

She cleans the kitchen and then folds some laundry before going into Daniel's room to tidy up. She has tried to mostly stay out of his room, wanting to give him the space she feels he needs, but she's sure that he won't mind coming home to a made bed.

In his room she picks up some dirty clothes off the floor, inordinately pleased that he is relaxed enough to begin behaving as he had done when he was six. She remembers arguing with him at least once a week about the fact that he couldn't get his clothes into the laundry hamper in the bathroom. "It's not rocket science and you are perfectly capable of doing it."

"Sometimes I'm thinking stuff and I forget," was his reply and it usually made her laugh.

She straightens his blue duvet and then she lifts the pillow and sees that his Billy Blanket is still stuffed under there. She smiles and thinks about folding it but then leaves it because she realizes he doesn't want her to know that he still sleeps with it.

As she goes to place the pillow back she notices the edge of a photograph under the blanket. She leans down and pulls it out. It is a photo of her and Michael and Evie—or at least it was. Megan recognizes her mother's living room with the ocean, a calm, flat stretch of blue, in the background. The photograph had originally been in the bottom of the cabinet in the living room where she keeps all her loose pictures that she has yet to put into albums. It was taken about six months ago when they had all been celebrating Connor's new research grant. She and Michael were both still a little dazed from lack of sleep because Evie was only two months old.

Michael hadn't minded the sleepless nights or the days when neither of them managed a shower. "I can't believe I was lucky enough to have a child. I never thought it would happen after my divorce," he said more than once.

In the photo, Michael is standing behind her, resting his hands on her shoulders, and Evie is in her arms. Megan recalls that her daughter was smiling her newly acquired smile at her grandfather, who Megan now remembers had just stuck his tongue out at her. Evie had let out a sudden, first giggle, making everyone else in the room laugh. Megan had wanted to bottle the happiness she'd felt that day so she would always be able to reclaim the feeling.

But as she looks at the photo that feeling is overshadowed by terror. She is hot and cold all at once. Both Evie and Michael have been eliminated from the picture, drawn over with thick, black marker. Only Michael's hands on her shoulders and half of one of Evie's hands remain. And stuck onto the picture, standing next to Megan, is Daniel. He has taken a photo of himself from six years ago, cut it out and pasted it onto the destroyed image. Megan almost wants to laugh because while the picture is a close-up of the top half of her body, the picture of Daniel has been taken from further away, and so she looks like a giant next to his six-year-old self.

She cannot place where the image of him is from. She has hundreds of photos of him, and after he was taken, she had asked her family to print out whatever they had. She has no idea when he would have gone through the bottom drawer and found the two pictures—one to ruin and one to save.

She sits down on his bed, feeling a little queasy. She understands him wanting to add himself, but the blacking out of Evie and Michael sends a chill down her spine. He has made them disappear.

He wants them to disappear. Megan can almost understand his feelings. Greg had told him over and over that she didn't want to be his mother anymore. Her having a new husband and child only serves to confirm that this is true regardless of how many times Megan explains what actually happened to Daniel.

She slides the picture back under the blanket and wipes her clammy hands on her pants. She replaces the pillow, unsure of what to do. She doesn't know if she should confront him or if she should just leave it, accepting that it's his way of dealing with how out of control he feels.

Going into Evie's room, she looks down at her sleeping daughter, who has recently found her thumb and now sucks it furiously in her sleep. Suddenly she is afraid for her, for what her older brother thinks of her, and for what he may be capable of doing.

She slumps down onto the couch in the living room and pulls her computer onto her lap. She would like to call Michael, but she knows he's busy with a new case and could be interviewing suspects or witnesses. She cannot call Olivia again and there is no way she would want to talk to her about this with Daniel in her house. She knows that she will have to mention this to Eliza next week, but she is almost certain that the therapist will tell her that he is just "trying to process everything."

She hates the way she feels, hates the idea that she is afraid of what he might do and of who he is now. She pictures Greg and imagines pushing her fist into his face. She doesn't know if the level of hate she feels for him will ever dissipate.

Opening her computer, she finds her Facebook page, hoping that Sandi is online. She would almost be happy to speak to Tom right now.

"Hey," she types.

"Hey," Sandi replies instantly.

"How are you?"

"I'm good, love, how are you?"

She thinks about how to tell Sandi what she's found. She hates the idea of discussing her son in a negative way but she knows she can count on Sandi to just listen and then offer advice.

"I found something," she finally types, and Sandi responds with a question mark.

"Daniel had a picture of me, Evie, and Michael under his pillow and he's blacked out Michael and Evie. I know that he's probably just acting out and he wouldn't really do anything to hurt Evie, but it feels... I feel like he's someone I don't know, someone I can't trust."

"Oh, babe, that's so hard. It must have really scared you."

"It did and now I don't really know what to do."

"Have you asked Tom? I know that sometimes it seems like he has more of a guy's perspective, and who wants to listen to men, right? But maybe he remembers being a twelve-year-old boy. I've only got daughters so I have no idea really."

Megan nods her head at this. She supposes she could call her brother or speak to James, but she doesn't want her family to know that things are this difficult with Daniel.

"I unfriended him."

"You did? Why?"

"He doesn't seem to be able to let go of the fact that I'm married again and have Evie. He thinks it's the reason I'm having such trouble with Daniel. I just didn't feel comfortable talking to him anymore."

"Fair enough."

"What do you think I should do? Should I ask Daniel about the photo?"

"Look, I kind of understand why he may feel that way, like he wishes Michael and Evie would disappear. I didn't know you and Tom weren't talking anymore but he and I still talk. It would be a dream for us to have our kids back."

"I know that and I feel terrible for... I guess for not being able to tell you it's just wonderful. It's not."

"Maybe you and he need some time alone—time just to be together without anyone else. Maybe you should go away with him, just the two of you so that you can really connect again."

"I wish I could, but I can't leave Evie. I'm still feeding her."

"Oh, right, I forgot about that. You can't express enough even for a few days?"

"No, I can't, and anyway I wouldn't want to leave her. I would have to come home again, and we would be right back where we started. Daniel is part of a family and he needs to get used to that."

"I understand but even just a day or two might help. It may give him the space he needs to talk to you, really talk to you."

"Maybe, but I don't think it's going to happen. I'm a mother to two children now. I can't leave Evie."

"I guess so, I just don't know what else to suggest. I have to go now but I'm thinking about you all the time and really hoping it gets better. xx."

Megan sighs, shutting down her computer. She wonders if Sandi is right, if some time alone with Daniel would help, but then she dismisses the suggestion. She is a mother to two children, not just one—she cannot simply abandon her daughter.

She hears the ping of a message on her phone. It's from Olivia, an image of Max and Daniel. They are both laughing at something they're watching on television. Daniel looks completely relaxed and at home with pizza slices piled on a plate in front of him. Olivia has texted:

They're having a blast.

CHAPTER THIRTY-THREE

Sunday, May 20, 2018

Five years since Daniel was taken

Megan opens her eyes and stretches across the bed. She runs her hand along the side where Michael normally sleeps, missing the feel of him next to her.

In a week's time he will sleep next to her every night for the rest of their lives but she wanted to be alone this morning, like all the other solitary years. "It's become something of a ritual," she explained. "I run and I think about him and then I get through the day."

"Wouldn't it be easier if I were there?"

"Next year you'll be with me but this year I need to do it alone for the last time. I can't really explain it properly but I don't actually want it to be easier. I feel like with each passing year it is getting a little easier to live my life without him, especially now that I have you. But I need the day to be hard, just a little hard. I want to devote some time to thinking about him and missing him."

"Okay," Michael had agreed, squeezing her hand.

Megan slides out of bed and dresses in her running gear. Today's run will be gentle, just like yesterday's run was.

"You can keep running," her doctor had said, "but you need to make it a gentler experience. You're thirty-seven now and that makes this pregnancy a little more complicated." Dr. Sakasky seems not to have aged since Megan last saw her eleven years ago, when she was pregnant with Daniel. She is still tall and slim, her skin unlined and her blond hair held back loosely in a ponytail. Megan had been surprised to find that she was still working in the same building, still using the same phone number. The allotted forty-five minutes for Megan's first appointment had ticked away as she filled in the last eleven years for the obstetrician while Dr. Sakasky shook her head and occasionally touched Megan's hand gently.

"You've been through so much, you've borne so much pain," she'd said. "Now it is time for a little bit of happiness, I think."

"I think," Megan had answered her, "but I am so afraid to believe."

When Megan had told Michael she needed to be alone, she hadn't added, "And next year we will have a five-month-old baby." She hadn't said that. It was a wonderful thought yet a terrible thought because a baby would make the day so much easier. A baby made you too busy to think much, a baby sapped your energy and your concentration. A baby might make her forget. The guilt already tore through her.

For her run Megan chooses a route that is long and flat and she hits her stride quickly. She feels like she could go forever. She has not told Michael about the baby yet because she wants it to be a surprise on their wedding night. She is conscious with each step that she is carrying precious cargo.

She is just over two months along and Dr. Sakasky is fairly confident that all is well, although she will have to go for more tests. When she first missed her period, she imagined that it was early menopause and she had been completely heartbroken. She hadn't tested until her period was nearly three weeks late, and then only because James had said, "What exactly is going on with your boobs, Megan?"

Walking back into her obstetrician's office had been a strange experience. Megan had paged through parenting magazines, casting surreptitious glances at the other women in the room, trying to gauge how far along they were. It was not a place she thought she would find herself again. She cannot help but compare it to her pregnancy with Daniel, which was not so much a surprise as a shock. Megan had already begun finding Greg's lightning-quick mood changes and obsession with knowing where she was all the time difficult to deal with. Stray thoughts of leaving him and starting again, of admitting her mistake, had begun to torment her. The pregnancy had changed everything.

"It will be the greatest thing that has ever happened to us," Greg had enthused and he had been right. Daniel was the greatest thing that ever happened to her. She had never felt so much love, but having a child had not changed who Greg was. He had, instead, become more controlling, more prone to outbursts, and more emotionally manipulative.

She thinks a simple lunch with Connor was the turning point for her. She knows that the afternoon she met her brother at an Italian restaurant was the afternoon that changed everything.

"Do you want a glass of wine?" Connor had asked as they sat down.

"I would love…" Megan had begun and then she had thought about Greg noticing the smell of wine on her breath, even though she knew she would brush her teeth straight away when she got home. She had imagined him sneering, "How nice that some people get to have long lunches and piss away their days while I work my ass off."

"No thanks," she had said to Connor. He had shrugged his shoulders and ordered a glass for himself. They had shared a salad to begin with. Connor's pasta had arrived soon afterward but Megan's had not. "Just start, I'm sure mine will be along soon."

"It's two orders of pasta, how hard can it be to get them out here together? Let me call our waiter." Connor had raised his hand to summon the waiter and Megan had felt herself shrink in her chair. "Don't make a fuss, Con, it's not a big deal."

Megan had looked down at her hands while her brother had spoken to the waiter, feeling herself flush. The waiter was a young man with thick forearms and a tattoo on his wrist. When Connor had finished speaking, she'd looked up at him and given him what she hoped was an ingratiating smile. She hadn't wanted him to be angry.

After he'd left, her brother had looked at her and given his head a slow shake. "What was that about, Megs?"

"What? What do you mean?"

"It looked like you were scared of him. He's a waiter who's paid to take our orders and get our food here at the right time. Why would you be afraid of him?"

"I just don't like people to be upset. I didn't feel like the confrontation."

"It's his job and he messed up. You would have been the first one to call him over and tell him to get his ass in gear before…"

"Before what, Connor?"

He'd forked some pasta into his mouth. Megan could see him buying time.

"Before you married that asshole," he'd said when he had swallowed.

"He's not…" Megan had started saying, treading her familiar path of justifying and defending her husband's behavior. But something had stopped her, and instead she had looked at her brother, letting herself, for the first time, be honest. "I don't know what to do, Con, it's just so awful."

The conversation that followed had started Megan down the track to divorce and to her finding her voice again.

She knows that this baby will be different because Michael is so very different. This baby will only bring joy. *If I don't lose it, if it's healthy, if the amniocentesis comes back with the all clear. If, if, if. It will be fine, everything's fine. Hang in there, little one.*

As she runs, Megan looks left and right at houses filled with swing sets and children's toys. She notices bicycles abandoned on lawns and hears a baby crying its parents awake. She cannot quite believe that she is here again, in this place of hope and delight. She cannot believe it and she feels guilty about it, but then everything that has happened to her this year has an aura of guilt around it.

She and Michael have begun looking for houses. "But what if he tries to find me again? How will he know where I am?"

"Megan, wherever we end up, our new address will be on every single database around the world. All he has to do is walk into any police station and tell them who he is, and they will find you."

Her son has lived apart from her for nearly half his life. She wonders if he remembers her at all, hopes he does, hopes he doesn't. Megan thinks about what kind of child he would be now. *Does he play a musical instrument? Does he roll his eyes like Olivia says Max does whenever Greg asks him to do something? Is he starting to go through puberty? Would I know him if I saw him? Would he know me?*

Back at home, feeling somewhat rejuvenated after her run, Megan showers and opens her laptop.

"Thinking of you, babe," Sandi has written in a message. *"Only one week to go until you change your life forever. Maybe it won't hurt so much to have lost him anymore."*

"Oh, Sandi, it can never stop hurting. We both know that. Thanks for thinking of me xx," she types for Sandi to read when she's back online.

"Thinking of you today, as always," Tom has written. She notices that he's online now.

"Thanks, Tom. How are you?" She and Tom have not spoken for a few months and she is surprised to hear from him. She had messaged him on the anniversary of Jemima's disappearance and received no acknowledgment or reply. She'd thought he was done speaking to her.

"I'm okay. Doing what I do, you know. I'm trying to get back into dating like you suggested."

"I'm glad, Tom."

"I don't know, it feels like I'm giving up hope of seeing Jemima again if I move on with my life. I don't want to move on without her."

"But you're not. All you're doing is trying to live your life. You're not going to stop looking."

"Will you ever stop looking?"

"You know the answer to that, Tom—no, I will never stop looking."

"What if you have another child?"

"I don't think having another child stops you loving your first child. Nothing will ever make me stop wanting him to come home to me."

"So, are you planning to have another kid?"

Megan sighs and looks around her apartment. She doesn't feel like having this conversation right now, doesn't want to have to lie about being pregnant, and she is certainly not going to admit to Tom that she is.

"Right now, all I'm planning to do is get married. I don't know what the future holds for me but I have to hope that one day Daniel will be home. It's what I hope for every day and what I will keep hoping for. Oh, there goes my phone. Sorry, I have to go. Thanks for thinking of me. Speak soon. X."

She watches the screen for a minute and finally Tom's message appears.

"Hope you have an easy day. x."

Getting off the couch, she goes to Daniel's room and sits on his bed. She smooths the sheets and pillow with her hands, touching where he once touched. Everything has remained the same: still, silent, and waiting for the child who is meant to be there to return. The room has such a sad, empty feel it makes it hard to breathe. She closes her eyes, imagines her little boy standing in front of her. She cannot stop the words escaping her mouth, feeling compelled to speak to him. "I wish you could be here to watch me get married, Daniel. I would love you to meet Michael and get to know him. I miss you so much but I have to take a step or two forward, I just have to. I hope that when you come home, you understand. I love you, my beautiful boy. I will never stop looking for you. Never."

She picks up his Billy Blanket and hugs it to her. It no longer smells of her son but she conjures up his face and tries to imagine him feeling her arms around him, her cheek next to his. When the tears come it feels as though they will never end, but finally she shakes herself and stands up. "Enough now," she tells herself, conscious of the little life inside her.

Her phone rings with her mother's usual call and Megan answers quickly. "Hi, Mum, I'm doing okay."

CHAPTER THIRTY-FOUR

Daniel—eleven years old

Daniel crouches in the bush, listening for the click buzz of the cricket he is trying to find. His shirt is thin and too short for him so he's feeling cold but he doesn't want to go back into the house for a sweater. He's wearing flip-flops because they're cheap. Dad always shakes his head and says, "Where do you think the money comes from, Daniel," when he tells him his shoes hurt, so it's easier just to wear flip-flops. It won't be that easy to do in winter when it's really cold, but it's okay for now. He looks down at the phone Dad has given him. It's nearly two o'clock and Dad said he would be back by three at the latest and that he wanted Daniel to finish the math work he'd set out for him.

His father won't let him go back to school again. Not after he told Victoria his mother wasn't really dead. Victoria had been his first friend in years and years and Daniel had made the mistake of forgetting the rules. Dad had been really, really angry. Victoria had told her mother and her mother had told another mother and someone had told the principal of the school and then his father had got a call.

Daniel had known it was all about to go wrong when the principal had called him into the office and Dad was there. He had to tell the principal he had been lying and his mother was really dead. Dad had taken him home right then, driven fast and angry, tires squealing, and when they'd got home, he'd turned to Daniel and said, "You remember the rules, don't you?"

Daniel had nodded and his father's fist had flown through the air, a wasp looking to sting, and landed on his cheek. It had felt like an explosion inside his head. He'd had a big, black bruise on his face for over a week.

They'd had to leave that night, sneaking out in the dark and driving for days. "You're never going to school again if you can't remember the rules," his father had said. Leaving Victoria had made him feel awful; not being allowed to go to school again had made him feel worse. Now they're here in Heddon Greta in a small shack with no heat and a broken stove.

"Look what you made happen, Daniel," he'd said when they got here.

Daniel is trying to be good, to stay out of his way, to not complain or ask for anything because he doesn't want to make him angry again.

He hears the leaves on the bush next to him rustle and thinks it may be the cricket whose green wings he spotted a few minutes ago, but then the bush rustles again and a wild rabbit darts out.

Daniel jumps and feels his heart race but then he laughs. He'll tell his father about the rabbit. He looks down at his phone again. It's very old but it has pictures from all the years he and his father have lived together. "If I let you have this, you can only call me—understand?" he'd said and Daniel had understood. He isn't going to break the rules again. It only has two sad little games on it but at least if something happens, he can call Dad.

Last night his father had shown him a picture on his computer of a blond woman. "What do you think of her?" he'd asked. Daniel had shrugged his shoulders.

"She's really nice, and she only lives in Newcastle. I might meet up with her one night."

Daniel doesn't like the idea of his father meeting another woman, liking another woman, and maybe one day marrying her. What would happen to him? If his mother hated him, another woman would hate him too and then his father would send him to foster care.

He sighs and walks back to the house. He can't let that happen. He's not going into foster care no matter what.

In the shack he pulls on one of his father's old sweaters and looks at his phone. He knows that he used to know his mother's cell phone number. He used to but not anymore.

"It doesn't matter," he says aloud as he hears the car pull up outside the shack. Nothing matters anyway.

CHAPTER THIRTY-FIVE

Six and a half weeks since Daniel's return

In the end, Megan doesn't mention the photograph to Daniel.

"He's acting out," Eliza had said when she'd explained it. "The fact that he is expressing his anger is a good thing. If he can express it, he won't allow it to fester. Be patient. You'll get there."

"I suppose I would feel the same way," Michael had said when she'd told him. "We're both watching him and that's all we can do. Hopefully he gets rid of it on his own."

So Megan tries not to worry, and over the next few days she has moments where she can see Daniel trying to fit into their family. He even asks her to teach him how to pick Evie up out of the crib so she feels safe. Evie loves being carried around by him and will spend her whole afternoon following him around, crawling after him into his room and even trying to get into the bathroom if he is in there.

"Mum," calls Daniel from his room one afternoon.

"What is it?" Megan shouts from the kitchen. "I'm in the middle of cutting up the chicken."

"Can you come get Evie? She's touching my stuff and I'm trying to do my homework." Megan realizes she must have forgotten to close the gate that keeps Evie downstairs. Evie knows she has to turn around and go backward down the stairs but she still needs help doing it so Megan is grateful that she's made it safely to her brother's room and stayed there.

She shakes her head and rinses off her hands. She goes into Daniel's room, where Evie has pulled all his shoes out of his cupboard. "Come on, little girl," she says, picking up her daughter, "leave your big brother alone to do his work."

"Yeah," he says, "leave your big brother alone."

Megan would like to jump for joy, but she bites down on her lip and goes back to the kitchen with Evie, giving her a teether to chew on and putting on a short DVD.

"It was like a normal family moment," she explains to Michael later, a smile on her face. "Like any other big brother irritated with a pesky little sister. I can't even explain how wonderful it felt, as though everything had just clicked into place."

The next day when she goes into his room to clean, she looks for the picture as she has done every day for a week and finds it gone. Her relief makes her cry.

"Shall we go out for a walk, Evie?" she asks her daughter, who is sitting next to her, her little hand clutching onto Megan's pants as she loads the washing machine. It is an unusually mild August day. Daniel will be thirteen soon and Megan wonders if he would like a big party or a small family celebration. She picks Evie up, eager to get out of the house with her daughter. For the past week, a driving cold wind has battered at the house, forcing Megan to keep Evie indoors.

When she opens the front door, there is a young man standing outside holding a large arrangement of soft-pink roses. "Megan Kade?" he asks, shifting the gum he is chewing to one side of his mouth.

"I am." Megan smiles, knowing that Michael is fond of gestures like these.

"Sign here."

Megan closes the front door, leaving Evie in the carriage as she takes the flowers to the kitchen. She searches for a vase and admires the beautiful arrangement that she will tell Michael tonight was unnecessary. They must have cost a fortune, especially at this time of year. When she finds the vase, she fills it with water and rests the bouquet inside, planning to arrange them properly when she and Evie get back from their walk. She catches sight of the little white card on the top and opens it, a smile playing on her lips until she reads the message.

I gave you every chance I could. Remember, Megan, this is on you. T

The words are shocking, cold, almost violating and Megan reaches for the kitchen counter, grabbing it. She rushes back to the front door and opens it, looking for the man who has delivered the flowers, but the street is empty. Who are they from? Who would send her flowers with a message like this? Who is angry enough at her to do this? Who is T? Could they be from Tom? The delivery man had called her Megan Kade—but Tom doesn't even know her new surname because she hasn't changed it on Facebook. He also doesn't know where she lives. She blocked Tom weeks ago—has he been searching for her address all this time just so he could send this hideous message?

She shuts the door quickly and locks it. She cannot leave the house now. She feels like whoever sent the flowers is watching her, like they are somewhere close. She hauls a complaining Evie out of her carriage and soothes her with a new toy she has been saving for when she wanted some time to herself. She needs time to think. *How did Tom get her address? What did the words mean? Was the man who delivered the flowers actually Tom? Is he in Sydney now? Has he been watching her all along?*

She calls Michael, who doesn't answer, and leaves him a voicemail, telling him it's urgent, noting her trembling hands. As she waits for Michael to call back, she looks up Tom on Facebook but his account has been deleted. She types his full name, Thomas Gregory, into Google and finds millions of results. She searches for images of "Thomas Gregory" and tries to find one that matches the man who delivered the flowers. If Tom sent the flowers, he would have had to give her address. She searches her memory for a time when she would have told him where she lived but cannot remember being specific, although she knows she talked about moving house.

Her cell rings, announcing a call from Michael. "What's up, babe?"

"I think Tom sent me some flowers."

"Tom? Oh, Tom, the guy from Facebook? You said you unfriended him."

"I did and I think he's upset or angry about it. I haven't heard from him since but now he's sent me flowers with this weird message on the card."

"What does it say?"

"It says, 'Remember, Megan, this is on you.'"

"What does that mean?"

"I don't know, Michael, I'm really frightened. I'm sure he wasn't happy that I've ended our relationship."

"No, I didn't like you talking to him, but I thought he was harmless."

"He has our address, Michael. I'm really scared. Tell me what to do, what do I do?"

"Okay, okay, let's just calm down. We have to think this through logically. Give me his full name and I'll see what I can do about finding him. Where does he live?"

"Queensland, I think he said. Yes, Far North Queensland, but I have no idea of exactly where." She spells out Tom's full name as she walks around the living area, checking the windows are closed and the door leading to the garden is locked.

"I'll call my contact there and see if there's anything to find out. The best-case scenario is that he's upset with you and trying to scare you. If I can find him, I'll make sure he knows not to contact you ever again."

"But why would he want to scare me? What could he be hoping to achieve? I'm sure that he's upset because I unfriended him but surely this is an overreaction?"

"Maybe. Maybe it's because he's lost his last link with you. He liked you and you rejected him and now you're not even his friend on Facebook. It's also possible that he's jealous."

"Jealous of what?"

"Jealous that your son has come home and his daughter is still missing."

Megan looks around at her house, at her daughter chewing on a toy. She is blessed to have Evie and to have her son back in her life. Is it possible that Tom is angry because she is no longer suffering as he is?

"Where did the flowers come from?"

Megan finds the small envelope that held the card but it's blank. She picks up the flowers and searches the wrapper for the name of a store but it too has nothing to offer. "I can't find anything."

"That's weird, you'd think there'd be a sticker advertising the store. Did you see the van when you signed for the flowers?"

"I may have but I wasn't exactly paying attention. I thought they were from you."

"Okay, never mind, I'm sure we'll get to the bottom of it. I'll get one of the tech guys to look into him as well, see if we can trace him through Facebook. They're pretty good at finding people online."

Michael's voice calms Megan down.

"Don't stay at home today. Why don't you take Evie and go and spend the day at your mother's flat? I'm not on night shift so I'll be home by five."

"Yes, great, good idea." Megan sighs.

She packs Evie's bag and puts her in the car. As she backs slowly out of the garage, she scans the street behind her, but aside from her neighbor, Mrs. Evans, no one is around.

When Daniel had returned home, she'd taken him over to Mrs. Evans to introduce him and had fumbled through an explanation of where Daniel had been, eventually settling on "living with his father overseas."

Now she slows down her car and opens the window. "Good morning, Mrs. Evans," she calls.

"Hello, Megan, hello, little... little, um..."

"Evie," supplies Megan. She has told Mrs. Evans her name many times before.

"Evie... that's right." Mrs. Evans walks closer to the car so she can peek inside at Evie, who throws her hands up when she sees her. "Clever little thing," laughs Mrs. Evans.

"Mrs. Evans, I just wondered if you'd seen a van out here this morning?"

"Oh yes, I see everything that goes on in this street. I saw that van and the man who jumped out holding that big bouquet of flowers. You're a lucky wife to have a husband send you something so beautiful. My Eddie never really was one for flowers, but he did like to come home loaded up with chocolates."

"Yes, I am," murmurs Megan.

Mrs. Evans is nearly ninety and has a tendency to repeat herself. Megan has heard about Eddie and the chocolates many times

"Did you happen to see the name of the florist on the van? Michael has forgotten it and I wanted to call and thank them."

Mrs. Evans removes her hat and stares up at the weak winter sunshine. "I don't think I did, no. It didn't have a name. It was just white. Of course, I could have simply forgotten it. I do tend to forget things now and again."

"Oh, well, thanks anyway. I'm sure I'll find it." Megan places her hand on the parking brake, getting ready to pull away.

"Of course, that man was here again," says Mrs. Evans.

"Which man?" asks Megan, feeling a chill go right through her.

"Oh, you know, brown hair, tall, and thin. I see him all the time now. He stands outside your house early in the morning. He just stands and stares up at the house. He looks very sad. Sometimes he looks like he's talking to himself but I can't hear what he's saying. He's very skinny, quite young, I think. I wave sometimes but he doesn't wave back, just scurries away."

"Scurries away where?" Megan asks, breathless.

"Oh, I don't know. I don't watch him after he doesn't wave, he's a bit of a rude bugger. I was going to tell you about him, of course. I mean, I have been meaning to but then I didn't see you and... it must have slipped my mind."

Megan's mind races, trying to process what Mrs. Evans is saying. A skinny young man? Megan cannot think of anyone she knows who looks like that. She doesn't understand how neither she nor Michael have seen him. Who on earth could he be? Is it Tom? Has Tom been watching her for weeks, or even months?

"He looks just like your boy," says Mrs. Evans.

"Just like my... oh, just like Daniel." Megan feels a weak laugh bubble up inside her. "Mrs. Evans, do you think it could be Daniel, maybe he comes outside in the morning?"

"Well... well, I suppose it could be, love. My eyes aren't what they used to be. Brain is still all there, mind you, except for sometimes, but I do need my glasses for even the smallest thing these days."

"I need mine more and more as well." Megan smiles. "We'd better go now. Evie and I are off to see her nana."

"Lovely, I'm looking forward to a visit from my grandson on the weekend—he's back from... um..."

"America?"

"Yes, that's it, America."

Megan pulls away from the curb and gives Mrs. Evans a wave. She has no idea why Daniel would be standing outside the house early in the morning. Whenever she goes to wake him for school, he is still in bed, but he must be getting up earlier than that. She is surprised she hasn't caught him when she gets up early with Evie. She knows she will have to speak to him about it. Perhaps he wasn't allowed out of the house when he lived with his father in case he was seen? Megan feels an overwhelming sense of sadness for her little boy. How will he ever leave his past behind?

I'm not going to think about that now, Megan admonishes herself.

"We're going to see Nana, Evie," Megan sings to her daughter.

As she turns the corner, she checks her rearview mirror and spots a white van behind her. For a moment her heart races but then at the intersection the van turns right when she turns left.

She shakes her head. *You're being paranoid and ridiculous. Paranoid and ridiculous.*

CHAPTER THIRTY-SIX

Monday, May 20, 2019

Six years since Daniel was taken

"Hey," says Michael as she opens her eyes.

Megan smiles.

"I don't know what you want to do today but I can leave you alone with Evie or I can take her out for a bit, if you like?"

"You really didn't have to take the day off, Michael."

"But I did and whatever I can do to make it easier, I'll do—just tell me."

Megan thinks about what she would like to do, how she would like to remember her son today.

"Six years is a long time," she says.

"I know. Evie's nearly five months old and it feels like she's been in our lives forever. I think I understand finally, like really understand, how impossible this must feel for you."

Megan nods. "I think I would like to go for a walk first, just alone. I might even run a little. And then maybe we could...I usually go through all the pictures I have of him. I would like to try and work a little in my studio as well. I haven't been in there since Evie was born and I think I'd like to have some time in there today."

"Whatever you need," says Michel.

Evie's cries fill the room and Megan turns the monitor's sound down. "She really wants to get up."

"I'll get her. You can feed her and I'll take her."

"Okay." Megan sits up in bed.

"Oh, and Megan," Michael says just before he leaves the room.

"Yes?"

"We're still looking for him. I called Tali yesterday and we had a chat and they're still looking for him."

"I know," says Megan. "I know."

CHAPTER THIRTY-SEVEN

Daniel—twelve years old

Daniel scratches inside his hair. "You've probably got lice," his father had said this morning. "You need to cut that hair, shave it off."

Daniel hadn't said anything to him. He likes his hair this long; it feels like he's turning into one of the animals that live in the bush out the back. A feral cat maybe. This morning he saw a fox nosing around by the garbage cans. It saw him too and growled, showing small pointy teeth. Daniel wished he could go closer and stroke its orange-red fur but the fox looked angry so he shouted and threw a stone at it instead. He wouldn't have liked to have to deal with a fox bite. His father wouldn't take him to the doctor and animal bites can get infected.

He looks down at the phone in his hand: it's way past lunchtime and his father isn't back from the store yet. Daniel sometimes feels like his stomach is trying to eat itself. He hasn't had any breakfast or lunch.

"I'll be back soon enough with a car full of food, stop whining," his father had said this morning.

He looks at the spot where the computer stands when it's in the house. He wishes his father wouldn't keep taking it. He's sick of having nothing to do when he's done with his work for the day. Sometimes he thinks about running away, about just leaving in the middle of the night and taking his chances. How hard could it be?

He hears the car pull up outside and gets up to go and help carry the groceries.

His father isn't alone. Daniel has to rub his eyes and look again because he can't believe there's another person with him. His heart beats faster as the idea that it might be a policeman occurs to him, but his father looks relaxed. He's smiling.

"Come over here and meet Steven, Daniel," he says. "Steve's going to stay with us for a bit. He's from the UK."

Daniel studies the young man, who smiles widely at him. His hair is long, not as long as his but long and messy, and his jeans are torn at the knees. "Hey, mate," he says and Daniel nods.

"Guess what I found out today?" says his father as they all unpack the groceries in the kitchen.

"What?"

"Your mother got married again. She got married and has already had another child."

"How did you find that out?" asks Daniel slowly, his heart sinking as the tears he thought he'd left behind long ago fill up his eyes.

"Saw it online."

"Why were you looking her up online?"

"I just like to see what she's doing sometimes."

"Can I look her up online? Can I talk to her?"

"No, Daniel, you know the answer to that is no."

CHAPTER THIRTY-EIGHT

Seven weeks since Daniel's return

Megan wakes out of a dream, disturbed by some sound she cannot identify. Sighing, she glances at the clock by her bed and reads the time through bleary eyes. Its four thirty and now that she's up, she's unlikely to get back to sleep.

She blinks and then stretches her arm onto Michael's side of the bed. He is working all night tonight, and will only be home in the morning. She hates it when he does the night shift, hates how empty the bed feels. Usually if she wakes before dawn, she will push up against him, waking him just enough for him to murmur, "Go back to sleep," and the sound of his voice will sometimes relax her enough to let her drift off again.

Now she lies and stares at the ceiling, going through what she needs to get done today. She has a lovely new babysitter named Emily starting next week so she can get out of the house without Evie every now and again. Megan smiles as she thinks about Evie, and she glances over at the monitor to see if her daughter has kicked off her blankets in her sleep. The nights are very cold but Evie moves too much to keep her blankets on, and Megan hates to think about her being cold.

She looks at the monitor for a moment before she registers exactly what she's seeing.

Evie's crib is empty.

She's not even aware of her body moving, and in seconds she is standing in her daughter's room, looking down at the empty crib. She puts her hands down to touch the still-warm mattress. "Evie," she says and then her heart accelerates into full-blown panic.

She switches on the light and lifts up the crib mattress, opens up the cupboard, looks under the crib, checks behind the changing table. "Evie, Evie," she says over and over again, but as if she is in a bad dream, her voice emerges only in a soft squeak. She cannot make her voice behave.

Evie cannot climb out of the crib. Surely, she cannot climb out of the crib? She's too young. The sides are too high.

A stray thought gives her a moment of peace. Maybe Michael came home early, heard her crying, picked her up, and took her to the living room?

Megan dashes down the stairs but finds the living room empty. Evie is not there, Michael is not there. "Daniel!" she calls, cursing the fact that her voice won't cooperate. She searches the house frantically, running up and down the stairs without stopping to think, checking under beds and in closed cupboards in case Evie has somehow locked herself inside. "Evie," she calls over and over. She runs back to her bedroom and grabs her cell phone. As she goes to press Michael's number, she sees there's a text message from him. It had come through at 11 p.m., after she had fallen asleep.

DNA finally came back. The body in the shack was not Greg. Call me when you get this.

"Not Greg? Not Greg. What? Where is she? Where is she?"

She rushes into Daniel's room and switches on the light, not caring if he is asleep. "Daniel, you need..." she begins but then she sees that his bed is also empty. Where is he? She whirls around and opens the cupboard where his clothes hang, silent and still. She gets on her knees and looks under his bed and his desk and then she looks at his side table where his phone is lying upside down. *He let go of it. He's never let go of his phone.*

She grabs it quickly and turns it over, pressing buttons to illuminate the screen.

The black square lights up. Megan sees the words, holds her breath, reads them, reads them again.

Now. Do it now.

The message has come from a phone number; no name identifies who it's from.

What? What? What? is all she can consciously think.

Panic makes her nauseous; her heart races. *My babies, where are my babies?* She runs back through the house to the front door. It's open. "No, no, no," she moans. And then she sees them. Daniel is standing in the pre-dawn light with Evie in his arms. "Oh, thank God," Megan says, and relieved laughter makes her weak at the knees. *What is he doing? Why is he out here? Is this what Mrs. Evans had seen before?*

Daniel turns and his eyes widen, panic spreading across his face. His feet are bare and he is dressed only in his thin pajamas. Evie is dressed in a warm onesie but it's not warm enough to be outside. The air is frigid.

"What are you doing out here?" she yells, relief turning to anger at the terrifying few minutes she has just gone through.

"Mum," says Daniel. He walks toward her. "Take her," he says, thrusting Evie at Megan. "Take her and run, Mum," he whispers urgently.

"What?" she asks, taking her daughter from him.

"Take her, please, Mum. Run, you have to run," Daniel pleads. His eyes shine with tears; his desperation is frightening.

"Why should I run? What's wrong?"

His eyes dart from left to right and then he moans a little. "Please, Mum, you're going to get . . . Please just run," he whispers hoarsely.

Megan jiggles Evie up and down a little as she begins to fuss. "Daniel, listen to me," she says quietly, certain he is in the middle of some kind of nightmare. "Let's go back inside and you can get into bed, it's warm in bed."

"No, Mum, please, please," he cries. His nose runs and tears drip off his chin.

"Don't you fucking move," Megan hears.

She looks behind Daniel into the gloom of the early morning. She thinks she may have imagined the whispered words. But then her eyes adjust to the low level of light, and as the words are repeated once more, she sees him as he walks toward her and her children.

Megan stiffens in horror.

"Don't you move an inch," he says. He is holding a small pistol in his hands and it is pointed not at her but at Daniel.

"G-Greg," stutters Megan. "Greg . . . Greg."

"Surprise," says Greg. "Aren't you happy to see me?"

CHAPTER THIRTY-NINE

"You were . . . the fire . . . you . . ."

But then she remembers the message from Michael on her phone. In her panic she hadn't been able to properly digest it. It wasn't Greg who got burned, who died, who was hurt. It wasn't Greg.

"You . . . you . . . you," mocks Greg. "Stupid bitch . . . I was never there. Some poor slob had to die for you, Megan. He had to die because you're an evil woman who doesn't know how to love anyone, not even her own son. Get over here, Daniel, now."

"Don't move," whispers Megan. "Please, Daniel, don't move." She risks a quick glance at her son, who is wringing his hands and bouncing on his feet. She can see that he has no idea who to listen to, no idea what to do.

"He doesn't love you anymore, Megan. He doesn't want to be with you. You never cared that he was gone. You just moved right on, didn't you? But maybe that's the difference between a man and a woman. Once a man loves you, he loves you forever. I was willing to love you forever."

The words feel familiar. She has heard them somewhere before. In the cold her shivering intensifies, her teeth chatter, and she feels her hands shake. Suddenly, she knows where she's read those words before.

"You're Tom," she states, the realization flooding her. Exhaustion and panic combine so that she feels numb and stupid, beyond stupid, for not having figured it out sooner, for believing that Tom was just another man devastated at the loss of his daughter.

"Who's Tom?" asks Daniel.

"Shut the hell up!" Greg shouts.

Megan sees her son flinch and then he takes a tiny step closer to her. A small, tiny, little step toward her.

"Yeah, I am," spits Greg, unaware of Daniel moving at all, his eyes focused on Megan. "Poor Tom, poor, poor Tom, whose wife has taken their little girl. You fell for Tom, didn't you, Megan? You liked him and you felt sorry for him and I think you may have even loved him. You should have agreed to meet him, Megan. You would have had a lovely surprise. Waiting for you would have been your husband and son, ready to try again, ready to be your family. I imagined it a thousand times. I knew how happy you would be and I wanted that for you because I have only ever wanted you to be happy. It's all I ever wanted. But instead you found yourself another man, or maybe you always had another man, even when we were married."

"What does he mean, Mum? What's he talking about?" asks Daniel. "Who's Tom?" he repeats, confusion across his face.

"What do you want, Greg? Why are you here?" Megan asks, her voice just above a squeak, knowing as she says the words that he can only be here to hurt her, to cause her pain. The gun makes that much very clear.

"I want what I've always wanted. I want to have a wife and son who love me and respect me. I tried, Megan, I really tried. Even after you rejected Tom, I gave you another chance. All you had to do was go away with Daniel for a couple of days, just a couple of days and it all would have been okay."

"A couple of days?" she repeats. "Tom never... You never told me to go away with Daniel for a couple of days... Sandi..." She stops talking. How does he know what Sandi advised her to do? She cocks her head a little in Daniel's direction, watches him take another small step toward her.

"Yes, Sandi said that," he says. "You liked Sandi, didn't you?"

He is no longer looking at Daniel, has seemingly forgotten he's there. Her stomach flips. All this time, she has been talking to him. She has only ever been talking to him. Only him. The connection she felt with Tom and Sandi was never real. They never existed. Everything has been a lie. She feels bile rise in her throat and swallows convulsively. *Idiot, idiot, idiot.*

"Don't you see? I gave you everything you wanted. I gave you a man to fall in love with and a woman to be friends with but they were all me. It's me you want to be with, me." Megan knows that he's waiting for her to tell him he's right. Even as he stands in front of her with a gun, he still believes they can be together again.

"No, I..." begins Megan and then she remembers a conversation with Michael about a time in his career when his life was at risk. He had gone into a service station and walked in on a man threatening the attendant with a knife. "I just kept him talking," she hears Michael say. "Sometimes all you need is to keep the person talking until you can figure out what to do."

"Who was in your house, Greg? Who was the person who died?" she asks.

"Ah, now that's the million-dollar question, isn't it? Who was in the shack? The horrible shack where I had to live with my son so you couldn't hunt us down and take him from me. Do you know how much I gave up for you, Megan? Do you realize how many people you've hurt? That poor bastard is just one more person who had to suffer for you. He had to pay with his life so I could make sure you never got to mess up another kid. All he wanted was a place to sleep for a couple of weeks and now he's dead. He's dead because of you, Megan. What other choice did I have?"

A face comes to Megan: a genial, smiling, young man on an adventure—a young man with a past. "Steven Hindley," she whispers. "The British backpacker."

"Well, well, look at you. Sleeping with a cop must have made you a bit smarter. Yeah, poor old Steve, he really shouldn't have accepted all of that whisky. He didn't even struggle when I put the pillow over his face, just went off to sleep like the idiot he was. Funny that he was the one who told me about fire and what it could do—that was his favorite subject. He was right about it too, it destroys *everything*, cleans it all up and leaves nothing. I had to light a few more just to enjoy the spectacle. I bet Steven never thought that fire would end up getting him."

"Steven? It was Steven?" gasps Daniel. "But you said he left. You said he left!" he yells. "You said he had to go and visit a girlfriend. You said he left." He is crying hard now, not even bothering to wipe his eyes, tears rolling down his cheek. "You said," he repeats, "you said, you said." He points his finger at his father as his face contorts with anger and despair. "You told me no one would be in there, that they wouldn't find anything, you lied, you lied." His hand shakes.

Please stop, Daniel, don't make him any angrier than he is.

"Shut the hell up!" screams Greg. "Just shut up. I had to do it because of her, it was all because of her."

Greg is out of control. An explosion is coming. He waves the gun around as he shouts, almost unaware he's holding it. The sick feeling in her stomach reminds her that she has felt this way before. He has reduced her to this feeling before. Someone is going to get hurt. They're going to get hurt.

She knows that she needs to keep him talking until she can get the three of them inside the house. Once they're inside she can get them to her bedroom and she can lock the door. Then she can take her children into the bathroom and lock that door as well. There will be two doors between Greg and her family. Surely he won't be able to get through two doors?

She goes through the route in her mind, her heart racing as though she and her children are already running up the stairs.

"Aaah," cries Evie, frustrated at being held so tightly, at being awake, at the fear shuddering through her mother's body. Megan swings her body, desperately trying to get her to quiet down.

She needs to get some help. She longs for a morning jogger or someone on the way to an early shift but the street is eerily empty and silent. She wishes Mrs. Evans was looking out of her window. It must have been Greg her neighbor was seeing all this time. He has been watching her and her family since the day Daniel came home. The thought makes Megan shudder.

You're their mother. Figure it out. You need to save these children.

"Why did you pretend to be Tom and Sandi, Greg? Why were you so kind to me online?" *Keep talking, keep him talking, keep talking.* "You hated me, Greg. Why did you want me back?" While Megan speaks, she touches the side of her phone, turning it to silent. Her hand is under Evie's bum and she doesn't think Greg can see that she is holding her phone.

Daniel is frozen in place now, eyes huge and head swiveling between his parents. His hands chase each other around in desperation. His tears keep falling.

I'm here, baby, I'm here and I'm not going to let anything happen to you. Hold on, beautiful boy, just hold on.

Megan uses her thumb to touch her phone, hoping that she has hit the dial button on Michael's number. If it's not him, it will be her mother, Connor, or James. They are the top four numbers that she dials and she prays that somehow, someone will answer and understand. But how could they possibly understand this?

"I didn't hate you, I never hated you! I love you. I'll always love you. I just wanted to make you happy!" yells Greg, throwing his hands around. His face is twisted with anguish and she can see the sheen of tears in his eyes.

"I was the perfect husband and you were too selfish to see it. We could have had such a wonderful life together. Even after you divorced me, I gave you another chance. I gave you Tom to fall in love with so that we could be together again but then you had to go and screw it all up. You had to marry that man and have that child as if Daniel and I had never existed. You tried to erase us,

Megan. What kind of woman does that? What kind of mother does that?"

"Greg, listen to me," says Megan as she slowly inches toward Daniel. He has stopped moving and she needs to get in front of him. She needs to shield him. As she moves, she turns her body a little, defending Evie. "We can sort this out. It can all be worked out so everyone is happy."

"No, I'm done with that. You don't understand that a woman like you needs to know the consequences of her actions. You can't have children, Megan, you're not fit to be a mother."

"Okay, Greg, I understand," says Megan as she slowly moves closer to Daniel.

Greg is still waving the gun around. His pupils are dilated and his movements are jerky. She tries to get Daniel to look at her without speaking. She needs to tell him to move behind her but he is crying and shaking and she can see he cannot think straight. The few steps between her and her son seem an impossibly great distance to cover.

"Megan . . . Megan, what's wrong?" comes Michael's quiet, tinny voice from her phone.

"Put the gun down, Greg!" Megan shouts.

"Who said that? Who are you talking to?"

"Put it down," shrieks Megan, her voice returning in full force. She will not let this man hurt her children. She will not.

She lunges for Daniel, grabbing him by his arm, pulling hard and shoving him toward the front door as she turns her back on Greg.

"Run, Daniel!" she screams, and together they stumble toward the front door. From a few streets away Megan thinks she can detect the sound of sirens but she knows it is probably wishful thinking. No one is going to save her children but her. She gives Daniel one more push and he falls into the house as she trips in after him.

What she feels then is not so much pain as a physical shock as the gun goes off and the smell of something burning fills the air.

She looks at Daniel and then she holds Evie out to him.

"Mum?" he says, tears streaming down his face. "Mum," he says as he grabs Evie from her and she falls forward.

The last thing Megan hears is Greg screaming her name.

Daniel saying, "Mum."

Evie crying.

And the sounds of sirens that have arrived . . . just a little too late.

CHAPTER FORTY

Daniel

One day later

"Do you understand the plan?" his father had asked him the day before the fire, the day before he'd sent him into the police station to tell them who he was, the day before everything changed.

"Yes," Daniel had said, just like he had said all the other times his father had gone over what would happen. "Yes, I understand, but I don't know what we're going to do with a baby. How are we going to raise a baby? She won't know us. She won't like us."

"Don't worry about that. I know how to take care of a baby. I took care of you, didn't I? All you need to do is make sure that she trusts you, that she likes you. Babies are stupid. They like anyone who's nice to them. Give her toys and talk to her. Show her pictures of me so she recognizes my face. Don't let them know what you're doing. Don't let them know how clever you are."

"Why can't we just go somewhere else? Why can't we leave without the baby? If Mum's had another child, she won't care where I am anymore."

"Don't call her Mum, she's not your mum. Now let's go through it again. You leave the house and you go to the spot I showed you under the big rock, and you wait there for me. I'll make sure your clothes smell like smoke before you leave. I'll come and get you once it's done and take you nearly all the way there. Tell them

I'm dead. Tell them about the fire. Tell them it was the hotplate. That thing's a piece of shit."

Daniel had nodded and nodded so his father wouldn't get angry. Now he remembers asking, "But what about Steven?"

"Steven wants to go back to Sydney to see some girl. I'll make sure he leaves before I do anything."

"Maybe he could help us. He showed me how to decorate my knife with a burning stick. Steven's good at fire."

"I don't want Steven involved. Only you and I can be involved. You make sure Megan trusts you; both her and that dickhead husband need to trust you."

"Do I call her Megan?"

"Of course not. Call her . . . call her Mum, but remember, she's not a good mother. She's a bad mother, a bad person, and everything she tells you about what happened when you were away is a lie. If she tells you she looked for you, it's a lie. If she tells you she wanted you home, it's a lie. She lies and she can't be allowed to get away with it—she has to pay for what she's done to you and to me. Her whole family are liars. Remember that, you're dealing with a family of outright liars and we have to protect that innocent child from them. Now do you remember the plan? They need to think I'm dead or they won't take you back to your mother. You have to tell them about the fire. Say it was started by the hotplate, say you tried to save me. Hide the SIM card for your phone in your underwear, don't let anyone see it. Take the phone apart the way I showed you and tell them you dropped it."

"What if you get hurt?" he remembers asking his father, because that had been all he was worried about. He didn't want to lose his father, even though sometimes, sometimes he hated him.

"Nothing is going to happen to me, Daniel. I'll just go back to the house and make sure the fire keeps burning. Once you're back with your mother, I'll contact you on the phone. Make sure you do what we talked about and tell everyone you lost the SIM. Don't let anyone catch you talking to me."

"I don't want to go back to her, Dad, she hates me."

"She sure does, and anyone who can hate her own child doesn't deserve to be a mother. You don't have to like her or be nice to her and you won't have to stay there a long time, a couple of months at the most, and then we'll have her child and we can leave the country again, start over somewhere fresh. I can get a real job and you can go to school."

Each phone call had been hard. "Does she trust you yet, does the baby trust you? She can't cry when you pick her up. Let me know when you're ready."

He hadn't been sure if he was going to take Evie to his father, not after the first time he'd seen her with his mother. He'd known that he and his father couldn't take care of Evie the way his mother did, and as the weeks had gone by, he'd started to wonder about the things his father had told him, about all the things he'd said his mother had or hadn't done.

In the middle of the night he would toss and turn in bed, clutching his stomach as anxiety gnawed away at him. He had no idea what to believe, no idea who to trust.

His first day at school had been a revelation. The other kids were supposed to be mean, to tease and taunt him and he was supposed to have to keep secrets like the last time he went to school. The other kids were supposed to pry and snigger but they hadn't. The teachers were supposed to tell him he was stupid because he hadn't been at school for such a long time, that he knew nothing. But he'd been right at the top of the class even though his father had told him to pretend he didn't understand. He couldn't resist getting the answer right or the way the math teacher clapped when he was the only one who could solve the problem. He couldn't resist the feeling it gave him.

And then he had felt guilty because he wasn't supposed to enjoy the school his mother sent him to or like eating the food his mother cooked or wish that he could talk to his uncle Connor about being a scientist. He was supposed to hate them all but he couldn't. He just couldn't.

He'd started to wonder and to think and eventually he realized that his father was the liar.

His father had been the liar all along.

He hadn't known what to do with that truth, with that reality, because it meant everything that had happened over the last six years had been a lie. Half his life had been a lie. His mother hadn't been tired of taking care of him, she hadn't stopped loving him, and she had looked for him. He hadn't wanted to believe any of the things she was telling him until he couldn't deny the truth anymore.

His father was the liar. He'd told the same lies over and over, making them part of who Daniel was until he believed everything he said. One lie on top of another, on top of another. Higher and higher went his father's skyscraper of lies.

But by the time Daniel had realized it, it was too late. He'd felt twisted up inside and he hadn't known what to do, hadn't known how to tell his mother what was really going on. Sometimes he'd gotten so close. He would open his mouth and try to make the words come out but he couldn't make it happen. The plan was in place and there was nothing he could do to stop it. His father wouldn't let him stop it and now... now none of them could ever go back.

In the other room Michael is crying and it scares Daniel to hear Michael cry because he's so tall and strong, but it also makes him feel it's fine for him to cry too. Evie is crying because she wants her mum. Daniel feels the tears slip down his face. He also wants his mum. He wants her to put her arms around him and tell him it's okay.

But nothing is okay.

How can it be okay?

EPILOGUE

Eight weeks later

Daniel kneels down and places the flowers he is carrying on the grave.

"They look good there, buddy," says Michael and Daniel nods.

"I like roses," he says, "they come in so many different colors."

"Do you want a little time alone?" asks Michael.

"I don't mind if you stay," says Daniel. He actually doesn't want to be alone. Graveyards are creepy.

Michael is carrying Evie and he puts her down on the grass. She toddles over to Daniel and pats him on the shoulder. "Dani, Dani," she says, repeating the first word that she has learned.

"Hey, Evie," Daniel says quietly.

Evie toddles away. She grabs at handfuls of grass and attempts to pull out the wildflowers growing freely around the graves before Michael stops her.

Daniel looks at the lettering on the grave, studying his father's name. Gregory Edward Stanthorpe, beloved son and father. Daniel had not wanted those words to be used when the gravestone was being made.

"I don't want people to know he was my father," he'd said to his grandparents. "I don't want anyone to know he was a father. He didn't deserve to be a father."

Daniel is ashamed of himself now when he thinks about the way his Granny Audrey's face had crumpled and she'd begun to cry.

They'd looked so different when Michael took him to visit them at the hotel they were staying at. They had only come for long enough to organize the funeral and bury their son. His grandmother had still looked young, still looked capable, when he had seen her for that one night over six years ago.

In the restaurant of the hotel Daniel had scanned the room for his grandparents and had completely missed them until a little old lady had waved him over. He had felt shock ripple through him at the idea that this thin, bent woman was his grandmother.

He hadn't wanted to discuss the funeral and he hadn't wanted to listen to them talk about what a wonderful man his father had been. "He made some mistakes," his grandfather had acknowledged, "but he was pushed to the very limit by his circumstance and we all need to think about that before we judge him."

"No, William, we can't make excuses anymore," his grandmother had said. "We simply can't. I'm sorry, Daniel, we're so sorry... I wish, I wish it could have been different. I wish I could have done it differently. We should have told the police... we should have," she'd said and then she had dissolved into tears.

Daniel had not known what to say to that but he had fervently wished that Michael had not politely moved a few tables away so he and his grandparents could talk.

Only when he had raised his voice and shouted, "I don't want people to know he was my father," had Michael returned and tried to shush them all into behaving.

"One day you may feel differently," Michael had said quietly, and even though he hadn't believed he ever would, he is grateful now that he just shook his head and walked away rather than keep arguing with his grandparents. It had felt like it was too late for apologies then, but now he's not so sure.

He doesn't know if he will ever speak to them again, if they will ever want to speak to him again. He had, as Michael told him weeks later, behaved badly, and Daniel had felt ashamed,

ashamed at himself for yelling at his sad grandmother and then for walking away.

"It was understandable," Michael had said. "You were traumatized, filled with grief, and afraid, but they had just lost their son."

"What should I do about it?" Daniel had asked, hating how whiny he sounded.

"Maybe a letter? I know they don't like emails but maybe you could write a letter and explain how things were, tell them you understand their grief. Maybe find a way to say something good about your father. They hadn't seen him for six years and now he's gone and they will never see him again. Try to give them something to hold on to, a memory or something positive."

"How can you want me to say something positive about him after everything he did? He was a . . . a monster. He stole my whole childhood, he stole . . . How can I say something positive?"

"I don't think he was a monster, Daniel. I think he was sick and delusional, and even though I do feel absolute hate and rage when I think of him, I try to keep reminding myself that he was mentally unstable. Only someone who was mentally unstable could have done what he did. That thought sometimes allows me to find a little peace. I'm not saying it always works but I do try. And in the end your grandparents are not really to blame for your father's sins. They've also been damaged and terribly hurt by what has happened."

Daniel is thinking about writing the letter, still thinking about it after all these weeks. The trouble is that every time he sits down to start it, he begins thinking about everything that happened and then the sadness comes and that's always followed by so much anger that he has to go down to the garage and punch the punching bag he and Michael use until he doesn't even have the energy to lift his arms, let alone write a letter to his grandparents. But he will get to it; he will try and give them something to hold on to. They deserve that at least.

As he looks at the gray granite stone, Daniel thinks that what he mostly felt all the years he was with his father was fear. He was afraid of his father dying and leaving him alone, afraid of the police finding him and sending him to foster care, afraid of seeing his mother again and having her tell him she didn't love him, and mostly he was afraid of never seeing his mother again.

He stands up, trying not to let the memories wash over him.

He looks around at all the other graves in the cemetery, feeling a heavy sadness for Steven, who had helped him with his homework and taught him how to make his own knife and who thought everything in Australia was amazing. And now he'll never get to do anything again.

He knows now that they were never going to just take Evie and go. All along it had only been about how much his father hated his and Evie's mother. It had all been about punishing her. Daniel has nightmares sometimes where he sees Evie in his father's arms and he sees what he's planning to do with his gun.

That final night he hadn't wanted to take Evie out of her crib.

The vibration of his phone had woken him out of a deep sleep just before dawn. He had looked at the text from his father and curled himself up in bed. He wouldn't do it. He couldn't do it. And then the phone had buzzed again with a call.

"I think this is wrong," he'd told his father in a whispered conversation. "I don't want to do it. Evie will be too sad. She'll miss Mum."

"Bring her out to me," his father had said. "Bring her out to me or I'm coming in there and everyone will end up dead."

Fear coursing through him, he had crept out with baby Evie in his arms, awake and alert, wide-eyed at being out of her crib in the dark. He'd hoped his mother would wake up, wished Michael would come home early from his night shift. When his father had stood up outside and waved the gun, Daniel had finally understood that he'd had it wrong. He had been entirely wrong. His father wasn't just a liar; he was something else as well, something awful and terrible and filled with hate.

He remembers the first shot, the one that hit his mother, and then his father's screams, "No, no, Megan, no."

Had he loved her? Had he hated her? Daniel doesn't believe his father knew the answer.

And then the sirens were in the street and there were police cars and lights everywhere and Evie was screaming but his mother was still. And his heart had simply broken. He hadn't ever understood what that meant before but now he knows it's a cracking-open feeling in your chest that squeezes the breath out of your lungs. He had stood, staring at his mother, at his mum, who had always loved him, who had never wanted to lose him, and who was now lost to him.

"Put it down, put the gun down, put the gun down," he had heard from one, two, three different places, and then more shots.

He had known the only thing he could do then was to save his sister. He had run upstairs to his bedroom with Evie, shut the door, held her on his lap, and waited. His ears had buzzed and his heart had raced and his tears had kept falling and the only thing he had been able to think about was keeping Evie safe, keeping his baby sister from harm. "Michael will come, Evie," he had kept saying as his sister screamed. "Michael will come."

And finally, Michael had come.

Daniel touches the gravestone. "Hey, Dad," he says and then he stands up and waves at Michael. "I'm done."

"Okay, buddy. Let's go then."

"Dani, Dani," says Evie from Michael's arms.

Daniel takes Evie from Michael and straps her into her car seat as she pats him and smiles. "Dani, Dani."

"Time to go and visit Mum," he tells Evie.

It's not a long drive to the hospital.

"Should we get her some more flowers?" asks Daniel as they pass the gift shop.

"Nah, don't worry about it. I think that painting is everything she needs."

Daniel looks at the small framed picture in his hands. It's of him and Evie, copied from a picture Michael took of the two of them on his phone. It had felt weird to stand in his mother's studio, to use her paints and canvas without her there. Weird but also right. He had been very careful to clean the brushes the way she taught him when he was little, to put everything back in place.

"Do you think she'll like it?" he asks Michael for the tenth time.

"No," says Michael. "I think she'll love it. I think it's amazing."

Megan has been in the hospital for two months now.

"The bullet hit her spine and veered off. We've repaired what we can but there has been a lot of trauma to the area. You need to prepare yourself and you need to prepare her for the fact that she may never walk again," the surgeon had told Michael and Daniel at the time.

Michael hadn't wanted him to listen, to hear, but Daniel had needed to know. He had grabbed Michael's hand and Michael had held on tight, and Daniel had managed to hide his tears in front of the doctor.

"But she'll live?" Daniel had asked.

"She'll live," she had said, and because she was wearing a white coat and she looked so capable, Daniel and Michael had believed her.

"What nonsense," Megan had said when they'd explained it to her. "I'll walk."

As they get out of the elevator, Michael puts Evie down and she toddles over to her mother's room, as familiar with this place as she is her own room at home. She comes with her grandmother every day to visit while Michael is at work, or with Emily, the new nanny.

Evie pushes at the hospital door, trying to open it. "Dani, Dani," she says because his name is the word she uses for everything right now.

Michael opens the door and Daniel pushes through, holding Evie's hand. The bed is empty, as is Megan's wheelchair.

Daniel's eyes dart wildly around the room. *Oh no, oh no, oh no.*

"Hello, darlings," she says.

Daniel turns around to see his mother. She is standing by the bathroom door, leaning heavily on two crutches. Relief makes him shudder and then he laughs.

"You're standing," says Michael, his voice filled with awe.

"She's standing," says Daniel.

"I'm standing," says Megan.

A LETTER FROM NICOLE

Hello,

For a long time, I was told to "write what you know," but that never really worked for me. Instead I write what I fear.

I write about families in crisis, about lives changing in the blink of an eye, and about people who somehow manage to survive very difficult situations.

I hope that you've connected with Megan and her family and their struggles. A child being taken from you is one of the very worst fears a mother has, and we are always so vigilant about strangers in our children's lives. I can only imagine how much worse it would be to have your child stolen by someone who you were once in love with, and how difficult that must be for the child who is taken. Those thoughts are what led me to write this novel. Most of us have either experienced or know someone who has gone through divorce, and this is one of the worst-case scenarios of what can happen when love turns and hearts are broken. I know that there are many parents around the world who are hoping desperately to be allowed to reconnect with their children. I have tried to write about this with the authenticity it deserves.

If you have enjoyed this novel, it would be lovely if you could take the time to leave a review. I read them all, and on days when I question whether or not I have another book in me, they lift me up and help me get back to work.

I would also love to hear from you. You can find me on Facebook and Twitter, and I'm always happy to connect with readers.

Thanks again for reading,
Nicole x

NicoleTrope

@nicoletrope

ACKNOWLEDGMENTS

I would like to thank Christina Demosthenous for her tireless and exceptional editing and for being there to celebrate every win with me. Thanks to Deandra Lupu for a detailed and amazing copyedit. I would also like to thank Kim Nash, Noelle Holten, and Sarah Hardy, publicity and social media wizards, for promoting my novels to the world. Thanks to Alexandra Holmes, Ellen Gleeson, Liz Hatherell, and to everyone who looks over the manuscript with fresh eyes. And, of course, to the whole team at Bookouture for their support. Thank you to Grand Central Publishing and Kirsiah McNamara for taking care of the paperback edition. Also thanks to Ivy Cheng and Morgan Swift for publicity and marketing.

I would also like to thank, as always, my mother for being my first reader.

Thanks also to David, Mikhayla, Isabella, and Jacob.

And once again, thank you to those who read, review, and blog about my work. You remind me why I choose to do this every day.

ABOUT THE AUTHOR

Nicole Trope is a former high school teacher with a master's degree in literature. Her first novel, *The Boy Under the Table*, was published in 2012 with Allen & Unwin in Australia. She went on to publish five more novels with Allen & Unwin before moving to Bookouture, where she has published five novels: *My Daughter's Secret*, *The Boy in The Photo*, *The Nowhere Girl*, *The Life She Left Behind*, and *The Girl Who Never Came Home*. She lives in Sydney with her husband and three children.